Atlas' Final Approach
By J. Channing

Book 4 of the Atlas Carter Saga

Red Team Ink
DBA of Zealot Solutions, Idaho LLC
5447 Kendall St.
Boise, ID 83706
Copyright© 2018 by Red Team Ink

For permission requests or information about discounts for special bulk purchases please contact: redteamink@gmail.com. Substantial discounts on bulk orders are available to corporations, professional associations, and small businesses.

Printed in The United States of America

ISBN: 978-1-7322129-0-9

Title: Atlas' Final Approach
Description: First Edition

Prologue

The Bwainhome
The Upper Dimensions

Captain Atlas Carter was losing control.

When he first thrust his hand into the beating heart of the Bwain mother ship, he'd done so because he'd wanted to die. Exiled in punishment for betraying the trust of the people he'd sworn to protect, witness to the murder of his wife, and captain of a doomed ship with a dying crew, the only thing he wanted to do when he'd first encountered the Endless Knot in a strange chamber at the top of the massive ship was to force his pain on the Bwain.

Rather than the death he expected however, he'd found salvation, both for the Bwain, and for himself. Connected to Bwain through the telepathic link known as the Bwainsong, he'd learned of the creatures' lonely journey through the stars as they searched for the home which their former slave masters, the First Ones, had taken from them. The *Bwainhome* had nourished the Bwain for millennia, grown with them, and led them to Earth many times, where they first encountered a brutal species that had evolved there known as homo sapiens.

After spending so much time aboard the alien craft, he came to realize that the *Bwainhome* was more than just a ship. There was a third mental presence bound within the Knot, one that whispered to darker aspects of his personality while he did his best to save lives and keep his fleet intact in the face of the greatest threat the universe had ever known. The *Bwainhome*'s voice was growing stronger even as his own body and mental state weakened. So much so in fact, that and it was becoming a constant struggle to steel himself against it.

"What is control?" the ship's deep voice murmured. There was no

sound in the telepathic link that Atlas used to communicate with the Bwain and control their ship. He communicated with emotion, imagery, and the memory of language, so when the *Bwainhome* itself spoke to him, it carried with it the sensation of a great creature sliding just under an ocean's surface. The Bwain sailed the galaxy in the decaying corpses of their former masters' ships, but the *Bwainhome*'s body was awakening, and what might happen when it fully arose from its millennia long slumber absolutely terrified him.

Atlas was steering the great ship through the higher dimensions that existed above the physical universe, taking it from Earth's orbit toward the place in physical space and time where a horde of First Ones had attacked a small fleet of human ships trapped in the vast emptiness of space. The ships carried the last survivors of the Sword Belt, the planetary system Carter had been ordered to protect. They were crewed by men and women who'd become his friends in the struggle to first overthrow a corrupt colonial administrator, then to resist the Bwain, and then finally to deal with the greater threat of the First Ones. The *Bwainhome* was consuming him, absorbing his soul into itself, and unless he abandoned himself and joined with the Knot completely, every one of his friends would die.

Carter flung the great ship back into the physical universe. A small part of his mind issued orders to Pandith, and then turning his fully concentration back to the matter at hand, he targeted the closest of the First Ones and fired.

The creature, an enormous slug-like thing with mucosal wings and a cluster of shuttles clutched in its maw, buckled and shook as the *Bwainhome*'s dimensional weaponry tore through its body and erased its existence from the physical universe. The *Bwainhome* had grown weapons that could do what human missiles and lasers could not. They were capable of attacking the bodies of creatures that existed simultaneously in all twelve dimensions of the universe. When the weapons fired, he could feel the *Bwainhome*'s nearly limitless power surge within him. He could travel anywhere in the universe in the blink of an eye, and grow any kind of tool or weapon imaginable with nothing more than a thought. He could hold the ultimate power in the universe in his hand, but that power would also tear him apart.

"*Control is restraint*," Atlas replied tersely as he refocused his thoughts. The feeling was one of forcing words through gritted teeth.

The Bwain were a collective consciousness, the thoughts of each individual united by the Endless Knot in the *Bwainhome*. When Carter had first joined with them, they'd known only how to charge into slaughter. He'd taught them to read their opponents, and how to develop tactics to defeat them. He'd shared with them lessons from his days as a young boxer training for what he thought would be Olympic glory on the streets of Belize City. Taught them how to bide their time, and how to pull an opponent in before they launched an attack. Unfortunately, he could still feel a tremendous amount of collective anger in the link, and it called to him.

Atlas had taken great pains to avoid unnecessary loss of life in his previous engagements with SSC fleets that were sent to destroy him, but after Admiral Nico had murdered the messenger Carter had sent with a message of peace just outside of Pluto, that pushed him one step too far. He unleashed his own and the Bwain's full fury upon the SSC fleet, striking the human ships at the speed of his thoughts, until a childhood memory somehow found its way into his consciousness.

"You win with control," Cazador had taunted him. His friend was hooking punches into either side of his body, harsh blows that a 14-year-old Atlas was powerless to defend against. Exhausted by the brutal training in the Belizean heat, his legs grew weak and unsteady, and his shoulders burned. Furious at Cazador's constant taunting, he abandoned his defense and threw a series of wild haymakers at Cazador's smirking face. Unfortunately, the none of the punches found their mark, and Cazador unleashed a brutal uppercut into Carter's solar plexus that dropped him to all fours and sent him crawling through the dust, gagging and panting wildly while Cazador simply laughed at his suffering.

"This is why I always win," Cazador said. "I know how to control you."

"*Control is a weakness,*" the Endless Knot's deep voice responded.

The ship's muscles, unused for millennia, contracted. Its rage tore apart the Bwain's former masters as the First Ones tried to surround the *Bwainhome*. These were Carter's muscles, his body, and he bent the ship to his will. For a moment, a brief passing of time in which he could have taken the ship to the far ends of the galaxy, he was united with the ship in utter fury.

Yet, even in that moment, a distant voice reached him. He had grown to love a woman after the death of his wife. She was looking into the eyes of one of the Bwain, trying to tell him that she was dying.

"Atlas, I'm sorry," Mephista said.

Death was a betrayal. He could not leave those he cared for behind ever again.

Roaring in pain, Atlas tried to rise up from the depths of the Endless Knot's visions. But it was too late, he'd become somehow both more *and* less than what he'd been.

"*I will control you,*" the *Bwainhome* intoned. Then it joined Atlas' screams to its own.

Chapter One

The Ninkovich
SSC Commanding Admiral Nico's Flagship
In orbit around Pluto near the SSC Kuiper Belt Research Facility

Admiral Vladislav Nico was the most powerful man in the universe. Not twelve hours earlier, a bloc of disaffected galactic senators from the outer planets who had grown weary of the constant Bwain attacks destroying their revenues, had voted to install him as the galactic president. Nico's loyal Sol Space Command Officers had arrested his sniveling predecessor, Nelson Kidewange, and imposed martial law on the Earth and its colonies in order to deal with the threat of Bwain invasion. Nico had never been a man of subtlety. His priorities were simple: eliminate the Bwain, destroy the traitorous Atlas Carter, and deal with the new threat that had emerged in the Sword Belt. He would accomplish these tasks with the same ruthless tenacity that had propelled him into command of the largest military machine that humanity had ever assembled.

There was one not so small problem with his plan however. Atlas Carter had just made a mockery of his fleet.

"Damage report!" Nico bellowed at his second in command. Captain Jansen was a professional who'd first served with Nico decades ago when the navy had put down separatists in a variety of skirmishes. She'd seen all facets of the hulking admiral's temper over her career, but even she blanched at Nico's tone.

"Sir, we've lost seven ships. Four more are inoperable. Casualties are..."

"I don't care how many men we lost!" Nico barked. His graveled voice, tinged with a hint of Russian accent, echoed off the walls of his vast bridge. "All I want to know right now is how the hell he did this!"

"Sir," his navigation officer called. "The Bwain ship seems to have some sort of a localized Alcubierre drive with apparently unlimited fuel. I've analyzed its course from the data we collected. It made 16 different jumps during the engagement."

"Sixteen?" Nico asked, stunned that it was even possible to do such a thing. "So...that's how he did it."

During the fight, it had seemed the Carter had been everywhere. The massive Bwain ship had never stayed in one place long enough for Nico's weapons to even scratch it, disappearing just as his fleet's missiles and lasers reached its previous location, only to reappear behind him to strike at his undefended rear. It was a coward's tactic, but whatever propulsion system the Bwain ship used gave Carter a formidable tactical advantage.

Human ships used an Alcubierre engine powered by antimatter to warp space time and pull themselves forward at faster-than-light speeds, but antimatter was incredibly precious, and extremely difficult to manufacture. Each ship in Nico's fleet received only two fuel pellets for an entire tour. One was for the outbound journey, and the other was for the return trip home. Antimatter limited Nico's tactical flexibility considerably, but if Carter had discovered a new way to travel faster than light, that would certainly change things.

"That's not all, Admiral. I've just received word that an antimatter theft was reported at the Martian facility," his communications officer reported.

"What?" Nico bellowed. He flung himself out of his captain's chair and began pacing back and forth between his crew's stations. His chest heaved against his tight uniform, and he balled his hands into fists. He felt claustrophobic and hamstrung.

"Thirty-six antimatter pellets were stolen by a man later identified from security footage as Aaron Granger."

"Do we know who he is and where he came from?" Nico asked.

"He was Captain Carter's Science Officer onboard the *Fates' Winds*. He has a son in the intelligence service."

Nico stopped and pulled at his jet black beard thoughtfully.

"That's how Carter made his jumps, Jansen. He must have captured one of the Alcubierre drives from Captain Decival's fleet and installed it on the Bwain ship," Nico said, his eyes narrowing as he considered the possibilities.

"Sir," Jansen interjected. "May I point out that Captain Carter has stated on more than one occasion that Decival has joined him to combat the new threat that Capra Falconi recorded in the Sword Belt?"

Nico spun and glared at Jansen. The admiral had stoked the flames of rebellion on Earth by painting Kidewange as weak in the face of the combined threat from Carter and the Bwain. It had been Kidewange who had urged caution, who'd demanded that Nico send a messenger to the Sword Belt to assess the true tactical situation. Capra Falconi had returned with warnings of a new alien species that seemed capable of far greater damage, and Carter had repeated those warnings, but it was clear from Falconi's dalliances with the reporter, Lana Delgato, that both men had been co-conspirators. Now he found himself wondering whether or not there were even more traitors among his officers.

"What are you suggesting, Jansen?" Nico asked. His tone of voice was a clear warning to everyone on the ship's bridge.

"What I'm suggesting is that with this unknown threat out there, and Carter's large stockpile of antimatter, the tactical situation has changed considerably. We may need to re-evaluate our threat response."

"Our mission is to destroy the Bwain and kill the traitor Atlas Carter!"

Nico shouted. "Is that clear?"

The captain was a good officer. She did not back down from Nico's humiliated rage.

"Sir, may I ask you to consider the possibility that Carter may be headed toward Earth to repeat his message even as we speak. With our strength reduced, he may have far better luck engendering fear in the populace than he would have had otherwise."

Nico stilled once more, considering Jansen's point. Carter's motives were at the heart of things, weren't they? The disgraced officer had tried to come back to SSC space after his betrayal and bargain, bringing tales of powerful aliens that, as much as Nico hated to admit it, looked as if they were true.

With a jerk, he turned back to his station and pulled up the recordings that Falconi had brought back from the Sword Belt. The newly discovered creatures were monstrous, gibbering white shapes that seemed as if they'd been assembled from a nightmare menagerie of sea creatures and insects. As Nico watched the images, the aliens dove into the planets of the Sword Belt, somehow absorbing the planets' matter into their own bodies, and through this process, they grew larger and more powerful than before.

Power was always the key. It was what separated men like Carter from men like Nico. Atlas Carter had come begging for Nico's help against these creatures, and if he was indeed making a run for the Earth, he'd soon come to realize that the help he was requesting would only come on Nico's terms.

"Set course for Earth orbit," Nico ordered. "We'll make our jump within the hour and leave the damaged vessels here for repairs."

"And your orders on arrival, sir?"

"We'll form a defensive perimeter. Jansen, you'll take command of the *Ninkovich* while I go to Johannesburg. I need to speak with my cabinet about this new threat."

*   *   *

Johannesburg, South Africa
The Office of the Galactic President

Phuri had always been able to read the desires of power. He'd begun life in the slums of Mumbai as a frail, malnourished boy, and had learned to survive by his wits. Over time, his petty thievery turned into the smuggling of various goods. He had a gift when it came to knowing when a customs officer would take a bribe, or when a politician would yield to pressure and order a crackdown. His skill at manipulating greed and fear had taken him from South Asia's backwaters, all the way to Latin America, where the connections he'd made with the *Narcos* had helped fund the campaign of Galactic Senator Sickyl Tannin. The plan had been to one day install Tannin as Galactic President. Unfortunately, Sickyl had proven to be a less than stellar partner in the scheme, and got them both cast into exile in the Sword Belt. There, trapped on Gertie, Phuri had bided his time.

When Phuri finally returned to Earth by tricking the SSC into thinking that Atlas Carter was a threat to its existence, he'd had only one choice if he wanted to regain the small amount of power and status he once held. He needed to turn his lie about Carter into the truth, but spreading that much misinformation required a heavy budget. It was only now that he'd been able to elevate Admiral Nico to the presidency that he was realizing the true extent of the debt he'd incurred with the *Narcos* who'd funded the coup. To make things worse, the *Narcos'* leader, a man called Cazador, was proving to be a much stronger adversary than he'd bargained for.

"What do you think these people's drug of choice is, eh?" the Belizean asked. Cazador was standing at the window of the Presidential Tower in the suite that had formerly belonged to Nico's predecessor, Nelson Kidewange. Two other *Narco* thugs flanked the man, saying little, but keeping their hands close to the knives and plasma pistols they wore at their belts.

"You'll get access to this market soon enough," Phuri assured him. "We need to begin the meeting with…"

"You know, *mijo*, you hold these meetings, but you rarely discuss anything of interest," Cazador noted casually.

"If you'd let me know which terms of our agreement you'd like to revise, I could have a more substantive discussion with you elsewhere at a later date, but not here," Phuri whispered as he glanced behind him at the SSC officers and senatorial aides who filled the room. They'd arrived at his request for an erstwhile planning session to discuss rooting out Kidewange's last loyalists from the upper echelons of the senate and navy. Cazador had not been invited, but had insisted on attending, and Phuri had spent most of the night worrying about what else Cazador wanted from him beyond repayments from the Galactic treasury at a generous interest rate.

"You may get your wish," Cazador said.

Phuri paled, nervous now about the true reason for Cazador's visit. He'd thought that the smugglers and criminals he'd dealt with his whole life had shown him all forms of greed and desire a man could possess, but this Cazador was somehow different. He had no overt need for money, or power, or drugs, or any of the levers that Phuri knew how to pull. A man who needed nothing and who had nothing to lose was by far the most dangerous to deal with. Now, and not for the first time, Phuri wondered who was manipulating whom in their arrangement.

"Mr. Vongsa, we're ready to start," an aide said.

"Ah, good. By all means," Cazador said in reply, although the comment was not addressed to him.

Phuri sighed, then turned to face the room.

"Ladies and gentlemen. No doubt you're wondering what the admiral's new government will look like, how it will integrate with civilian authority, and when martial law will end. This will come as soon as the Bwain threat we face is completely eliminated and the Earth's safety has been ensured."

"With all due respect, the intelligence we've seen doesn't point to the same conclusions you've been feeding us," the acting trade minister responded as she glanced down at her notes. An SSC captain added his voice in agreement.

"She's right. I've seen the footage of these new aliens that the messenger ship captured in the Sword Belt. That threat is several orders of magnitude higher than one defector on a Bwain ship."

"Is Carter even really a defector? We've heard rumors that he was trying to make peace before Nico launched his strike." The colonial administrator was not fully convinced, and his voice reflected the doubt many in the room seemed to share.

"Now I can assure all of you that...," Phuri began, but he was quickly interrupted.

"Shhhhhh...," Cazador sounded as he held a finger to his lips.

Several of the attendees stiffened in shock as Cazador turned to face the room. It had taken Phuri himself a long time to steel himself against the man's appearance, and he sympathized with their reaction. Wrinkled knots of scar tissue cut down from Cazador's temple along the left side of his face before disappearing into his light-tan suit. The man's left hand seemed formed from raw muscle, and he stared at the room from one brown eye and a second that was clouded and useless from the burns that had wrecked his body. Cazador could have hidden his wounds. He could have had his skin repaired, his eye regrown, but he had chosen not to, and that fact alone was enough to give pause to those who encountered him.

"Who is this man?" another officer asked bluntly as hushed murmurs filled the room. "Nico informed all of us that we were only to trust those who he introduced to us personally."

"Allow me to introduce myself. I'm the man who's funding your new government, and I'm here today because I have questions about the way you conduct your business," Cazador said rather casually. What he lacked in appearance, he more than made up for with deadly confidence.

Nervous laughter filled the room. These were men who'd spent their lives navigating the currents of power after all, so what did they have to fear from some petty drug dealer?

"And what's that supposed to mean?" the officer in charge of Earth's outer defenses asked. "You want a higher price for cocaine?"

"Your Admiral Nico put up very little resistance to this Carter fellow, no?"

Phuri pinched the bridge of his nose. Cazador was revealing that he had access to classified SSC intelligence data, which destroyed any illusion he'd tried to maintain of having an informational advantage over the man. Thankfully, no one offered any reply.

"Judging by your silence, I assume that we're agreed on that fact," Cazador said, pausing for a moment to let that particular realization sink in a little. "So Carter, a man who our friend Phuri here has told us is a traitor, a man who was exiled for gross dereliction of duty, was able to single-handedly take on the most hardened fleet we had to offer...and he defeated them as though they were mere flies to be swatted away on a summer day. If he hadn't suddenly decided to retreat for some reason known only to him, then there's no telling how much damage he could have done."

Silence filled the suite. Even though many of the officers in the room were newly installed to their posts, they did not like being humiliated in this fashion. Phuri needed to move the meeting along.

"Where are you going with this?" Phuri asked.

Cazador smiled. Though the side of his face that remained intact could have been considered handsome, the only thing those in the room could focus on was the grotesque pulling of the misshapen skin under his dead eye.

"I am very glad you asked, *mijo*. Because in exchange for the continued funding of this government, my associates and I would like to be given the weapons Carter possesses," Cazador said evenly.

"That's preposterous," an officer cried out.

"SSC intelligence and scientists will recover and study the weaponry to improve the fleet," another said.

While arguments flew around the room, Phuri realized just how badly he'd miscalculated Cazador. The man wasn't content to simply gain the ability to ship drugs beyond Earth for the *Narcos*. He was thinking much, much bigger. While Phuri's plan all along had been to supplant Admiral Nico's brutality with a more pliable president at the first opportunity, he'd never factored in having to counter Cazador as well.

"This is a new era, where we will be open and transparent about exactly who we are, and exactly how we make decisions," Cazador shouted to the assemblage. "I leave nothing behind the curtain, and I expect the same in return. We deal straight with one another, and things will go well."

One of furious officers screamed at Phuri. "This wasn't what you promised us! When the admiral arrives..."

"Your admiral was beaten by a single Bwain ship," Cazador interjected. "It's better to think about who is truly strong among you."

"I think we all know what real strength is, and we know exactly who you are," the trade minister said.

"Good. Because I'm the man who taught Atlas Carter how to fight," Cazador's said as his expression suddenly turned deadly serious, and he glared hard at them with his one remaining eye.

* * *

LaGrange Station Alpha
Outside of the Moon's orbit

"Ms. Delgato, is there gonna be a war?" one of the students asked.

Lana was pacing the small living quarters of the SSC's gravity research station. The cramped habitat module held a few couches and chairs positioned around a circular holotable that doubled as a dining area, with a set of beanbag chairs and ten decorated hatches that led to each graduate student's private quarters. The module could have been a grad school dorm anywhere on Earth, except for the large electroglass window at one end that provided the room with an incredible view of the moon. She could have spent hours studying the gray and black beauty of its cratered surface, but instead she paced while her reporter's mind tried to understand what she'd just experienced.

"You're sure it's not a weapon? You're not lying?" she asked.

"No, it's not," a different student answered. This one's name was Hansel, a Swedish post-grad studying physics. She could only remember his name because he was pale blonde to the point where he almost seemed like some sort of an albino, and he looked perfectly at home on a space station away from any sunlight.

"The gravity drive was just a prototype propulsion system. It's built on the concept of an SSC inducer, which uses quantum fluctuation to generate thrust. We tuned the drive to only be able to generate thrust by producing gravitons, which react against the gravitational fabric of the universe and generate a thrust greater than any other sub-light-speed method of travel."

"It's the first time anyone's ever been able to generate gravitons. The gravitons are incredibly hard to isolate, and...," another girl added, but then she trailed off when it seemed that Lana was not really interested in hearing more.

Lana had been introduced to her earlier, but she couldn't remember the girl's name. They kept speaking in technicalities about their experiments and completely missing the point she was trying to make, which frustrated her to no end.

"That doesn't matter right now," Lana said impatiently.

"It does," Hansel said quickly. "Until our class no one had been able to..."

"No, it's *you* who doesn't understand," Lana said firmly, cutting him off before he could launch into their grandiose list of accomplishments. "The real question is, why did Carter want your experiment so badly that he sent Pandith and the Bwain here to hold us all at gunpoint until you handed over the gravity drive?"

"Because he's at war with the SSC?" one of the students offered.

"But that's the thing. He's not at war with them. Pandith said that the Bwain have masters, and that they're back now," Lana said as she returned to her original question. "That has to be why they want the gravity drive."

"But gravity isn't a weapon. It's a physical law," Hansel said.

"I think you're right," Lana said, as she continued to pace and think out loud. "Carter doesn't want a war at all, but the SSC has to have one. It's the only way that they can justify the coup against President Kidewange, and Admiral Nico taking his place. It's why Pandith had to sneak all the way here, and why he had to have the Bwain with him. Whatever they're doing, the SSC won't help them."

"Our project is due in two weeks. If we don't get it back, we'll all be flunked," Hansel said as he single-mindedly continued to focus on the missing gravity drive that they'd all worked so hard on.

"I'm sure there's a clause in our tuition contract for acts of theft," another student answered.

"So, is there gonna be a war?" the girl asked again.

"Not if we can stop it," Lana said.

"But even if what that Pandith guy said was true, what would we be able to do about it?" Hansel asked.

That was what Lana was trying to figure out. She'd simply been a reporter looking to do background research on Majorana particles when she'd stumbled onto the conspiracy against Atlas Carter. Phuri's thugs had been pursuing her on Earth ever since she'd started looking into Aaron Granger's Majorana research. It's how she had come across Ensign Capra Falconi, the messenger who'd revealed that all was not as it seemed in the SSC's propaganda against Captain Carter. And, before he'd stolen the gravity drive, Pandith had given her even more hints of the truth.

Whatever was happening outside of Station Alpha, the story was as big as the universe, and she was stuck here. Unless...

"Where's your shuttle? Can any one of you fly it?" she asked, the excitement causing her voice to rise.

"Yeah, we can," Hansel said. "But uhhh..."

"But what?" she cried. "We need to get back to Earth. Let's go, where's the airlock?"

"That Pandith guy stole our shuttle," the girl informed her. Lana stared at her blankly for a moment as her momentary excitement suddenly faded.

"The next supply shuttle will be here in a week," another student offered.

"A week! Whatever's happening out there will be six days over by then!" Lana nearly shouted.

"We could send a distress call," the girl suggested. "There's a big base on Luna. The SSC would be here in a few hours."

"The SSC are the last people we want to see right now. They'll arrest all of us without even thinking." Lana's mind raced as she tried to find some kind of solution.

"They wouldn't do that. They couldn't," Hansel protested naïvely.

For a moment, Lana thought of Captain Agricourt, her first informant, and wondered what had happened to him. Phuri had undoubtedly disposed of him, just like so many others she'd never hear about.

"Yes, they will," Lana said firmly. Her voice indicated there was no room for doubt. "What kind of broadcasting facilities do you have here?"

"They're pretty limited," one of the other students replied. We've got laser to the Earth and Moon, but other than that, just low-power antennas."

"It'll have to be good enough," Lana mused.

"Good enough for what?" one of the students asked.

"Good enough to tell the truth."

* * *

SSC Galactic Headquarters
Cape Canaveral, Florida

The driver who took Admiral Nico down the steeply sloping tunnel that ran beneath the waters of the SSC headquarters on Cape Canaveral had been trained to ask no questions and observe nothing. Lights flashed by every six meters, illuminating the four lanes of the massive concrete silo in which she spent the majority of her waking life. She noted the various branches that led to the upper levels with their numerous offices and research facilities, and the elevators that led to classified launch platforms that rose from the sea only at night. At the deepest level, protected even from a planetary bombardment, were the intelligence, command and control facilities. The driver kept her hands on the steering wheel at the positions of 10 a.m. and 2 p.m. Her eyes never left the road, and yet somewhere beneath all the discipline, she was worried.

The rumors that had come with the return of the admiral's fleet were devastating. Atlas Carter had damaged fully a quarter of the admiral's ships without taking any casualties in return. Even worse were the whispers that the fight against Carter had become personal. Messengers hinted that Nico was ignoring a new, larger threat in order to pursue his vendetta against the rogue captain.

"So what have you heard in the Cape lately?" Nico asked, his deep voice dragging the driver's attention back into focus.

"Sir?" she asked. She'd been popping her ears to equalize the pressure as they passed two miles underground. The air here was warm and humid, a constant reminder of the massive weight of the ocean above. She needed time to think. Nico was legendary for both his rash temper and his ruthlessness. His eyes smoldered in the dim light now, as if probing her loyalty on the spot, and she needed to give him the proper answer.

"Come now, you must have some sense of the people's mood," Nico continued.

"I'm afraid I don't get topside very often. We aren't permitted to communicate with anyone but our superiors while on duty," she said carefully. It was a lie, mixed with the truth. She'd been going topside multiple times a day, and while she only interacted with military personnel, she did still hear the whispers about what was going on.

"Well, your adherence to your duty is admirable," Nico said, but she couldn't tell if his response was sarcastic or sincere.

When she glanced in the rearview mirror, Nico was crushing an empty water bottle in his hand. The admiral wore a pistol at his hip, as if he was standing at permanent battle stations, and his chest heaved with each breath, almost like an animal that was readying itself for the kill.

After they came to a stop at the executive lift, she exited the vehicle and moved quickly to open Nico's door as the honor guard that lined the approach to the elevator snapped to attention.

"I think you'll do quite well, sir," she said, but then she closed her eyes in a flicker of embarrassment. It was against protocol for a driver to speak at all. When she opened her eyes a moment later, she found Nico standing beside her, smiling. His heavy brow loomed over his face, casting all but his teeth in shadow.

"The key to being a good hunter is to show no mercy. Always remember that," he said.

"Yes sir, I will," she said as she took a step back and snapped him a salute, which he casually returned before he turned and strode through the lines of marines that led to the elevator.

* * *

Phuri savored the anger boiling on Nico's face. It was comforting to know that among all the members of his conspiracy at least Nico remained predictable. The admiral stood in the doorway of his private quarters, processing the fact that he'd found Phuri waiting for him in an area that was supposed to have been off limits.

"You!" Nico growled as he stalked forward, grasping for Phuri's throat. Phuri backed away until he knocked into a bar filled with glittering bottles of Russian vodka. His hands rose to his throat to prevent the bigger man from choking him, but they were no match for Nico's strength. Nico clamped down on his neck like a vise, driving him backward against the bar.

"Admiral, your heroism is being broadcast across the planet," Phuri panted.

"You told me to engage Carter!" Nico yelled in his rage. "You told me that it was an important show of strength, and that the battle would be over quickly. You wanted me humiliated!"

Lifting Phuri up by the jaw, Nico slammed him backward onto the bar top. Bottles crashed down around him, shattering, and the clear musk of vodka filled the air. Feeling his own fingers crushing against his throat, Phuri choked out his next words.

"The battle...went ill...but our plan...has worked," Phuri gasped.

The realization seemed to clear away the bloom of Nico's anger. Just as Phuri's vision began to narrow, the big admiral released him. Phuri slumped down onto the bar top gasping. He'd known what Nico would do. The admiral had needed to take out his anger at the embarrassment he'd been subjected to, and now he would be pliable for what Phuri needed.

"I came here to tell you that you're still the president of the Galactic Senate, and High Admiral of Sol Space Command, no matter what happened in your engagement with Carter," he said as he rubbed at his throat, fighting against its stiffness.

"So you're saying that I should still trust you after all this?" Nico sneered.

Phuri slipped gingerly down to the concrete floor. Glass crunched underneath his boots.

"I'm saying you should trust the people, those in the senate who are supporting you, and your officers and backers."

"Yes, this Cazador...your friend from the shadows. He left me a message on my private exchange, which no one has access to. Who is this man?"

"He's the one who funded our efforts," Phuri answered as he continued to massage his throat.

"And where does his money come from?"

"Smuggling. Narcotics from South America mostly," Phuri explained. An inquisitive look settled on Nico's face as he studied his aide.

"Another of Carter's enemies then?"

"You could say that," Phuri said. He knew that getting Nico to calm down and talk was key to restoring some semblance of control. "Cazador was the man who secured Carter's oath not to intervene when the *Narcos'* army took Belize city."

Nico's heavy eyebrows rose.

"That was why we court-martialed Carter," he realized. "I'd never heard this part of the story."

"Cazador had bought off Carter's under-officers, but Carter himself had command of the SSC forces off of the city's coast and couldn't be bought, so Cazador kidnapped Carter's wife Aída and forced Carter to do nothing while his home city fell."

Nico rubbed the thick beard at his jaw, considering what he'd just learned.

"I think I might just like this man after all, and after what happened at Pluto, it looks like the *Narcos* can be of some use to us. Carter is well armed, with a fleet's worth of antimatter at his disposal. He could strike anywhere."

"Thanks to Cazador, we have an unlimited war chest, and I have no doubt that you're up to the challenge of finding and eliminating Carter," Phuri replied in a voice long accustomed to placating men with large egos and narrow focus.

"When the time comes, I will crush Carter like an insect," Nico said through gritted teeth. "As for right now, my place is here. We need to consolidate power to prepare for these new Bwain weapons."

Phuri bit his lip as the gears of his mind started spinning. Without a counterbalance to Cazador, the calculus of power in the government would swing irrevocably toward the *Narcos*. With Nico's temper, it was only a matter of time until either he or Cazador moved against the other. If he could just locate Carter, and perhaps get a message to the man that his old nemesis Cazador had returned, perhaps he'd be able to tip the scales to his own advantage.

"May I offer a suggestion?" Phuri asked.

"Speak," Nico said, cocking his eyebrow at the much smaller man.

"We came to power through fear, and that fear will remain as long as Carter is at large. The people will want action. They'll want you to find him and kill him."

"You're a fool, Phuri. I don't have the antimatter to waste searching the entire galaxy."

"Think of the prestige though! You'd be a hero for generations."

Nico resumed stroking his beard as he considered Phuri's suggestion. The man's immense ego was such an easy lever to pull that Phuri felt a momentary pang of embarrassment for him.

"This Cazador...he could fund the production of more antimatter, couldn't he?" Nico asked.

"Of course, Admiral. Anything you'd require."

"Then maybe the people's wish will be granted. I want to meet this Cazador person. Take me to him, but I'm warning you Phuri," he growled as he stepped closer to the small man once more. "I put very little trust in you, and I will trust him even less. If either of you try to supplant me, I will break you with my bare hands."

Phuri put on an act of protest as Nico swept him out of his quarters and toward the lift, but he had to fight to keep his satisfaction from breaking through to reveal itself on his face. Nico would bring him to Carter, and Carter would eliminate Cazador. Then, when all was said and done, Phuri would stand alone in his rightful place.

Poor Nico. He'd never learn that his predictability meant that he could be controlled, and that control was the key to power.

Chapter Two

SSC Cruiser Tranquility
Drifting in unexplored space near a gravity anomaly
1,340 light years from Earth

The First One that tore through the *Tranquility's* hull and breached Captain Mephista's bridge was enormous. Its skin pulsed against the blackness of space with a cold white light, and dozens of mouths ringed its head, opening to bare teeth that wriggled like centipede legs as the creature consumed the decompressing atmosphere. One of the beast's tentacles dissolved the hull above her, exposing her crew to the black void of space. Mephista was flung upward toward the creature in the force caused by the decompression, and then quickly jerked to a stop, saved for the moment by the tether that connected her EVO suit to the captain's chair on the bridge.

"Aft decks are compromised!" a panicked voice reported through her implant. "They've breached...aaaghh!"

"...inoperable. The Bwain are dying!" another voice screamed.

Mephista rolled to face the creature that was destroying her ship. The First Ones were nightmarish, shape-shifting aliens drawn from another dimension to consume the universe's matter. She'd once dared to hope that they had a chance to fight them, but now as she stared into the thousand slavering eyes of the creature above her, she knew that she'd been mistaken.

Her helmsman's tether suddenly snapped, and he flew screaming toward the First One's ravenous white flesh. The restraints had been designed for antigravity situations, not explosive depressurizations. They'd only hold for so long. When his suit impacted the creature, it seemed for a moment as if the nav officer was still there in flashbulb silhouette before he instantly dissolved. A thin web of what had once been a human being wrinkled across the disgusting creature's skin while it eagerly continued to pull itself closer to the rest of her crew.

Mephista had spent half her life crippled after escaping a Bwain attack in a damaged EVO suit, and as the *Tranquility* collapsed around her, she felt the void pulling at her once more.

"Weapons systems are offline!" another doomed member of the fleet cried.

"Mayday! Mayday! This is the *Maru*. We have lost all propulsion. We are dead in space and abandoning..."

"Captain, I'm coming for you! Don't you give up!"

Something pounded against the arm of her EVO suit. One of the Bwain was clinging to the railing beside her. The bird-like aliens had begun as enemies but quickly turned into humanity's allies in the fight against the First Ones. More importantly, they were Mephista's only link to talk to Carter. He was able to communicate to the creatures telepathically, and had stationed them on the human ships to act as his personal radio communications system.

This Bwain, seconds from death, was trying to tell her something, doing its best to mouth English syllables through its beak. The aliens were best described as feathered dinosaurs. They were small lizard-like creatures covered with chameleon-like feathers, ending at a neck that somewhat resembled that of a turkey vulture. They were grotesque enough without decompression. Exposed to the vacuum, the creature's scale-feathered skin sizzled as the pressure of the fluids in its body tried to equalize with the void of space.

"I don't understand!" Mephista cried.

The Bwain held on, its beak and purple tongue still working, desperate to make itself understood, but there was no air between them for sound, no lips to read. Mephista found herself growing more and more angry at this waste of life, and at Carter who had abandoned both her and the fleet when they needed him the most.

"Where are you?" she demanded. "Where are you, you son-of-a-bitch?"

The poor alien's eyes ruptured first. Vitreous fluid crystallized instantly and flowed upward toward the First One. Its skin then split down its fingers. A froth of blood lifted from its muscles, and then froze. The creature was convulsing, boiling and freezing at the same time. It's bloody grip finally, mercifully, loosened, and the alien slipped upward to join the body of one of its former masters.

Long ago, the First Ones had discovered the Bwain and made the creatures their slaves. She had no idea how long either the Bwain or the First Ones lived, and she wondered if the First One gibbering above her had any memory at all of its latest meal.

All around her, holoscreens still flickered with their automatic reports. Members of her crew were triggering their suit inducers, trying to get through the airlock and away from the First One. The *Tranquility* clung to its last shreds of momentary life, but it was a fool's hope.

That was her last thought as she stared into the hideous face of the First One. It was a bloody mess, flashing red and pink before her. She pulled her plasma pistol from the holster at her side, and then reached for the latch of her tether. If she was going to die, then at least she'd die fighting. It was all she'd ever been good at.

"I'm sorry Atlas. I wish things could have been different for us," she said as she flew upward from her dying bridge.

* * *

The Dauntless
Refugee fleet flagship

"I don't care about my safety, damn it!" Hal Yellowknife bellowed to the young SSC marine blocking the cargo hold's exit. "I need to get up to that damn shuttle bay and see what the hell's goin' on up there!"

"I'm sorry, but I'm under orders to keep all civilians in the hold, and…" the boy began, as if reciting a lesson in one of the SSC's academic classes.

"Son, don't you know there's a war on?"

"But if we're attacked, there could be a depressurization event, and…" the marine reasoned, but Hal wouldn't back down.

"If we're attacked, then we're gonna fight back, and we're gonna use the weapons that *my* factories built, so I need to get the hell up there and see how we're doin'," Hal growled with frustration.

The boy was using his combat EVO suit to block the cargo hold's exit. He was maybe eighteen or nineteen years old, and slightly green from the constant shifts in the ship's trajectory as the *Dauntless'* evasive maneuvers flung the helpless civilians all around the deck. At least five-hundred of them were crammed in the hold with Hal, all of them refugees from the colony planet Gertie. They were tired, dirty, and scared, and the one thing they needed right now more than anything was just a small glimmer of hope.

The ship lurched to the left, and then quickly to the right. Hal widened his stance and stayed on his feet while everyone around him tumbled. Danielle Hoff, the fleet's navigation officer, must have been desperate to avoid the First Ones. She was throwing the ship into maneuvers without regard to its passengers and crew. Years of stumbling home drunk had given Hal an uncanny sense of balance, and the motion sickness that was debilitating those around him barely registered with him. He had a job to do, and come hell or high water, he was going to do it.

The marine blocking his path suddenly slapped his hand over his mouth, and then his eyes widened for just a quick moment before he bent over and puked all over the deck.

"Don't worry son, you'll get your sea legs someday," Hal said, patting the boy's back in sympathy as he passed by him and left the cargo hold.

"Mr. Yellowknife!" the marine managed to call out before he turned away and puked once again.

"I'm not goin' back in there, so don't even bother with all that crap about orders," Hal said without turning back as he hurried down the corridor. "I need to get to my factories!"

As the colony engineer for the Sword Belt, Hal had been in charge of the nanofactories that made colonial life possible. The factories collected raw materials using a fleet of microscopic robots programmed to harvest raw materials at the molecular level. The material those robots brought back was sorted for assembly in 3-D printing stations that could manufacture everything from a pair of socks to repair parts for an orbital cruiser...if they were provided with the right component molecules. Captain Carter had enough foresight to transport Hal's factories from Gertie to the fleet before the First Ones came. Thanks to a little telepathic intervention from the Bwain, those factories were now converting waste and spare parts into weapons that could fight the First Ones. Hal needed to know how those weapons were performing, and if the fleet needed more, then he'd make more, and that was all there was to it.

"Hal!" a voice said as an arm clamped down on his shoulder.

Angry, Hal turned, ready to punch the young marine. Instead, he found his assistant Kilver clinging to him. The boy was green-faced, just as motion sick as the others were, but he'd gamely followed Hal down the corridor. Kilver had been a farmer on Gertie before Tannin's militia had killed his parents. With no one else to turn to, he'd attached himself to Hal, and he quickly proved himself to be a natural engineer. Without Kilver, the fleet wouldn't have even half the supplies that it currently had.

"You sure you're gonna be ok?" Hal asked with a look of concern.

His assistant tried to straighten to his full height just as the ship veered to starboard. He and Hal both flew into the side of the bulkhead. Somehow, Hal managed to stay on his feet, but Kilver fell down to his knees beside him.

"I guess it doesn't matter," Hal said as he lifted his assistant back to his feet. "Come on kid, we got someplace we need to be, and we're runnin' outta time."

Red lights indicating battle stations flashed in the hallways as they jogged down the corridor and through bulkheads to get to the shuttle bay. Hal had stationed the *Dauntless'* factories in the ship's main shuttle bay in order to easily process any asteroids or other material that could be harvested, although the fleet hadn't had time to collect any materials before the First Ones arrived.

"So, what's the plan? How are we gonna get the weapons to the other ships?" Kilver asked. Even though there was fear in his voice, there was also an eagerness to get the job done, regardless of his own discomfort.

Hal slowed down for a moment. He had never been good with planning ahead, and up to now he'd been focused exclusively on getting to the factories. Glancing around, he found a storage locker and thumbed it open. Rifling through the contents, he dug out a radio and keyed the transmitter as they continued on toward the shuttle bay.

"Danny Xiao, do you read me? Danny, it's Hal," he called.

Static and shouting flowed from the speaker:

"...all around me. Need to..."

"Mayday! Mayday! This is the *Excelsior*. We have lost propulsion. Need immediate..."

"My Bwain are dying over here! Where the hell is Carter?"

Hal tried not to notice Kilver's grim look as they neared the shuttle bay. It was the same worry that gnawed at him now as well. Despite their best efforts, there might not be anything they could do to save their friends.

They cycled through an airlock into the *Dauntless'* massive shuttle bay. The hold had been designed to carry close to a hundred tender craft for a larger fleet, and yet it was largely empty. The plan to defend the fleet had been to use the Bwain weapons Hal's factories had produced and mount the devices on the fleet's shuttles, to keep the First Ones away from the civilians on the larger ships. Now, though, every single small craft that could fly was out in space. From the chatter on the radio, it didn't sound like it was going well at all. For the moment, all he could do was to get back to work on cranking out weapons to fight those things.

His factories were tucked in the near corner of the bay, four gray rectangles two meters high and ten deep that housed the fusing apparatus that printed whatever Hal programmed. Beside the printing stations, what looked like a mountain of sand littered the floor. This was a mix of carbyne steel, plastic, precious metals, and other resources scavenged by his nanobots.

Ever since Captain Carter had somehow triggered the *Bwainhome* to intervene in Hal's production, his factories hadn't needed those materials to complete their production tasks. The dimensional weapons the devices now produced looked like some sort of a strange undersea coral, and for all Hal could tell, the raw materials were being culled from some other dimension on a quantum level. The conveyors leading out of the factories were full of the strange glittering things.

"My god Kilver, there's hundreds of 'em!" Hal exclaimed.

"Looks like they've been busy," Kilver replied as he took it all in.

"We need to get the next wave of shuttles prepped," Hal said as he pushed the radio toward Kilver. "Here, use this and find Danny. We need to..."

"Hal...," Kilver said as he stared in shock toward the bay's clear electroglass barriers.

Hal turned to see what he was looking at, and he blanched visibly at what he saw. The devastation that was going on outside the ship was absolutely staggering. Pieces of shuttles and ships littered the space all around them. A fine mist of gasses and leaking atmosphere seemed to spread like a small nebula between those ships that were still operating under their own power.

"Oh my god," Hal muttered as an icy chill ran down his spine. The scale of the destruction was incredible. Somehow, the *Dauntless* had survived, at least for now, but the fleet had been utterly devastated. Speechless, he stood and watched the disgusting shapes of the First Ones weaving their way through the battle.

"Are we gonna die out here?" Kilver asked.

Hal squinted, seeing shuttles and human ships in pursuit.

"I don't know kid, but we're sure as hell not gonna go down without a fight," Hal promised. "Come on, we've got work to do."

* * *

The Bwain were dying, and Lieutenant Bryon Purcell was killing them. One by one the creatures slumped out of the copilot's seat beside him and crumpled to the deck as he piloted his shuttle through the battle between the overmatched refugee fleet and the First Ones. The strange dimensional weapons that the *Bwainhome* had built for the fleet could only be fired through the Bwain's telepathic abilities. Through some psychic resistance or mental warfare on the part of the First Ones, every five or six shots from the shimmering glass stalactites mounted to the nose of his shuttle were fatal to his copilots.

The Bwain had been cultivated to be the First Ones' slaves for billions of years. Fighting their masters did not come easily, and they were giving their lives en masse for a chance at freedom. Their sacrifice was in its own way an act of courage, but for a weapons officer who could put none of his training to use, it was also agony to sacrifice others for something he should have been able to do himself.

"There, right there," he said as he pointed through his shuttle's electroglass.

The target was a smaller First One that could have been a mix between a jellyfish and some kind of enormous grasping octopus. It had shot out a proboscis to feast on a disabled shuttle, and as the Bwain unleashed another shot from the alien weapon, it sent out a stream of multicolored energy directly at the creature's head.

The shot struck the First One square in the center of its mouth. For just a brief moment, nothing happened, but then the First One suddenly flashed a series of wounded colors. It reared back from its meal, seeming almost to cough, and then began folding in on itself. As it shrank and shuddered, other First Ones swept toward it. Instead of providing aid to it however, they tore its weakened form apart before the creature could vanish from existence.

"Jesus, your masters are horrible," Bryon said to the Bwain that was sitting beside him. "New target, dead ahead."

After several seconds, Bryon noticed the weapon had stayed cold. When he glanced over, he found the Bwain slumped in the chair with its head dangling on its scaled chest. The weapons worked incredibly well against the First Ones, but that effectiveness came at a price.

A small gnarled hand pulled the body out of the seat and onto the shuttle deck where it joined four more. The next alien took its seat, and Bryon's odd cannon charged again, but this was his last Bwain. If he was going to keep fighting, he'd have to figure out how to fire the cannon himself. Unfortunately, the way the fight was going up to now, it looked as though he just might have to.

"Mayday! Mayday! This is the *Carpathian*," a desperate navigation officer's voice called through Bryon's earpiece. "We need help. Can anyone get to us in time?"

With only a limited amount of alien weapons available to the fleet, Captains Decival and Mephista had planned to use the armed shuttles as a perimeter to keep the First Ones away from the ships carrying the evacuated civilians for as long as possible. The First Ones had broken through the gravity anomaly in such a mass that they had shredded the humans' defensive perimeter, and even though the First Ones were taking losses, they'd already consumed nearly a third of the fleet.

"Shuttle wing alpha," Bryon called. "Whoever's left, we need to get to the *Carpathian*. It's a refugee ship and...oh no..."

On his holos, Bryon watched as a First One shaped like a blunt shark's snout knifed through the middle of the *Carpathian*. The ship split in two, spilling atmosphere and bodies into the void that the spinning First One swept against itself.

Furious, Bryon punched the console in front of him. Again and again his glove smashed his controls. He was powerless to protect anyone. It'd all been for nothing.

A small leathery hand rested on his forearm. He stared at the Bwain. The aliens were normally quite shy, and this one shocked him. It was almost as if the Bwain was trying to comfort him, when he'd been the one killing them.

"We're gonna die out here, little buddy. I'm so sorry," Bryon said.

He didn't really expect the alien to answer. As a rule they weren't very talkative, but this one seemed suddenly different. It puffed up its chest, and its feathers rippled from the deep blue of the copilot's seat to a green and brown camouflage that was closer to its native coloring.

"That one," the Bwain rasped. The voice didn't sound like the alien's normal speech at all. It spoke as if someone else was trying to talk to him, someone whom he'd thought had abandoned the fleet.

Bryon enlarged his holodisplays to understand the Bwain's target.

"That's the *Tranquility!*" he cried out in shock.

The ship Bryon's shuttle had been assigned to was in tatters. A First One had latched on to its stern and was worming its way forward. Another had sliced through the upper decks, and to his horror he could see the individual bridge crew just meters from being consumed.

"Oh no you don't, you son of a bitch! Not today. Not after all this," Bryon said as he turned the shuttle and sent it streaking toward the battered ship.

* * *

Atlas' Final Approach

The Bwainhome

"Pandith, go," the Bwain standing in his shuttle's hatch croaked.

Had he taken a minute to reflect on it, he would have noticed something strange in the creature's voice. It had spoken with the pain of a struggle, even anguish. Pandith had originally been assigned to the Sword Belt as the *Fates' Winds'* environmental engineer, tasked with maintaining not only the crew's health but also their emotional well-being. Yet, since he'd served under Captain Carter, his empathy had hardened into a focused resolve to keep his friends alive and defeat the First Ones, no matter the cost.

That focus was why he didn't notice the Bwain's struggling voice until the shuttle's hatch was already sealed, and his co-pilot, Aaron Granger, was launching the craft through the strange membrane that kept the void of space outside of the *Bwainhome*'s shuttle bay.

"Something's wrong," Pandith said. Some old instinct caused him to half turn, as if he could see behind the shuttle and back to the *Bwainhome*.

"With what?" Granger asked. "Are the inducers malfunctioning?"

"No, something's wrong with the captain," Pandith said. When he faced forward once more, the carnage before him overwhelmed him, and any worry he'd been feeling for his captain suddenly vanished. The First Ones were shredding the human fleet, consuming shuttles and larger ships in great mouthfuls. Though many of the hideous aliens were being hit by the dimensional weapons, there were far too many creatures to stop them all. Pandith and Granger were piloting the only weapon that could defeat the First Ones, but he didn't know if they had arrived in time.

"Powering up the gravity drive," Pandith called.

On his exterior cameras, the experimental apparatus looked like a ring of

36

eight rocket engines mounted to the rear of an ordinary maintenance shuttle. Aside from the massive inducers at the craft's nose that were designed to counter the gravity drive's thrust, the shuttle Pandith was steering into the midst of the battle could just have easily been a normal craft.

"I'm getting a surge in propulsion. Compensating inducers," Granger reported. His voice seemed steady, but adrenaline was coursing through him as his heart pounded hard in his chest.

Pandith watched the holos as the gravity drive nudged toward the battle. Below and to their left, one of the capital ships was listing badly as a First One with a half-dozen chitinous claws hacked at the ship's exterior. A shuttle angled itself to fire one of Hal's weapons, but the First One lashed out with some kind of studded tail and pierced the tiny craft, absorbing it in seconds.

Something was off here too, and he couldn't put his finger on just what it was until he opened up the drive's throttle. The craft rocketed through the holographic representation of the battle in the blink of an eye.

"Cut the drive! We're going too fast!" Granger practically shouted.

Panicked, Pandith cut power to the *Gravity Drive*. His restraints dug into his shoulders as Granger used the craft's inducers to slow the ship. They'd crossed the entire anomaly in less than a second.

"How the hell are we supposed to aim the drive if it goes that fast?" Pandith asked.

The science officer stared at him, wide-eyed. After the *Fates' Winds'* navigation officer Danielle Hoff had discovered that gravity affected the First Ones, Captain Carter had led them on a desperate stealth mission to steal the experiment and return it to the battle. He had been so caught up in the effort to capture the craft and get back to the fleet, that he hadn't even thought of how to use the engine as a weapon.

"I need to calculate the propulsion force," Granger said.

On his holoscreens, Pandith found a crabbed First One shuddering in their direction.

"It sees us," he whispered. Somehow, a creature without eyes was staring right into Pandith's soul. He felt its lurching hunger, its greed to consume the very molecules that made up his existence.

"Granger, give me maximum induction toward that thing," Pandith said.

"Have you lost your mind?"

"Just do it!"

"You're gonna get us killed!" Granger protested, but then with a grunt he followed Pandith's instructions.

He nudged the *Gravity Drive* back into operation. There was a shuddering as the shuttle compensated, but it was still moving toward the First One. If he could just keep the drive at low power, he could aim its thrust. There was only one problem.

"It's getting closer!" Granger called. "One thousand kilometers and closing."

"How fast do gravitons propagate?" Pandith asked.

"Eight hundred kilometers!"

"How quickly though?"

"I don't know. My field was in Majorana research. I think they propagate at the speed of light though."

Pandith's heart sank. The gravitons should have passed through the First One by now, but so far, nothing had.

"Hey, look! Something's happening!" Granger said excitedly as he leaned a bit closer to the holoscreen.

On their screens, the blurry representation of the crab-like First One had become a mottled red. The creature's skin flickered and peeled back as if it were a marshmallow held too close to a flame.

"It's working!" Pandith cried. "It's working!"

The creature seemed to hesitate at the last moment, realizing that its hunger was killing it, but its flight was too late. As Pandith watched, its shape split apart, collapsing into a wisp of escaping gases.

"We just need to calculate the thrust, and we can sweep every single one of these things away," Granger exclaimed. Already his scientist's mind was making a series of quick analyses of what they'd just seen.

"Attention, all ships," Pandith called out through the comms system. "We're back with the gravity drive, and it works! Just hang in there as best as you can, and we're gonna see what we can do about givin' these bastards a one-way ticket straight back to hell."

* * *

The Dauntless

On board what had once been the flagship of the fleet sent to destroy Captain Carter, Lieutenant Danielle Hoff felt a twinge of hope flicker in her chest. She had been watching the First Ones consume ship after ship of the ragged fleet she'd been assigned to protect, while she desperately tried to keep the civilian ships out of harm's way. Her intense vigil had gone on for so long that, for a moment, Pandith's excitement in her cochlear implant didn't even register.

Then she shifted her gaze from her failed attempts at plotting escape vectors, and saw a tiny shuttle on the main holoscreen with an ungainly ring of what looked like ancient chemical boosters mounted to its rear. The shuttle was sweeping its apparatus in all directions, almost as if it were spinning out of control.

"What's he doing?" Captain Decival's voice rang out above the noise of the chaos around him. "What's going on? Have you sustained damage?"

Danielle checked her instruments.

"No, he hasn't Captain. He's replicating an anomaly," Danielle reported.

"An anomaly? What do you mean?" Decival asked, not taking his eyes off of the main holoscreen for even a second.

"Gravity travels in waves," Danielle explained. "In the anomalies, those waves were propagated by the remnants of former stars, or micro black holes, or any other number of natural phenomena that emit gravitons in all directions. Pandith and Granger are replicating the anomaly by directing their gravitons in all directions."

"So...what? They're basically trying to build us a new anomaly to repel those bastards?" Decival asked.

"That's exactly what they're doing, and it's working too! Look!" the ship's science officer called.

On the holoscreens, the fleet had no formation to speak of at this point, with its shuttles scattered in all directions and its larger cruisers and frigates cycling through evasive maneuvers at their top induction speeds.

Everywhere Danielle looked the creatures were separating from the human ships and pulling away from the battle.

"I don't know what the hell you're doin' but keep on doin' it!" Bryon practically shouted over the comms channel. There was a sense of both hope and elation in his voice that was quickly spreading throughout what was left of the fleet.

"Attention! All fleet ships that are still mobile are hereby ordered to move into a close formation around the gravity drive shuttle. I want all the shuttles that are still active to form a defensive ring around the larger ships, and someone get me a damage report!" Captain Decival ordered, once more sounding like a veteran military commander with years of experience.

"Copy that, Captain," Danielle acknowledged. Using the mental interface that all navigation officers had with the ship's computers, Danielle transmitted courses and final positions to all the ships in the fleet. Less than half were still able to operate under their own power, but at least they had survived the assault, and that was what mattered more than anything.

She watched the ships until they had formed a ragged perimeter within Pandith and Granger's protection. The little shuttle was still gyrating in what she could only have imagined was a nausea-inducing spin, but it had saved them. Captain Carter's plan had actually saved them.

"The fleet is secure, sir," she croaked.

A wave of emotion filled her. The pain of the foot she'd lost in the first Bwain attack rose once more up her leg. Exhausted, she let her head drop and studied the protective bulb that the ship's doctors had fixed around her ankle as her new foot regrew, while her eyes quickly blurred with tears of relief.

When she'd first come to the Sword Belt she never thought that she'd have been able to protect anyone, nor had she ever really cared about anyone else. Captain Carter had changed that. She believed in herself now, and she wanted to help. She rubbed the tears away that had been forming in her eyes, and then glanced around for the Bwain that Captain Carter had stationed on every ship.

When she spotted the aliens huddled in a shuddering mass in the corner of the bridge, she got up and limped over toward them.

"Captain?" she asked.

The Bwain had tucked their heads under their wings, and she faced a half-dozen thinly feathered spines. Gingerly, she reached out and shook the bony shoulder of the closest alien.

"Can I speak with Captain Carter?" she asked.

The creature's long neck shifted, and it lifted its stalk-like head to face her. The Bwain's vulture faces were difficult to read, but she thought she saw pain in the creature's glassy eyes.

"Bwainslayer gone," it squawked.

Chapter Three

LaGrange Station Alpha
Outside of the Moon's orbit

Lana fixed her hair as best she could, combing her fingers up under the back of her skull to give herself more volume for the camera. Then she stared into the hololens, smiled her best anchor's smile, and tapped the button to record.

"This is Lana Delgato, reporting from LaGrange Station Alpha in orbit around the moon. What I'm about to tell you may, for some of you, be shocking. To be honest, this is a dangerous story to report, and it may be the only time that you hear from me but..."

Her breath caught as the reality of the risk she was taking started to sink in. She thought of the protestors she'd seen on Earth, the men who had pursued her, and Phuri's oily smile as he had tried to convince her that Nico's government was going to do the right thing. It steeled her resolve, and she quickly rediscovered her voice.

"...but the truth needs to be told, and that truth isn't just that President Kidewange was the victim of a coup. It's that the fear of the Bwain and of Captain Atlas Carter that led to that coup was based on a falsehood."

"I met one of Captain Carter's crew recently. It was a man by the name of Pandith. Captain Carter brought him here to get the gravity drive from this research station, and he could have used the same technology that he used to infiltrate Sol space to launch a crippling blow against the SSC, but he didn't. When Pandith took the gravity drive from this research station, he could have killed me and the students living here, but he didn't."

"You've heard a lot of warmongering, but the truth is that Atlas Carter is working with the Bwain in an effort to protect the Earth. The messenger who took Carter to the Sword Belt, Capra Falconi, never believed that Carter wanted anything more than to do his job. And yes, this man once let his own home city fall to the *Narcos*, but if he was such a threat, then wouldn't he have used his power by now?"

She paused for a moment, thinking once again about everything she knew about the situation.

"Pandith told me that an alien race far more powerful than the Bwain has been discovered in the Sword Belt, and that the struggle to defeat them is so important that humans have joined with the Bwain in order to defeat the new threat, in spite of the SSC going to war against Captain Carter. I have, no way at the present time to verify this information, but I do know that Carter went to extraordinary lengths not to harm the sailors on the first fleet that Nico sent after him."

"So I call on Admiral Nico and all officers in the SSC who are loyal to the Earth to investigate. As for the people of Earth, we are not puppets to be manipulated. We are people who have a say in our government, and it's time that we took up that voice! Demand answers from your leaders. Demand to know what they know, and keep fighting until you discover the truth."

"Thank you. This is Lana Delgato, signing off."

She held her smile for a moment longer, and then toggled off the recording.

"What's gonna happen now?" Hansel asked.

Lana's eyes focused beyond the camera, studying the brilliant whites and grays of the moon.

"I don't know," she said with a heavy sigh. "I guess we'll just have to wait and see, and hope for the best."

* * *

The Fates' Winds
In Orbit around the obelisk
1,339 light years away from Earth

When Aric Keith died on the *Fates' Winds,* he'd almost welcomed his death. He'd been a failure as the ship's temporary captain, and although he'd found some measure of redemption, those past failures would have just continued to haunt him. Unfortunately, the First Ones would not allow death to claim him.

Using the ship's own nanorobotic technology that was originally intended to repair carbyne steel hulls, they reconstructed his body. Electric filaments inside his skull kept his mind functioning, and polymers moved his muscles at the whim of his new masters. Exposed to the void of space, he needed no breath in his lungs, no a tongue to speak, and no eyes to see the obelisk that was hovering out in space near the ruined hull of the ship. Though the First Ones had departed for the moment, he was not permitted to look away from the abominable construction.

The massive, white-gray pillar was a seam torn in space that led to the upper dimensions where the First Ones had made their home for trillions of years after leaving the physical universe. Driven nearly mad by their incorporeal existences and longing for the sense of physical touch, they'd returned to the universe through the obelisk to consume all the matter they could find. They had only kept Aric Keith alive because he had the misfortune to be the engineer on the *Fates Winds,* and possessed the expertise to keep the ship's damaged reactor operating. The obelisk fed on the reactor's radiation, and was slowly growing stronger all the time.

Aric had no idea how long he'd been a slave to the First Ones, but it had been a long while since a new First One had been birthed by the obelisk. A part of him prayed that they'd abandoned him, and that they would soon end his torture completely.

It was one thing for the First Ones to have dominion over his body. They forced the nanobots forming his muscles to move, and he moved with them. When he tried to resist, when he felt their attention slip from him long enough to allow him to pass a word of warning to the fleet, he did so. The First Ones also gave him pain, but he was already dead and had little to fear from pain. He'd thought for a time that he could endure long enough to find some way to sabotage the creatures, but The Ancient, the First Ones' vile leader, had been hiding the full extent of his control.

Too late, Aric had realized that The Ancient was capable of reading the synapses that it had rebuilt. Aric's engineer's mind had drifted to the location of Earth, its defenses, Captain Carter's likely tactics against the First Ones, and numerous other things, and The Ancient had captured every last thought.

When the entire mass of creatures had departed the obelisk at lightning speed, he had no doubt that they were on their way to Earth to consume not only the planet, but the whole solar system. Gradually, as Aric felt The Ancient's mental hold on his muscles diminish, he tested out his partial freedom.

His frozen boot moved a few inches of his own accord. His arms raised and lowered, and he could squat down, grasp the cutting torch fixed to the open locker at his feet. While his initial efforts to move his thumb failed, the nanos eventually did their job. The torch's blue flame sparked, and for a moment he paused with the torch held in front of him, thinking that perhaps he deserved this endless penance for dooming his entire species.

He glanced up at the obelisk a last time, studying its malevolent lightning, and the sickening shimmer of its mucosal whiteness. If this was to be the new order, he would not want to be its slave for millennia like the Bwain.

His ruined lips screamed as he drove the torch into his abdomen and tried to end what semblance of life he still had left.

* * *

Earth

Nico said little on the shuttle from Canaveral to Johannesburg, though the admiral's brooding anger was palpable. Phuri watched the late afternoon shadows crawl through the cabin as day slipped into night. Flashing lights burned alongside of them as the admiral's escort fighters guided them through the darkness. Although his eyes were heavy, Phuri couldn't sleep. If the plan he was considering was going to work, it would require a very careful manipulation of the three most dangerous men he had ever known. Nico's anger would be easily directed into any number of mistakes, but Cazador's intelligence was another matter entirely, and he still had Atlas Carter to deal with as well.

Not for the first time, Phuri wondered if it wouldn't be better to simply lose himself in the obscurity that was offered by the Earth's teaming masses. The funds he'd hidden upon his exile to the Sword Belt remained intact, so if worse came to worst, he could retire to some forgotten corner of the planet with his accumulated wealth and leave the concerns of the planet to bigger men. He had no doubt however that if he did manage to get away, Cazador would hunt him down in order to end any potential threat that he might pose. The place between Phuri's rock and a hard place was growing more and more uncomfortable.

The sunrise over Africa surprised him, breaking over the horizon with a sudden flash as the shuttle descended toward the presidential tower. The grounds that had been filled with thousands of protestors just a few days ago were now only sparsely populated by military personnel. The SSC marines were patrolling a large perimeter around the building, and he couldn't help but wonder if they were under Nico's orders, or Cazador's.

When the shuttle hatch opened, an aide jogged up the ramp, followed by one of Cazador's thugs. The men were easily recognizable. Every one of their tanned scalps were close shaven, and they moved through the heat with the slow prowl of an animal waiting for its time to strike.

"I'd like to get to my quarters," Nico said to the aide. "Inform the Cabinet that we'll need to meet in an hour."

"You need to see the hunter, right away," the thug said.

"That's not what the admiral said. Please move out of the way," Phuri responded as he stepped forward toward the ramp.

Before he saw it coming, he was doubled over from a punch to his stomach. Gagging and breathless, he leaned against the shuttle bulkhead to try and keep his balance while Nico laughed.

"You don't give the orders here," Cazador's enforcer said.

"That *was* a bit harsh, but I'd be lying if I said I hadn't thought about doing it myself," Nico said. "Why don't you tell me what's going on?"

"A reporter that's somehow connected to this weasel has been broadcasting lies about you and Carter. The hunter is not pleased. Come, I'll take you to him."

* * *

They found Cazador in the tower's lecture hall. He was sitting alone, watching a Spanish-accented woman narrate a story about Carter's resistance to the alien threat. Security footage of an SSC officer stealing what looked like a modified shuttle from a small space station was crudely intercut with the video.

"That's Lana Delgato," Phuri noted as they saw the images flash before them.

"Indeed it is," Cazador said without turning around. "You told me you could handle her, and yet here she is on the screen for all to see, not handled at all."

Phuri glared at the man who had sucker-punched him on the shuttle.

"I'm not the one who allowed her to escape Cape Canaveral," he said defensively.

"You should have killed her," Cazador replied.

"That's enough about a reporter," Nico growled. "Why am I here exactly? What's so urgent that I had to see you right this second?"

At the admiral's tone, Cazador stood and turned. He offered a small bow and a smile when Nico gave no reaction to his appearance.

"I believe, Mr. President, that this is the first time we are meeting in person."

"It is, and I'd like to make it the last. Why'd you ask me to meet you here?" Nico demanded once again. He had no desire to exchange pleasantries with this criminal, nor did he wish to be around him any more than was necessary.

"I have a business proposition that I'd like you to consider."

"Phuri mentioned that you'd be willing to fund more antimatter production in exchange for Captain Carter's head."

"Did he?" Cazador asked with a hint of a smile. "Well, it appears that our misguided little friend here doesn't entirely understand my position."

Phuri studied both men, trying to get a read on them. Nico seemed strangely calm. He couldn't predict if the man's anger would erupt unexpectedly, or if he'd developed a new reserve of self-control. As for

Cazador, he seemed almost jovial.

"Then let's hear what you have in mind," Nico said.

"These aliens that Carter is fighting. In exchange for funding your government, I would like access to their technology, but more specifically their weapon technology."

In all his time with the admiral, Phuri had never heard the man laugh, so the deep barking that now emanated from his chest came as a bit of a shock.

Smiling, Nico waved away Cazador's offer and turned to leave.

"You already have your customs inspections waived for off-planet shipments. I will not negotiate on military matters," the admiral said flatly, the mirth already gone from his eyes.

"I see, but what about civilian concerns?" Cazador called as Nico strode towards the doorway.

"The people only want safety. No *Narco* can deliver that," Nico said, spitting out the word with unbridled contempt.

"Perhaps not, but what if we *Narcos* spread this reporter's broadcast, just as we did our lies about Carter? Would it take long for people to question you and your sudden rise to power?"

Nico froze just as he was about to reach the door, and his nostrils flared dangerously as he slowly turned.

"Are you threatening me?" Nico asked as his hand fell to the plasma pistol at his waist. Instantly, a ring of armed men stepped out of the auditorium's shadows with the flat look of men who'd long ago ceased caring about the taking of a life.

"Well, I'm sorry you feel that way, but just so you know...I don't threaten. I do business. Threats are for people who are afraid to get their hands dirty," Cazador explained with a serpent-like smile. Nico stared hard at him for a moment, but Cazador's expression didn't change in the slightest. Most other men would have shown some sign of weakness or uncertainty, but this man showed none at all.

"What do you want?" Nico growled.

"I want you to go to the Sword Belt and bring me back those creatures' weapons. In exchange, I will fund all the antimatter production you require. Give me the ability to ensure that certain promises made to me by your government will remain in effect, and you will never hear from me again."

"So you basically want an insurance policy."

"Well, I am a businessman after all," Cazador protested, spreading his hands outward in a gesture of innocence. "What businessman wouldn't want to reduce the amount of risk in their business dealings. Besides, why would I want to harm my best trading partner?"

"And why would I give you the ability to do so?" Nico asked.

"Admiral...your government will be bankrupt in a week without my assistance? To any reasonable man, I would think that would be enough of a reason," Cazador said far too casually for Nico's liking. "Besides, even if you should turn down my generous offer, it will change nothing for us. We'll continue to do business, just as we always have, and when your government inevitably falls and the world devolves into a state of utter chaos, business will just continue to get better and better without any form of organized government to get in our way."

Nico's good humor was gone, replaced by the fuming anger of a child who'd just lost a game. Phuri was standing there taking it all in, and a chill ran down his spine. Cazador was far more formidable than he'd initially thought, and he'd be absolutely unstoppable unless he could somehow reach Atlas Carter.

"Fine, you have a deal," Nico growled.

"Admiral, we may want to consider remaining...," Phuri cautioned, but Nico didn't want to hear it.

"No tricks this time, Phuri. You're coming with me this time," he growled as he pushed Phuri back up the aisle.

On their way out, he paused to glare at the attendants who opened the entrance to the amphitheater.

"And get someone after that damn reporter!" he snapped.

* * *

LaGrange Station Alpha
Lunar Orbit

When the research station's airlock opened, Lana half-expected to see the two men who had pursued her from Madrid to Florida burst into the habitat. Instead, she was greeted by a group of soldiers in black combat suits with electroglass faceplates that shielded their faces from view. The soldiers fanned out into the habitat module, their plasma rifles crackling with charge as the barrels swept the terrified students and herded them into a circle. These were exactly the kind of men Nico would send Lana thought to herself. They were nothing but heartless robots who were *just following orders*. Looking around her, she couldn't help but to think that she'd failed in her efforts to warn the solar system of the terrible mistake they were making.

"Are you the reporter?" a machined voice crackled from the lead soldier's helmet speaker. The man's visor swiveled toward her, and Lana had no doubt that he was conducting a scan of her face that confirmed her biometrics as he spoke. She could only see her expression reflected in the golden shimmer of his faceplate, and she found that she looked much more defiant than she felt.

"Journalist's rights are protected by Galactic Senate Resolution, and...hey! Let go of me!!!" she exclaimed as two of the soldiers seized her arms.

As she struggled to get free, their leader shouldered his rifle, and then drew a long strip of glistening metal from his belt. The soldiers holding her forced out her arms in front of her, and the leader set the metal against her wrists. A spark from his suit triggered the spider-steel to form a loop that cinched itself down painfully against her skin. There were no handcuff locks to be picked, and no way to cut the steel unless a particular frequency of electrical charge was delivered to the cuffs a second time. She was now the SSC's prisoner, with no hope of escape.

"Come on you guys, you're makin' a huge mistake here," Lana protested.

"Lana Delgato," the man's voice growled through his helmet's speaker, "By order of Galactic President Vladislav Nico, you are hereby placed under arrest for suspicion of treason. If you..."

"So we're under martial law now, are we?" she demanded, cutting him off before he could finish. This was new information, and despite the seriousness of her situation, she couldn't tamp down her natural curiosity.

"If you attempt to resist, we will incapacitate you during your extradition to Cape Canaveral," the man finished without acknowledging her question.

"Galactic Senate Resolution 85-42...," she said defiantly, but strong hands gripped her tightly in a warning that it'd be better if she closed her mouth, and kept it closed.

Their leader stepped closer to her. She tried to back away, but she had nowhere to go. The cold metal of his helmet pressed against her temple, and he stayed like that for a moment before he finally spoke.

"None of that matters now," his voice growled menacingly through the speaker.

His helmet lingered against the side of her head for a moment, and though she could see nothing through the gold plating, she had the oddest sensation that the man's expression was changing, and that he was actually thinking about something.

A few moments later he pulled back and nodded to the soldiers that were holding her. They shoved her forward and frog-marched her toward the airlock. She emerged facing the rifle barrels of another five-soldier team that was stationed on their shuttle.

"Does Nico consider the truth that dangerous?" Lana dared to ask.

As before, the soldiers said nothing. The two assigned to her pushed her down into a jump seat next to a small porthole, cinched her restraints, and then stepped back as the airlock sealed shut. A series of thumps shook the hull, and then Lana felt the craft floating free and turning. She strained to see any faces at the station's observation window as the shuttle pivoted, but the moon's reflection shone so brightly off the glass that she couldn't make out any of the students.

A few steps away from her, the detachment's leader reached up, unlatched his collar, and lifted off his helmet. The red flame of his hair was shaved into a soldier's buzz cut, high and tight, and his piercing green eyes seemed to glow against his white skin.

"Tell command that we have her," he ordered.

"Where are you taking me?" she asked.

Rather than answer, the soldier stared out the set of portholes on the far side of the shuttle. Straining to duck down, she could just make out the brilliant green and blue of Earth in the distance.

"It's so bright," she muttered to herself. In her rush to escape the planet, she hadn't had a chance to look back and admire the view. She half-smiled at the irony that it was Nico who was finally showing her the beauty that he was trying to destroy, but the thought of his injustice suddenly infuriated her, and she lashed out at her captors.

"Did any of you ever think to question what Nico says, or do you just accept every lie he tells you like good little soldiers?" she demanded.

Helmets tilted toward the detachment's leader, but the man said nothing. Lana noticed for the first time that the soldiers bore no rank or service insignia on their uniforms. It was obviously some special intelligence unit what was likely composed of nothing but brainwashed fanatics, but she still felt the need to try.

"Nico's gonna get you all killed. He's gonna get all of us killed. I saw the footage Capra Falconi recorded in the Sword Belt. Carter is right. We've got a hell of a lot bigger problem headed our way than the Bwain ever thought of being."

The soldiers gave no indication that they heard her. The man across from her studied his home planet.

"But Nico needs you to believe the Bwain are the issue. He needs to keep everyone afraid, so he can stay in power. That's always what happens when you..."

Suddenly the shuttle lurched violently to one side. Lana's head whipped down as a burst of curses filtered from a pilot on the flight deck.

"What are you doing?" the detachment's leader said as he grabbed ahold of one of the hand rails and reached for his helmet.

"Sergeant, you need to see this," a voice called back.

The young officer ducked through the low hatch that led to the shuttle's bridge. Lana turned to her window, trying to make sense of the shapes that were appearing before her in the blackness of space, but before she could understand what she was seeing, the sergeant's boots pounded back down the gangway and he was leaning over her.

"What's happening?" she asked, suddenly more terrified of what was outside the shuttle than whatever fate Nico had planned for her.

"You're gonna tell me everything you know about Atlas Carter," the man demanded. "Right now!"

* * *

The Fates' Winds

Aric's pain was instant, but dull. So many of his body's nerves had died, that the torch felt no worse than a toothache as it carved upward through his stomach toward his heart. What remained of his organs superheated and ran boiling over his cold, shaking hands. Nanobots spilled in a golden pool at his feet and began crawling back up his boots, and yet he was still standing.

The First Ones had even taken the ability to end his own suffering from him, but he'd show them. He'd drive the torch straight through what was left of his brain, melting whatever connections the First Ones had made so he could end the nightmare once and for all. He withdrew the torch, held it in front of his face, and then froze. The torch sputtered until Aric's thumb slid up and turned it off. He then watched in horror as his arm wheeled back and hurled the torch out into space.

"ARIC KEITH, YOU WILL NOT DEFY US!" a rasping metallic voice roared in his mind. He could not stop his head from turning toward the onrushing streak of hideous white shapes that filled the sky.

The First Ones were returning to bend him once more to their will. The nanobots crawled up his thighs and into his abdomen to repair the damage that he'd done. His body shuddered for a moment in a reflex that would have been a sob, but then he fell still once more as he looked out into space and studied the First Ones. It was then that he realized that something had changed.

The creatures that circled his ship were damaged. Their bodies were swollen with red and black scarring, as if they'd been charred in battle. As Aric watched, a ropy creature that looked like a coil of intestines flickered a baleful red. In the blink of an eye, its neighbors turned on it, dug their grasping suckers into its body, and shredded their fellow First One for whatever nourishment it gave them. The sight was barbaric, but even so, Aric's frigid cheeks rose in a smile.

It had been eons since the First Ones had possessed physical form, so they were weak against this dimension's gravity. If they didn't feed constantly, they would succumb to its pressure and be forced back into their ethereal existence in the upper dimensions, reduced once more to nothing more than shades of thought.

For the first time, Aric felt the fear of dissolution within their minds.

"WHAT IS THIS WEAPON YOUR CARTER HAS?" The Ancient demanded.

The leader of the First Ones wore the body of a narwhale crossed with a centipede. A seething mass of tentacles protruding underneath a skirt of white chitin gave the creature the appearance of some bastardized war galley, and its painfully white figurehead ending at a fiercely armored head studded by a single cyclopean eye. Yet, when confronted with this hideous creature, Aric's heart rose.

"He beat you, didn't he?" Aric asked through his thoughts.

A trickle of electric pain wormed through him, but Aric had long ago reached the point where pain no longer mattered.

"YOU WILL ANSWER ME!"

Against his will, Aric's hollowed body twisted back to the reactor. His frozen hand tapped a holocontrol that ramped up the reactor's power output. An arc of white lightning shot out toward the *Fates' Winds* from the obelisk, and then more threads connected to the wounded First Ones. The creatures hungrily absorbed the nourishment he was giving them as they bathed in the lightning's sickly glow.

"I wasn't there. How would I know what sort of weapons he has?" Aric asked.

He never should have been so flippant, but the fact that Carter had found a way to harm the First Ones was grounds for celebration.

Suddenly, he fell down onto the deck in a crumpled heap, his body jerking uncontrollably as the pain shot through him. His limbs jerked and stretched in unnatural directions as The Ancient burrowed into him, seeking out his very soul. He writhed and jerked until strips of his freeze-dried uniform, as well as the skin and muscle under it started to peel away, and a steady stream of nanobots spurted from his broken nose.

Then, the pain suddenly stopped. Images of the gravity drive flooded Aric's mind, and before he could even think of resisting, The Ancient ripped the related thoughts from him. The gravity drive was an experimental system. Aric had only heard of it in passing the last time he had transited through the Luna Station, but The Ancient took in everything he knew about it.

"THERE IS ONLY ONE OF THESE?" The Ancient seemed to laugh. *"AND CARTER HAS BROUGHT IT HERE?"*

"No, there are hundreds," Aric said, but it was already too late. The Ancient could see his thoughts.

"YOU HAVE NO SECRETS FROM US. YOU WOULD STAB US IN THE BACK WITH YOUR GRAVITY. YOUR GRAVITY IS NOTHING. THERE IS NOTHING THAT CAN STOP US. WE MADE THIS UNIVERSE, AND WE WILL REMAKE IT," The Ancient said, its thoughts roaring through Aric's being like searing fire.

"Captain Carter will stop you," Aric said, but the words sounded more like a plea than a threat.

"CARTER IS A FOOL!" The Ancient cried. The massive creature slipped toward one of the most wounded of its kin, a creature studded with flippers and the body of a mole, that was flickering, trying to gulp from the nourishing lightning that flashed from the obelisk.

"WE WILL CONSUME YOUR PLANET!" The Ancient roared. As it did, it grasped the flipper scales of the wounded First One and began tearing them from the creature one by one. The wounded First One bit and snapped defensively, but it was too weak to fight back, and was slowly consumed.

"IN THIS MANNER WE WILL CONSUME YOUR EARTH, ARIC KEITH."

"It doesn't matter. He'll stop you there too," Aric responded dully.

"NO, ARIC KEITH. WE HAVE LEARNED WHAT YOU CALL TACTICS. WE WILL DRAW HIM OUT, AND THEN WE WILL STRIKE WHERE HE LEAST EXPECTS IT."

Chapter Four

The Refugee Fleet
Shuttle Tiderian on approach to the Dauntless

After taking up the role of supply officer for the fleet, Danny Xiao had been responsible for providing all the supplies and equipment needed to survive in space. He'd helped evacuate the colonists from the doomed planet Gertie, shuttled supplies back and forth between ships when it had looked like the fleet would be on a thousand-year voyage to the closest star, worked around the clock to distribute the weapons that Hal's machines were cranking out, and even fought the First Ones himself with a desperate crew of Bwain. Despite these accomplishments, his job had never been harder than it was in the aftermath of the fleet's "victory" against the First Ones.

"Aaaghh!" one of the shuttle passengers behind him screamed. "Oh god, just kill me already!"

Danny glanced back through the hatch at the wounded he was ferrying to one of the intact cruisers. He had no medic on board, and had long ago run out of first aid supplies. Even though he was pressing the shuttle's inducers to the limit, he knew that some of the civilians and sailors he'd rescued from the foundering hulk of the *Maru* wouldn't survive.

"Just cut 'em off and be done with it!" the man howled.

Nearly a quarter of the fleet had been destroyed and roughly twenty-thousand lives had been lost in thirty minutes of frantic fighting. Survivors were being evacuated from the damaged vessels while the wounded ships were being stripped down for every useful component that could help the survivors. Though there had been a time back on Judgment when his guilt and self-loathing would have caused him to turn his back on the fleet, now all he could think of was saving as many people as he could.

"Please!"

The *Dauntless'* massive hull filled his viewscreen. The flagship hadn't suffered any damage and was serving as the main hub for the wounded. Danny tapped a holocontrol to set the auto-pilot, slipped off his restraints, and then wormed his way down from the flight deck to the cabin.

Writhing on the deck in the arms of a half-dozen other colonists was a young man in his twenties, maybe a year older than Danny. The man's legs had been severed at the shins, and though someone had been able to apply a tourniquet to them, blood loss wasn't the poor colonist's biggest worry.

What looked like a white mucous was inching up from the stumps on the man's legs. Danny had shuttled enough of the wounded that he recognized the aftermath of physical contact with a First One. He had soon come to learn that a quick death from the creatures or exposure to space was much better than being consumed by the First Ones' leftover acids.

The man sat up and seized Danny's shoulder.

"Cut 'em off!" he begged. "I can't take it anymore!"

"Please! Please, you have to do something!" a woman holding the man's hand cried.

Danny was bone-tired and barely able to think, but he'd always had a mind for organization. He intimately knew where each compartment in the shuttle was located, what the stowing regulations were, and how the cargo and material were laid out.

He turned to a locker behind him, thumbed open the code, and pulled out a cutting torch. The wounded man's eyes pleaded with him when he knelt down and sparked the torch.

"Are you sure?" Danny asked.

The man nodded, then wadded up the collar of his dirty shirt into his mouth.

At the first touch of the plasma torch the man groaned and jerked his leg upward. Danny's blade slipped easily through the flesh, but before Danny could stop the plasma made contact with the First One's residue.

"What are you doing?" the woman screamed.

Given new energy, the gangrenous shape surged up the wounded colonist's thigh as the man howled and thrashed with the pain.

"Hold him!" Danny cried. "Hold him!"

The other colonists helped to press the wounded man down on the deck. Danny sparked the torch once more, cutting at the closer leg to him. The man's flesh bubbled and seared, but the torch was designed to cut through carbyne steel hulls of the heaviest battle cruisers. It separated the man's knee from his thigh in the blink of an eye, but even that short time had been too slow.

On the leg opposite the one he'd been working on, the First One's essence had climbed through the man's pelvis. It left behind a slumping tangle of organs that looked as if they'd been chopped cleanly open. No blood leaked from him, and the man seemed beyond pain.

"I'm sorry, Danny said. The colonist stared at Danny for a long second before his eyes rolled back and his head dropped limp.

"Stand back, stand back!" a voice called. The colonists pressed against the shuttle walls as the First One's remains climbed up the victim's torso. Before the blob could do anything far more dangerous, a stream of violet fireballs washed over the victim's remains. The dimensional plasma shimmered and sank into what remained of the First One, dissolving its disgusting trail.

Danny looked up, surprised to see a familiar face lurching above the two Bwain that had come on board.

"I'm sorry Danny," Danielle Hoff said. She was balanced on her one good foot, with the bulb that was protecting her regrown leg on the other. As the medics behind her rushed through the shuttle's airlock to tend to the other wounded, she couldn't stop staring at the half-corpse below her – and the leg that Danny had severed.

"I am too," Danny said as he climbed wearily to his feet. "It was too many of us."

"It was," she said, and then she was embracing him, letting what must have been weeks of tension sink out in the ferocity of her grasp.

"I don't think I can take much more of this," Danny said as he returned her hug.

"We might have to," she replied.

"What do you mean?" Danny asked as he let go of her and leaned back to look into her eyes.

"Something's wrong with Captain Carter. We need to get to the *Bwainhome*."

* * *

"What's wrong with them?" Pandith's voice asked in Granger's ear. The science officer was staring at the clutch of Bwain seated across from him on Danny's shuttle, but "seated" was the wrong word. The aliens were slumped over, nearly catatonic, and they were shuddering as if locked in some kind of dream.

"I have no idea," Granger said, shrugging his shoulders slightly.

"That's why we need you, Granger," Hal Yellowknife said. "If there's something going on with the Majorana radiation, or the Bwainsong..."

"It could be something the First Ones are doing to 'em," Bryon Purcell called through their implants. "We hit them good with the help of our little buddies, and then they hit back at the little buddies."

"If that's true, then we need to be on alert," Danielle added.

Granger stared through the electroglass viewscreen as the *Bwainhome* loomed before the shuttle. He was nervous about leaving Pandith alone in the *Gravity Drive*, but worse was the feeling that he should have seen something like this coming. If he'd been able to figure out how to track the Bwainsong's telepathic projections through the Majorana radiation they gave off, the First Ones would have been able to do the same thing. Their powers and knowledge dwarfed anything the human scientists had developed, so it was a foregone conclusion that they'd figure it out sooner rather than later.

His thoughts drifted back to Kaylee Wyatoshi and the stories the poor girl had shared with the crew of the *Fates' Winds* after Captain Carter had rescued her. Though the Bwain fascinated him as research subjects, he had spent enough time with them on the *Bwainhome* to begin to feel an affection for them. If that meant he was losing his scientific objectivity, then maybe it was about damn time.

"Pandith, if the First Ones are waging mental warfare on the Bwain, then you're our only defense," Granger said.

"With all the caffeine Danny brought me, I should be well stocked," Pandith quipped in an effort to relieve some of the stress that hung over their conversation. Sadly, no one on their private transmission seemed to find it funny. After running for over twenty-four hours on minimal sleep as the fleet tried to regroup, it was difficult to release any kind of tension. Worse yet was the fact that Carter had fallen silent.

"I mean, he brought the *Bwainhome* here, so we know he's still in there. You saw him, Granger," Hal said as he anxiously listened to the transmissions.

"He did take longer to come back for me and Pandith than he should have taken, but I haven't seen him since…," Granger said, his voice trailing off in a silent sigh.

"Since before the First Ones attacked," Pandith finished for him.

Danny slid the shuttle through the membrane that guarded the *Bwainhome*'s atmosphere from the vacuum of space, and brought the shuttle down to rest gently on the deck of the alien ship.

"You don't think that was part of the attack, do you? Could they have gotten to the captain?" he asked as he unbuckled his restraints.

"I don't know, but we need to find out," Granger said tentatively.

*   *   *

The Bwainhome

"Something's off here," Hal Yellowknife said as their rescue party stepped down the shuttle ramp and onto the *Bwainhome*'s deck.

The vast shuttle bay looked like a chasm that had been carved into fleshy rock. The chamber could have fit an entire frigate with room to spare, and the Bwain's dimensional fighters spread out in disorganized rows in all directions. This was Danielle's first time setting foot on the alien ship, and while the others had been back and forth multiple times, she was experiencing everything through new eyes.

"What was it like before?" she asked.

The group was following Granger toward an entrance that resembled an esophagus that irised open and led them upward through a milky orange light.

"When the captain first arrived, he told us that the ship seemed like it was almost dead. It was dark, and most of the cabins weren't in use. They weren't when Pandith and I surveyed the ship either, but then things started changing. Chambers that hadn't been in use for what looked like thousands of years were all of a sudden brand new. It made the weapons for us, and it took care of the Bwain as well," Granger said, but then he paused a moment to examine something that had caught his attention.

"It started helping us is what it did. It was like it picked a side," Hal added.

Danielle ran her hand along the wall beside her. The ship's material was warm, and it gave the impression that it clung to her skin for just a moment too long.

It was hard work limping on the protective boot around her re-growing foot, even with Danny helping with her to walk. It'd taken her a while to realize what had been bothering her about the ship, but she finally figured it out. It wasn't the alien materials and construction, or even the strange lighting. It was the fact that they were alone.

"There don't seem to be any Bwain anywhere," she noted.

"She's right," Hal whispered as he glanced around nervously.

"That's weird. They're usually all over the place," Granger added.

"It's almost like the ship's waiting for something," Danny said.

"I don't know if I wanna find out what that something is. Let's hurry up and get where we're goin'," Hal said nervously as he started forward once again.

Seeing the ship from the outside gave Danielle no sense of the utter vastness that was to be found within. As they wound up a dizzying array of corridors, they came across great rooms that looked like they were rookeries for the Bwain, thin corridors that would not fit a human, and pulsing veins that lined the walls. They were all empty however, and the more they walked, the more they began to worry about what had happened to cause that emptiness.

"Shhh!" Hal suddenly hissed as he stopped short. "Do you hear that?"

The group stilled for a moment. Straining to hear what he was talking about, Danielle could just barely make out what sounded like a low moan.

"How far are we?" Granger asked.

"I think another two or three decks," Hal said with a nervous frown. "It's hard to tell. Every time I come over here I feel like the ship's different."

"Wait, so we don't even know where we're goin' in this thing?" Danielle asked.

"No, we do...sorta. The ship always gets us where we need to go somehow," Granger replied as he continued to observe the odd mutations in the ship's surfaces.

They turned up what looked like a stone staircase that warmed Danielle's foot. Finally, the ship's deck opened out, leading to a cavernous space and a ramp that sloped upward toward a strange sight. The ramp stopped at the entrance to a brightly lit room, but above the room, instead of more of the pinkish-orange hull, there was the deep black of space.

"Where the hell's the roof?" Danielle asked as she eyed the darkness nervously.

"That's not what I'm worried about. Look," Hal said as he pointed above them.

At this distance, Danielle had assumed that the dim blackness spilling out from the chamber was a natural coloring of the ship, but as they climbed higher, she realized that she was seeing thousands of Bwain that had laid down in a prone position on their approach to the chamber.

"How many of 'em live in this thing?" she asked.

"I don't think they even know," Danny said.

"Millions," Granger answered vaguely, as he spun around on his heels, trying to take it all in.

"Well, however many there are, this feels like all of 'em," Hal said as he gingerly stepped through the creatures.

The Bwain spread out from the chamber in all directions for several kilometers at least. They seemed to not even notice the humans passing through them. Even when Danielle accidentally trod on a talon or feather, they didn't move at all.

"Are they still alive?" she asked.

No one knew the answer. Even worse, no one knew what the creatures would do without Carter commanding them. Danielle ran her hand over the pistol she'd absently slapped to her hip before leaving the *Dauntless* with Danny. If the Bwain turned hostile, would the humans be able to do anything at all to defend themselves?

Danielle was sweating as she climbed the steep ramp with Danny's help. They wound higher and higher underneath the strange sky, finally arriving at a chamber that seemed suspended in mid-air beneath the shifting artwork of the universe.

"Get ready you guys. There's a lot in this room that we don't understand," Granger cautioned them before they stepped into the chamber.

As they entered Danielle raised her hand to protect her eyes at the sight of the Endless Knot. The Knot gave off no heat, but it was incredibly bright. It twisted and writhed against itself in a constant interlocking pattern that, if you focused long enough, seemed to almost form some manner of speech. Focusing on the Knot for more than a few seconds however was next to impossible. Like the First Ones, it blurred at the edges. It was a part of this dimension, but it was bound to the others as well.

As they made their way further inside, the Bwain suddenly erupted with agitation. They sputtered and screeched, their ragged coats splitting into different bright colors that had to mean fear or nervousness. Danielle's hand dropped to her pistol as she spun around, trying to figure out what had startled the Bwain, but they seemed to be surging in all directions. One of the diminutive bird things darted toward her, clutching at her hand.

"Bwainslayer…," it hissed. "Save…"

"What are they saying?" she called. She drew the pistol out of reflex, but it was clear that to shoot one of the creatures would be suicide. They didn't seem hostile as they milled in waves around the Knot. They were just scared.

"That's what they call the Captain!" Granger said as he held back a pair of the creatures who were trying to break into the human's circle. "It's some sort of a legend of theirs."

"So he's their god?" Danielle asked.

"I don't know. He had trouble explaining it to us, so I'm not really sure what it's all about," Granger explained.

"Yeah well, none of that matters right now," Hal said anxiously. "We need to find him so we can find out what the hell's goin' on in here."

Frantic, Danielle turned back to the Knot's cold light. Hundreds of Bwain were filling the chamber, and though the tallest Bwain's head reached just over her waist, they were making it harder to see in the strange room.

She pushed closer to the Knot. If this strange orb was how Captain Carter communicated with them and controlled the ship, then logically he would probably be somewhere close to it. She expected to feel warmth from the bright light the Endless Knot was emanating, but a cold shiver ran through her. For just a brief moment she had a vision of the deep, endless darkness of space, but the sensation passed rather quickly. Rubbing her arms, she began circumnavigating the phenomena, pushing the Bwain aside until she stumbled over a pair of legs at the edge of the Knot.

"I found him! He's over here!" she called.

Carter was lying on the floor with his torso up off the floor, and his arms and head somehow suspended in the Knot.

"What happened to him? Was he trying to go inside that thing?" Danny asked.

"I don't know," Danielle said as she unsteadily knelt down beside him.

Atlas' Final Approach

"He doesn't look conscious. Captain, can you hear me?"

"We need to get him outta there!" Hal said. He reached forward and seized Carter's belt, but Granger quickly clamped down on his hand to stop him.

"What the hell are you doin'?" Hal cried.

"We don't know what it'll do to him if we just yank him outta there like that. For all we know, it could kill him!" Granger said. Hal stared hard at him for a moment, and then pulled his hand back.

Just then, a Bwain shuffled between them. This one seemed somehow older. Its head and throat were flecked with gray, and there were bare spots in its feathers, exposing scaled patches of skin.

"Stay," the Bwain cawed.

"What does it want?" Danielle asked.

"Stay," another of the Bwain repeated, and then dozens of hoarse alien throats started chanting the word in unison.

"I think that's pretty clear," Granger answered.

"Well, I don't care. He was ours first!" Hal grumbled as he lurched toward Carter's prone body and grabbed ahold of it once more.

With a grunt, he pulled back away from the Knot, and for a moment, it seemed as though it didn't want to release his body. Danielle was watching closely as it all played out, and even though she couldn't be sure, it almost seemed as though there were currents in the Knot that were trying to tighten their grip on the captain's arms. Hal grunted hard one last time, and then fell backward with Carter's limp body on top of him.

The captain's appearance shocked her. The SSC uniform Carter had been wearing since his arrival in the Sword Belt months ago was worn, threadbare at his chest and throat. The last time she'd seen her captain in person, he'd had a heavy layer of muscle over his tall frame, but now he seemed shrunken, as if his muscles were atrophying at an accelerated rate. His face was pale and drawn, and his skin was mottled with bruises and marks from ruptured capillaries.

"My god, he's wasting away," Danny said in a tight voice. This was not an image of the captain he had ever seen, and seeing Carter lying there looking the way he did made him realize how long the man had been fighting for their survival.

"Hal, you could have killed him doing that!" Granger said angrily, but then he stopped himself and took a deep breath to control his anger.

"Killed him? It's that thing that was killing him, and you know it!" Hal responded shakily.

"Stay! Stay!" the Bwain chanted.

Danielle looked back and forth between Carter and the Bwain. The aliens were closing in on Carter, fluttering their wings in an agitated manner, and flashing a fiery combination of colors.

"STAY!" they hissed again. "STAY!"

Carter's body convulsed beneath them, and his limbs snapped against the deck.

"Captain, wake up!" she pleaded.

The Bwain were plucking and scratching at her. She drew her pistol once more, uncertain of what was going on, or what she should do.

Atlas' Final Approach

"His skin is tingling, like he's holding a charge or somethin'," Hal said.

"Come on Captain, you gotta wake up now!" Danielle pleaded. "We need you!"

* * *

The Bwainsong

Atlas Carter was everywhere and nowhere. His body, if it could still be called that, raced along fissures in space and time, leaking into other dimensions where he could only dimly grasp the shapes and structures that moved around him. The warmth of every star and the frigid cold of the deepest space both filled his heart. His perspective rose higher and higher until he felt as if he were striding across the galaxy, staring down at the universe and seeing its pattern for the first time. All molecules in the universe thrummed with the same rhythm. Their movements were echoes of each other, bound together in a writhing 12-dimensional shape that curled and twisted in and out of the different dimensions in the same shape as the great Endless Knot.

"It's all one," Carter said as he marveled at the complexity of it all.

"Yes," the Bwainhome answered.

"This is why you wanted to keep me here? To show me this?"

"To talk. Ask us what you will."

"You made this?" Carter asked.

"No. We found it."

"But where did it come from? Who made it?" Carter asked, hoping to somehow begin to understand this strange alien race and the ship that had sustained their lives for countless generations.

"This is the question we left to seek."

"But you didn't leave. You stayed," he said as he felt the collective memory of the Bwainsong tugging at him.

"We were one people. No longer."

A crushing wave of exhaustion filled him as millennia passed before his eyes in a heartbeat. He saw a group of *Bwainhomes* that had been chosen to stay behind as the other First Ones traveled to other dimensions. They had been tasked with paving the way for their brethren's eventual return to the physical universe.

The *Bwainhomes* kept the First Ones' slaves alive, traversed the stars out of idle curiosity, watched a billion suns and planets live and die, and found a small, blue planet that would come to be known as Earth, where life could potentially evolve.

Over time, the *Bwainhome* realized that its existence was no longer life. It had lost its purpose, and thus, its will to live.

Two more visions came to him then. First was the battle against his old ship, the *Fates' Winds*, and then a distorted view of him stumbling into the Endless Knot's chamber for the first time.

"You know what we seek. Come with us."

Atlas felt the ship's muscles as if he were a feeble man remembering his former strength.

"You're tired," he observed dully.

"We are all tired. We will rest soon," the Bwainsong thrummed back at him in response.

For a moment, Atlas considered the descent into oblivion. He could release himself and his own consciousness to join with that of the Bwainsong, giving them his experience and knowledge as his consciousness continued on within their culture. He felt their longing, their calling out to him. They'd never had another mind or perspective with them, and their thirst to learn was insatiable. The ship's hunger was killing him however, and as that realization suddenly presented itself, it pulled him back from the precipice.

"My job isn't finished," Atlas said as he forced the temptation from his mind.

He'd felt anger before in the Bwainsong, but the sensation that flooded him now was akin to desperation. Again he saw the smoking rooftops of Belize City, felt his hand push forward on his helicopter's throttle as the craft surged toward the battle-scarred streets. A part of him knew that Cazador's *Narcos* had already won, and that he was being shown yet another of the visions the ship used to communicate. Even so, his heart broke once more as the air cleared and he saw his wife Aída struggling to break free of Cazador's grasp. Her red dress fluttered on the roof of their house...and then she was gone. In the blink of an eye she was lost within the fireball that was created by one of the *Narcos'* tanks when it fired at his home, and his heart was torn open anew.

"SAVE!" the entire Bwainsong demanded.

"But you're asking me to give up my life," Carter protested through his agony.

"SAVE!"

Another flash of memories came to him. It was the crew of the *Fates' Winds*. They were bickering, but at the same time they were joining together into a cohesive unit that worked together for the greater good. Then the vision changed again. The citizens of Gertie were rising up against Tannin. Then one last vision came to him. It was the vision of a moonlit night with Captain Mephista's head resting on his chest.

"We have none of this. We cannot live without it," the Bwainsong called to him. The ripple of longing they were feeling coursed through him, filling his being with the unfulfilled desires of the Bwain, and the *Bwainhome.*

A calm sadness filled him as he realized that his destiny all along had been to reach this moment. He was the Bwainslayer, the captain of a force more powerful than the universe had ever known. It was his duty to stop the First Ones.

"Yes," Carter said with strengthened resolve. "Yes, I will save...but not yet."

* * *

The Tranquility

Captain Mephista closed her eyes and reached for her helmet seal. Her ship and crew were dead. The First Ones had destroyed everything, and Carter had abandoned her. The only right thing to do was to die with whatever dignity she could muster.

"Mephista," a small voice said in her ear.

Her hands paused against the helmet release. The void of space cradled her body inside her EVO suit. It would welcome her quickly into its cold breath. There would be little pain.

"Mephista, I'm hurt."

The voice that came through the captain's implant was the frightened whisper of a young girl.

Mephista's eyes opened. She was facing the hole in her hull where the slavering First One had been poised to devour her, but instead of its gibbering white flesh, she saw only blackness. Small caltrops spun through the debris outside the ship, and it took her a moment to realize that they were the drifting husks of her crew, doomed to drift in the cold void of space until the end of time.

"You have to find me. Please...," Kaylee said.

"I don't know how," Mephista replied. Her own voice in her helmet sounded murky, somehow muted.

Kaylee Wyatoshi had been a comfort girl on an illegal mining freighter before Captain Carter had rescued her. Watching the shy, damaged girl blossom on board the *Tranquility* had been one of Mephista's true joys. For a time, Kaylee had helped her remember her own life before a Bwain attack had left her crippled.

"I'm scared," Kaylee said in a broken voice as she started sobbing.

Mephista shook her head, trying to clear it. If Kaylee was alive, she couldn't just abandon her and leave her to die.

Twisting around to face the deck, Mephista gathered her tether and pulled herself toward where the carbyne mesh was attached to her captain's chair. Without the use of her legs, Mephista had kept the ship's gravity turned off, and had become adept at navigating in zero-G. She had also made use of a few shortcuts, like the oxygen bottles she stored under her chair. When she finally reached the chair, she grabbed one of the bottles, aimed the nozzle, and then jetted off toward the airlock.

"I'm coming Kaylee," she said. "Just hold on. Tell me where you are."

Somehow, the *Tranquility* still had power, and Mephista was able to cycle through the airlock and into the corridors that led from the bridge. As she did, the ship lurched. Wracked by venting and depressurization, its movement sent Mephista flying against one of the bulkheads. She saw stars for a moment as her forehead knocked against her helmet, but a few moments later she was on the move once again.

"It's dark here," Kaylee said.

"Were you in the infirmary? Were you sleeping in there when we got attacked?" Mephista asked, trying to focus her thoughts on where the girl would most likely be.

After Pandith and Granger had revived Kaylee, the girl had been afraid to leave the infirmary. When her nightmares had wracked her on the *Tranquility*, she usually made her way to the infirmary. Being surrounded by doctors and nurses made her feel secure, and allowed her to get the sleep she needed.

"I don't know...," Kaylee answered with hesitation.

Mephista tried to locate the transmission, but something was wrong with her helmet. Normally it would have been able to give a direction arrow on her heads-up display, but the system had crashed.

"Is there anyone else alive? Anyone near the infirmary?" Mephista asked on the open comms channel.

Silence crackled through Mephista's earpiece. She had no idea how long it had been since the attack, or if the fleet had even survived. She remembered the last Bwain trying desperately to make itself understood, and then she wondered if it had been Atlas trying to say goodbye.

The ship lurched again. Mephista's shoulder brushed against the bulkhead, but she was making good progress toward the infirmary at the center of the ship. The key to maneuvering in zero-G was to develop a rhythm. Pick a target, launch from a handrail, adjust course at your next target, and keep going. Swing your arms, work your shoulders. Just keep going.

"I'm coming, Kaylee. Just hang in there sweetie," Mephista called, frustrated by her slow progress.

"Please hurry!" Kaylee cried through her sobbing.

The ship rocked again, harder this time. A fissure broke through the hull beside her, sucking atmosphere from the corridor in a freezing torrent. Mephista locked her arm around a handrail while she waited for the atmosphere to finish venting, and then she resumed her search.

"Kaylee, are there beds where you are?" Mephista asked.

"I don't know."

"Were you with the doctors? Is there anyone else there?"

"There are lots of us," the girl whispered.

Mephista redoubled her efforts. Kaylee's voice seemed farther away than before. Her suit's life support could be failing, or she could be in a pocket of radiation.

"Kaylee, just keep talking," Mephista said. "I'll find you."

Mephista tapped the control band at her wrist, signaling her suit to go to local voice commands.

"Reboot HUD display. Show source of most recent transmission," she instructed. After a moment, a blurred holoimage overlaid itself on her visor's electroglass. Mephista expected to see a map of the ship in front of her, but what she saw instead was a series of shattered pieces floating in a glowing hulk. The *Tranquility* was utterly destroyed.

"This doesn't make sense," Mephista said aloud into her helmet as she studied the images.

The lights in her corridor were burning steadily. The airlock that led to the supply hold was still functioning properly, but if they no longer had physical connection to the onboard reactor, then how were they powered?

"But it will," Kaylee whispered.

Mephista flung herself across the floor of the hold, using the deck grating to grab purchase and build speed. The next compartment on this deck would be the galley, and then the med bay. She'd start there and work deck by deck if she had to. Her suit's biogel was constantly recycling her oxygen, and her inducers were all working at full capacity.

"What do you mean, Kaylee?" Mephista asked. "Just keep talking."

The airlock ring before her flashed green. Mephista heaved open the heavy carbyne steel door, sealed it behind herself, then unlocked the hatch on the other side. Instead of the long tables of the officer's galley she expected, she floated into an empty void.

"Inducers," she said. At the command, the small induction thrusters at the joints of her suit worked to stall her drift. She tilted her helmet up and down, horrified at the brutal severing of her ship's bow from its middle decks. The bodies of her crew were spilling from hatches and corridors by the hundreds, a slow-motion waterfall of faces frozen in horror and shock. She watched as their skin sizzled and burned, their flailing arms useless to swim through the inky currents.

Swallowing, Mephista triggered her inducers and began crossing through the bodies toward the next section of her ship.

"Kaylee, I'm coming!" Mephista said

"No, you aren't. You left me to die," the girl said, sounding almost...what? Petulant? Accusing?

A body spun into Mephista, knocking her momentarily off course. It was a man who looked like her former weapons officer. But that man had died in the first battle with the First Ones days ago. He couldn't have been here.

"I'm coming," Mephista called as she sloughed off the corpse and jetted forward.

On a deck above her, a small figure was waving. Mephista angled her course upward through the debris. The figure was a young girl with thick dark hair. Her face was a pale skull that once had been meticulously painted with a geisha's makeup.

"Kaylee, where's your suit? Put on your suit!" Mephista called desperately.

"It's too late. I have to go now," the girl said without emotion.

"No!" Mephista cried. She rammed her suit's inducers to full, trying to reach the girl who'd been so desperately calling out to her. Despite Mephista's increased speed, the far section of the *Tranquility* was drifting farther away from her.

"Goodbye," Kaylee said in a soft whisper.

The girl turned away from Mephista, revealing her raw spine and a chunk of gray lung where her flesh had been ripped away. She was just another body floating in space, a frozen memory.

"Kaylee, please!" Mephista screamed as she jolted awake.

Blurred faces loomed above her. A hand pressed against her shoulders, and another held her arms as she tried to fight the restraints.

"It's all right, ma'am. It's over now," Lieutenant Purcell said as he loomed over her to make sure she was ok.

"Where's Kaylee? Where are we?" the captain asked, trying to gather her thoughts.

"We're on the *Dauntless*," Bryon said. "I found you in the wreckage, remember?"

Mephista blinked and tried to focus. She was in a med bay, lying on a firm mattress in the middle of hundreds of other patients.

"And the ship?"

Bryon's face, normally never far from a smile, was sober and drawn. The young weapons officer looked exhausted.

"The *Tranquility* was destroyed. There were a few survivors, but Kaylee...," he said, but then he felt silent when the words just wouldn't come.

Mephista had little range of motion from her restraints, but she managed to wedge her hand into Bryon's.

"She didn't make it?" Mephista asked in a coarse whisper.

"No ma'am, she didn't."

She closed her eyes and took a heavy breath as the tears started to flow.

"I was dreaming about her just now," Mephista said in a broken voice. She sniffed and tried to stop the flow of tears, but it was no use.

"I still see her too," Bryon said. "Granger had a theory that she was linked to the Bwainsong in some way after they'd tried to take over her mind. Maybe she's still out there with us somewhere, like an echo."

"Wherever she is, I hope she's finally found the peace she deserves," Mephista said as he started to remove the restraints from her arms and waist. When she opened her eyes, Bryon was maneuvering himself so that he could lift her.

On the opposite side, she noticed that another set of eyes was watching her. A curious Bwain tilted its head toward her in a birdlike gesture of viewing her out of first one eye, and then the other.

"I'm not sure I'm ready," she said, still feeling somewhat disoriented after such an abrupt awakening.

"I know ma'am, but Captain Carter needs you," Bryon said as he hefted her up into his arms. The look of shock on her face gave him the first genuine smile he'd had in a while.

"Atlas? He's back? He's really back?" she asked, not really sure she'd heard him correctly.

"You could say that, but there's something happening to him. We don't really know what's goin' on. All I know is that he needs you now probably more than he ever has."

* * *

The Dauntless

"I've never seen any human brainwaves that look like this," Captain Decival's harried medical examiner said as he examined the scan. The man was so tired after three days of processing thousands of the fleet's wounded that he was swaying on his feet. "I mean, there's nothing I can do, at least for right now. I have no idea what's happening to him, much less how to stop it."

Decival stared down at Carter. The unconscious man's cheeks were sunken under a sheaf of gray stubble. Carter's eyes roved frantically under their lids, and every so often his limbs would shudder. Whether the only man who had the power to truly protect the remaining fleet was alive, or would ever recover from what was happening to him, was at this point an open question. Unfortunately, they didn't have the luxury of time when the First Ones could strike back at any moment.

"We need to pull him out of this. What do we know for sure?" Decival asked the nearby crew members.

"We found him inside the Endless Knot," Danielle said.

"The Bwain didn't want him to leave either," Hal added.

"Why not? What were the Bwain doing to him?" Decival demanded.

"To be honest, I don't think it was the Bwain. I think it might have been the ship itself using the Bwain," Granger explained. He knew his theory sounded strange, but there had been some discussion about that possibility some time back when Carter had asked him and Pandith to learn more about the ship.

"His neural activity is off the charts. There's been a few theories floating around for a while now that the human mind is capable of operating at a higher capacity, but nothing like this," the doctor added.

"Do you think it's hostile?" Decival asked. He was worried now about more than just the First Ones. The Bwain had nearly turned violent when Carter's friends had pulled him from the ship. The creatures that had been assigned to the *Dauntless* appeared sullen and lethargic now, but when Carter had first been brought aboard they'd been scratching and clawing to try to get near him.

"Doubtful. He's been in command of their ship and in constant communication with them, so I can't see why they'd try to attack him like this, especially when it'd have been so easy to do it physically once he was unconscious. If anything, I think they're talking to him," Granger theorized. "If I can borrow your science team, I'll be able to fashion Majorana radiation detectors. The Bwain's telepathic patterns operate cross-dimensionally, but Pandith and I were able to track 'em via Majorana radiation once before. Maybe we can use the radiation to communicate with the captain."

"Back on Gertie, Tannin used mushrooms to communicate with the Bwain," Hal explained as he glanced over at Danny. "I don't suppose there are any of those left, are there?"

"Beats me. I'm not a smuggler anymore, but we could ask the colonists," Danny suggested.

"It's a long shot, but at least it's a shot," Hal said.

"You know, we might have another option," Julie said.

"Julie, no!" Danielle blurted.

Decival turned to his navigation officer. She'd refused a painkiller for her foot from the doctor, and he could see the ache in her face, but she would not leave her captain's side. Decival was impressed. In all the time he'd served under Admiral Nico, he'd never once felt the same level of commitment to the man. No matter what the rest of the SSC said, he knew he'd made the right choice in surrendering to Carter when he'd first entered the Sword Belt.

"Go ahead, Ensign," Decival said.

"Sir, Aric Keith is still alive on the *Fates' Winds*," Julie replied. "We've received sporadic transmissions from him, enough to know that he's able to talk to the First Ones. So maybe..."

"You think he could talk to the captain?" Granger asked.

"It's possible, but when Julie and I discussed it, I thought we'd decided that it was too dangerous. Isn't what we decided?" Danielle asked, giving Julie a stern look. Julie looked abashed, but she continued to press the idea.

"I mean, at least it's an option. What other choice do we have at this point? We're sorta stuck between a rock and a hard place here."

The crew turned toward Decival, waiting for his orders. The captain considered himself and his crew extremely well trained. He'd been placed in command of the strike group tasked with taking out Atlas Carter because of his record of training crews and handling the tactical challenges that the Bwain had thrown at him. Now he had to decide what to do with a damaged fleet, thousands of civilians, and the fact that his best asset was functionally brain dead.

"I want each of you to get started on your options right away and report back to me within four hours," Decival said. "We'll reconvene then in my cabin."

"Captain that's not a lot of time," Granger noted uneasily.

"No, it's not. The First Ones could come back at any moment though, so time is something that's in short supply at the moment," Decival reminded them.

As was his habit, Decival stiffened in salute to indicate that the meeting had ended. The other crewmen returned his salute and left the med bay, but Decival lingered behind for a moment. The doctor tapped a holocontrol and then shuffled toward his next patient, leaving Decival alone with the man who'd outwitted him in battle, and had proven to be an effective leader.

"Why are they holding on to you like this?" Decival asked softly.

The wasted man under the sheet offered no answer, so after a few moments Decival turned to leave. As he turned around, he was startled by a woman, a young officer, and a Bwain who'd slipped silently into the room behind him.

"They're holding onto him because they need him," Mephista said, answering his question.

* * *

Johannesburg

Cazador scratched at the scar tissue on his neck while he watched the orbital shuttle carrying Admiral Nico and Phuri streak toward the heavens. The left side of his body irritated him constantly thanks to the mass of inflexible tissue from his burns pulling and pinching whenever he moved. His fingers and arms felt too tight, and every blink of his stilled eye was a painful reminder of the day so long ago when he had risen high up the *Narcos'* ladder. He'd been a fixer for the cartels in Belize City, but as they'd prepared their assault against the last free state in South America, Cazador had worked on the problems of righteous government officials, gathering intelligence about the SSC's dispositions, and smuggling supplies and fighters into the city.

The final key had been Atlas Carter, Cazador's childhood friend. As youths they'd shared their first cups of cane liquor together, trained and boxed together, and charmed women together. When Carter had married his wife *Aida,* Cazador stood beside him as his best man.

It was Carter's heart that had given Cazador control over him. It had been Aída that had allowed Cazador to finally gain his obedience, and in a way, the act had saddened him. Cazador had taught Carter how to box, how to move his feet, and how to get up after a kidney shot. He'd also advised Carter to join the navy as a way to escape his surroundings. His encouragement however was not an attempt to push his friend to rise above his humble beginnings. His plan all along was to use him as a source of information about the SCC, so he could further aid the *Narcos'* in their illegal activities.

Cazador had taken Aída in order to guarantee that Carter kept his promise to not act against the cartels with the SSC forces at his command when they took Belize city. It had at once been a betrayal, and an acceptance of how far their paths had diverged.

Cazador turned and rode the great tower's elevator down to the underground warren of offices and facilities where the true business of governing the galaxy was conducted. Several stories below the surface, he stepped out into a spacious hallway that was flanked with guards. His smile had returned by the time he stopped at the suite that would normally be used for visiting dignitaries who wished to remain out of sight. The guards unsealed the doors for him as he approached, and he entered a brightly lit grand foyer. The chamber boasted marble flooring, a granite fountain, and cultivated vines crawling up the walls.

His footfalls echoed across the stone, but no one came to greet Cazador as he circled the fountain and entered the inner chambers. The next room was a parlor, furnished with extravagant couches and a glittering wet bar at the rear of the room. Cazador drifted there, and looked over the selection as he searched for a bottle of Pasion Azteca. Unfortunately, all he could find was a bottle of Don Julio, so that would have to do for the moment.

He lifted the glass stopper, poured himself a shot of tequila, and then turned to find a man waiting for him in the doorway.

"Make yourself at home," Nelson Kidewange commented in a voice dripping with sarcasm as he entered the room. "I should have snuck up behind you and strangled you."

The deposed Galactic President was a native South African, going elegantly gray with a broad forehead and intelligent eyes, but his anger was unmistakable.

"And maybe I should have had you executed," Cazador countered, as he held the glass up to examine its contents in the light.

"But you've settled for executing the planet instead."

Cazador nosed his drink, and then sipped the buttery smooth sourness. He pointed at Kidewange with a free finger.

"You know, you have a strong reputation as an intellectual. It is a shame that these fearful times require a stronger hand."

"Phuri's already come down here to taunt me enough. What do you want?"

"I want to discuss policy with you. Forming coalitions, gathering power, and things of that nature," Cazador said evenly as he studied the former Galactic President.

"Then you should be talking to Nico and his lapdog Phuri," Kidewange spat as he spun and started for the door to his bed chamber.

"If I move against them, what should I know?" Cazador called after him.

The former president froze. When he turned, his face was calm and calculating.

"You've just taken power not two days ago, and now you want them out?

Why?" Kidewange asked, genuinely curious to hear the answer despite his barely contained anger.

"They are both small men," Cazador replied. "They dream small. To be in charge of something is not the same as having power. It is not the same as realizing a vision."

"So that's why you kept me alive. You want a puppet if Nico and Phuri split from your interests," the former president said.

Cazador smiled as he lifted a glass to offer Kidewange a drink, but the other man declined with a wave of his hand.

"I am afraid that Phuri didn't fully understand my associates' and my terms for helping him when he returned to the planet," Cazador said.

"He worked with you before?"

"He was an errand boy. Nothing but a messenger who informed Sickyl Tannin of our interests. When he and Tannin were exiled however, well…let's just say that his value to us diminished considerably. He had little in the line of leverage when he returned, but he can be rather clever at times. He and that gorilla Nico know nothing of power, or of what it takes to hold it. I believe that you my good sir would be more pragmatic."

"And what about Captain Carter?" Kidewange asked.

"Atlas Carter and I are intimately acquainted, and I can assure you that I have nothing to fear from that man," Cazador said as he lifted his chin with a slight jerk. Whether it was an automatic response to the discomfort of his scar-tightened face, or a gesture to assert his confidence, Kidewange could not tell for sure.

"I think I'll take my chances. Atlas Carter has beaten our fleets three times now, so for all the power that you claim to have, I don't think you can hold a candle to a man like that."

Cazador chuckled, circling toward Kidewange while his tequila sloshed in his glass.

"He's become quite powerful if he can defeat your SSC fleets so easily, but do you know what real power is? No, I don't suppose you would. You've worn the trappings of power, but you've never truly understood what it is to wield it."

Kidewange glared at him angrily, but Cazador didn't even blink.

"And you do?" he asked finally.

"Power is the willingness to send men to their deaths to fulfil your vision, and their willingness to die for your vision because they fear meeting their death at your hand far more than they fear meeting it elsewhere. That, my friend, is true power."

"That's not power. That's nothing but domination through fear," Kidewange protested.

"Call it what you wish, but the end result is still the same. Anyway, I suggest you reconsider my offer. Sleep on it. Perhaps when you've had a chance to think it over, you'll change your mind," Cazador said as he casually turned and walked back toward the bar.

"What makes you think I'd do that?" he asked, but Cazador didn't respond. He simply sat down at the bar and poured himself another drink.

The former president's frustration at his current situation was boiling over, but he held his tongue and turned to walk away. Behind him, he thought he could hear Cazador chuckling quietly to himself at the bar. There was something unsettling about the man. Perhaps it was his infuriatingly calm demeanor, or the apparent smugness with which he spoke, but the man was dangerous. Was he more dangerous than Nico and Phuri? That he didn't know, but the thought of Nico being in power frightened him far less than the thought of Cazador having that power. Perhaps he already did, and Nico and Phuri were simply his puppets. He didn't know, but for right now at least he'd chosen to put his faith in Nico and the SSC.

* * *

The refugee fleet

"We've got twelve ships at full combat readiness, fourteen with significant damage, and the rest have been...," Danielle said, but then she paused for a moment, stunned at the information she had received at her station on the *Dauntless*' bridge.

"KIA," Bryon Purcell finished for her somberly.

"Which, with all due respect, is what we'll all become if we go anywhere near that obelisk," Decival's adjutant offered.

Decival studied the faces surrounding him. A mix of Carter's crew, his own officers, and a scattered group of men and women representing the colonists were all watching him with a great deal of concern etched on their faces. Every minute they spent without acting was a minute more the First Ones might be able to use to their advantage.

"Sir, there are approximately fifteen-thousand civilians on board the remaining ships," Danny added.

"What's our ration situation?" Decival asked his adjutant.

"Without knowing how long we're going to be out here, I'd recommend going to half-rations immediately. We weren't prepared for this level of support when we entered the system."

"And that's really the question, isn't it? Just how long are we gonna be out here? Lieutenant Xiao, have you finished distributing the antimatter?" Decival asked.

"Yes, Captain. We've got enough for one trip for each of the damaged ships and two for those remaining."

"And our shuttles?" Decival asked.

"We're down to about three-hundred after that last attack. It's not a lot, but it'll have to do," Bryon answered.

"Mr. Yellowknife, your weapons situation?"

"Production, runnin' ok, but I don't know for how much longer without...," the engineer said, but didn't finish. He didn't have to, because everyone was thinking the exact same thing.

"Without Captain Carter," Decival acknowledged. "Mr Granger, what's the status on your end?"

"I've tried broadcasting Majorana radiation. It might be theoretically possible to communicate in that fashion, but it would take me years to understand how to make a simple word," he explained, clearly frustrated at his inability to find a solution.

"It's all right, Mr. Granger. We can only do so much with the time we have, and it was a long shot anyway," Decival said consolingly. "Lieutenant Xiao, what about the mushrooms?"

"If there were any, there aren't any more. Not on the ships we've got left anyway," Danny said.

"Which leaves us with the *Fates' Winds* and Aric Keith," Decival concluded.

"That's a suicide mission," his adjutant stated bluntly.

Decival turned to study one of the holoscreens that was displaying the status of what was left of the fleet, and then zoomed out just how little distance he'd managed to put between his ships and the obelisk in the first place.

"We could go back home and start churning out those Bwain weapons in a place where we have more resources," his adjutant offered.

"I think you're forgettin' that we're all considered traitors by the SSC," Hal commented. "They'd probably start shootin' at us the second we arrived in the system."

"Well we can't just leave Captain Carter like this," Ensign Ford added. "If we take him too far from the *Bwainhome,* we don't know what'll happen to him."

"Or we could take the fight right to those bastards," Mephista said firmly. "We've got the gravity drive and the Bwain weapons, and now that the Bwain are acting at least somewhat normally again, we can be fairly sure that they'll cooperate."

"Are you sure you're not letting your personal feelings for Captain Carter affect your thinking?" Decival asked.

"No, that's not it at all. This is personal for all of us now," Mephista answered truthfully.

Decival glanced around and noted that most were nodding their heads in agreement.

"All right, here's what I'd like to do. Mr. Xiao, get your shuttles ready for some heavy duty. Ensign Ford, I'd like you to prepare to lead the damaged ships back to Earth. Mr. Granger, I'd like you to get the gravity drive ready."

"So what exactly are we gonna do, sir?" Bryon asked.

"We're gonna send our wounded and the colonists back home, and then we're gonna go after that damn obelisk. It's time to put the First Ones in their place."

Chapter Five

The Ninkovich
En route to the Sword Belt

"We're gonna flush Carter out like a rat from a burning barn. And then when the second wing arrives...," the admiral said as he lifted his boot and stomped it back down on the deck.

"Understood, sir. I'll be prepared," his weapons officer responded with a salute before he turned and returned to his station.

Phuri had watched Nico drill his officers relentlessly in the days since the fleet had begun its Alcubierre jump. Taking advantage of the nearly weeklong journey to the Sword Belt, Nico had worked through different formations and navigation solutions to account for the Bwain ship's ability to make short, faster-than-light jumps. The admiral's plan was to keep his ships in a formation of two concentric spheres, with the outer sphere of ships ready to engage anything that appeared in front of them, and the inner sphere targeting the center of the formation and providing fire support to the opposite side. Based on the measurements of the Bwain ship, the formation would allow no empty space for Carter to surprise them.

The admiral hunched his bulk on one arm of his elevated chair on the bridge, appearing almost as if he were fighting stomach problems. The electroglass that ringed the bridge looked out on the gray void at the interior of the Alcubierre bubble. It had been days of tense travel for the fleet, and Phuri hadn't seen the admiral sleep more than a few hours each day.

What worried Phuri more than Nico's disposition, or the soundness of the admiral's tactics, was the fact that Phuri had been out of contact with Earth for several days. With antimatter at a premium, he wouldn't even be able to send a message to Earth until the engagement was concluded, so at a minimum, Cazador would have nearly two weeks to operate behind his back. Then there was the matter of their victory not being anything close to certain. As a result, Phuri had taken to pacing the *Ninkovich*'s corridors, trying to work through the situation in his mind so he could figure out the best scenario for survival.

At 03:40, the admiral finally lifted himself from the bridge and turned for the airlock. Phuri had been drowsing, but the sudden movement startled him. Getting to his feet, he hurried through the hatch next to Nico.

Nico's coal-black eyes glared with suspicion. He still thought Phuri and Cazador were in league with one another, and nothing Phuri had to say would change his mind. Phuri's only hope was that Nico would value power more highly than revenge.

"A word, Admiral?" Phuri called as Nico stomped down the corridor in the direction of the officer's quarters, but Nico said nothing, forcing Phuri to pursue him.

"I've had a thought that may benefit both of us," he said. Nico barely deigned to turn his head.

"I could space you right here and now," the admiral said. "It would be an interesting experiment to see what happens to a human body inside an Alcubierre bubble."

"Admiral, aren't we past all of that yet? Remember how far we've come together."

The hulking officer turned at the hatch that led to the officers' recreation room. He glared for a moment, and then his expression suddenly softened a bit.

"Maybe I've been too hard on you. Come."

The flagship's officers room was more like a country club than spaceship, with polished wood, soft carpet, and a number of couches and recliners where the ship's officers could spend their downtime. There were about twenty or so officers in there at the moment who all sprang to attention when their admiral made his appearance, but Nico ignored them as he stalked across the carpet and into the next room. Phuri followed close behind, and soon found himself in a locker room that smelled of talcum powder and aftershave. For a moment, Phuri felt the pangs of bitterness over his exile on Gertie, but he did his best to push it away. The past was the past, and right now he needed to think about his future.

Nico stopped at the first locker, thumbed it open, and stripped to don his workout clothes while Phuri stood awkwardly beside him.

"What did you want to tell me?" Nico asked.

"Are we..."

"Of course we're secure. No one is admitted into the locker room once I've arrived."

Nico pulled up his shorts, slipped on a tight shirt that clung to his chest, and led Phuri through another door into the gym. The admiral stepped onto a row of treadmills, then began pounding out a slow, deliberate pace.

"Talk," he grunted.

"This won't be easy for us to discuss, but know that I bring it up from the standpoint of our larger goals," Phuri said.

"*Our* larger goals, or perhaps you mean *your* larger goals," Nico commented.

"No, and that's my point. You and I together brought down Kidewange and installed you in his place."

"Yes, I'm familiar with my own history," Nico said as the whine of the treadmill grew louder.

"I'm just saying...you should consider that in your dealings with Cazador."

"And what dealings have I had with him may I ask?" Nico asked.

"I'm sure you know by now."

"No, I don't. What I do know is that *you* have dealt with him. *You* took his money, and now he asks for weapons that he could use to stand against my fleet. Now, tell me again why I should trust you?"

"Because, he's acting on his own. I had nothing to do with this. It wasn't part of the deal."

"I'll eliminate him when I go after the cartels in Central and South America. There's no way in hell I'd give that man any weapons, alien or otherwise," Nico said. Sweat was now beginning to glisten on his forehead, and a dark line ran down his spine, but he continued his punishing pace.

"I'm not worried about that. What I'm worried about is the people, and where their sentiments lie when we return," Phuri explained.

"People value their own skins. Once the threat from Carter and the Bwain has been eliminated, they'll be so grateful to us that they'll forget all about Kidewange and the coup, and they'll want nothing to do with some filthy drug runner from Central America."

"That's exactly what I wanted to discuss. While we used Carter's threat to fuel the coup, that threat has already served its purpose. We're in power now, so we no longer need him. What we need to do now is to plan for what we may find waiting for us when we get back home, because while we're out here chasing down Carter, Cazador may have already decided that he no longer needs us."

Nico sprinted on as if he hadn't heard. His massive legs surged faster and faster and his arms pumped hard as his breath came in gasps between his teeth. A few moments later, the admiral balled up his fist and punched the stop button. He let the momentum carry him to the end of the conveyor belt, and then he leaped off of the end of it before turning to stomp toward Phuri.

Phuri backed against the wall, his hands raised in case Nico should strike him, but the big man simply stood there with his chest heaving in front of him.

"Carter is a dead man, and so is Cazador when I get back to Earth," he growled through clenched teeth. There was a tense moment where Phuri wasn't sure what was going to happen next, but he breathed a sigh of relief when the admiral suddenly grabbed his towel and wiped the sweat from his forehead.

He slapped the towel back over his shoulder, and slammed through the door to the showers without another word, leaving Phuri standing there with the smell of the admiral's sweat still lingering in his nostrils.

* * *

The Gravity Drive

"I've never led a vanguard before," Pandith said. The computers in his shuttle routed his comment to his former shipmates while the *Gravity Drive* cycled up to full power. It was strange knowing that he'd be at the very front of an assault on the obelisk itself. A part of him was terrified, especially as he watched the *Bwainhome* slip behind him, but he knew this was their only real chance at survival. If they failed to seize this opportunity, then the First Ones would continue to devour everything in their path, until there was no life left at all in the physical universe.

"Well, up until a week or so ago I'd never killed a trans-dimensional being either, but there's a first time for everything," Bryon called back to him over the comm link.

Pandith laughed. On his holoscreen, Bryon's shuttles were spread in an arc behind him with Captain Decival's cruisers behind the shuttles. The plan was simple. Pandith would take up a position close enough to the obelisk to be able to reach it with the gravitons, but far enough away that the First Ones wouldn't notice his presence until it was too late. As best as he and Granger could calculate, that meant that he'd be four million kilometers from the obelisk, which was approximately where the Sword Belt's sun had once been.

"Do you remember when we came through The Gates?" Danny asked.

"Which time?" Danielle asked.

"I guess all of 'em. They were so beautiful, and now these things have just...they've just destroyed everything," he said with a touch of nostalgia and sadness in his voice. So much had been lost in such a short period of time. Sometimes it didn't even seem real, and he desperately wished it wasn't.

The Gates had been a vast nebula left over from what had been a binary star's explosion millennia ago. They'd marked the edge of human-explored space, but now they were gone, consumed by the First Ones, along with the rest of the system.

"How are you doin' out there, Mr. Pandith?" Captain Decival asked over the comm link.

"Course and speed are good, sir. At present course and speed, I should be in position in thirty-one point seven minutes," Pandith reported as he checked the data before him.

"Copy that. Decival to the fleet. I want everyone keeping their eyes open. If these things are coming at us, then we need to know," Captain Decival ordered, his voice rang with confidence. They had all needed some time to regroup after the devastating losses from the recent battle with the First Ones. Even the small respite that they'd been granted had allowed them time to focus on the wounded, make necessary repairs, and get some much-needed rest.

"The Bwain seem calm, sir. No concerns at this point," Bryon reported.

At the mention of the Bwain, a question rose in Pandith's mind.

"Sir, has there been any change in Captain Carter's status?" he asked over the comm.

"Unfortunately, no. He's still catatonic," Decival said with a concerned look.

"You know, in our crew psychology classes we discussed traumatic catatonia," Pandith noted.

"There weren't any signs of trauma though. None that we could find anyway," Danielle offered.

"But from what you described, it sounds like something happened to him. You said he doesn't look healthy, and he's been totally unresponsive," Pandith said.

"But what would have traumatized him?" Granger asked.

"That's just it. He would have had to have seen or done something that...," Pandith said, but he quickly fell silent as he studied the images on his holoscreen. "Hang on a second."

"What is it, Mr. Poth?" Captain Decival asked.

"I've got multiple signatures approaching, but they're nowhere near where they should be!" Pandith said, trying to keep the panic from his voice.

* * *

The Ninkovich

It had been a six-day journey, and there wasn't a day that went by that Admiral Nico hadn't imagined what he would do to Atlas Carter when he finally confronted him.

Running on the treadmill or working on his jujutsu in the training room were the only activities that released his pent-up energy and stilled his mind. In these moments, he imagined a variety of tactical scenarios involving how he could defend the Earth and her colonies with a depleted fleet, and then he drilled his crews on each of the various scenarios he had considered. He put himself in the position of having nearly unlimited antimatter and the ability to flit back and forth from system to system causing damage, and so he drilled his crew to anticipate every potential offensive and defensive maneuver that would be applicable when facing an opponent with superior maneuverability.

With all this battle readiness, the last thing Admiral Nico ever imagined that he'd find upon their arrival in the Sword Belt was nothing but empty space.

"I don't understand, sir," his navigation officer said as she stared up at an empty holoscreen. "The coordinates check out. This is the Sword Belt, but there's nothing here. I don't understand."

"Well, check again. They have to be here somewhere. It's the only logical place," Nico growled, though he himself was suddenly experiencing some doubt as to the situation. What if Capra Falconi had been correct after all? What if there were creatures so powerful that they could consume an entire solar system? Was such a thing even possible?

"Sir, all of our star maps check out. This *is* the Sword Belt, or what used to be the Sword Belt anyway. In our present location, we should be in orbit around the system's sun," his navigation officer reported from her station on the bridge.

Glaring into emptiness where he thought he'd find an opponent, Nico gripped the arm of his chair and flexed his muscles as he dug his fingers into it.

"I'm picking up some very strange readings on the sensors, but nothing that would allow us to determine exactly what happened here," his science officer reported.

The admiral hadn't told his crew anything about what Falconi had reported upon his return, because the security risk would have been far too great. Now he wondered to himself if he'd made a mistake.

"Do you know what they say about discretion and valor, Admiral?" Phuri asked from behind him.

"Whatever did this, we will find it and kill it, but that's not our first priority," Nico grumbled as he stared at the images before him and listened to the random reports from his officers.

"Admiral, how should we proceed?" his science officer asked when Nico stopped responding to the reports and fell silent for several moments.

"Conduct a deep scan," he ordered. "It's time to bring Carter out of the shadows."

A deep scan was a pulse of electromagnetic radiation that streaked through the surrounding space in all directions. Any of the frequency and spectra that were reflected back could be analyzed by the science team based on its signatures.

As a hunter, Nico didn't like being blind, but the tactical situation didn't worry him much. He was as prepared for Carter's fleet as he could possibly be.

"Admiral, I'm showing hard targets on the scan. There's fifteen 'em, with a number of smaller craft about two million kilometers behind our position. I'm detecting carbyne steel in the targets, sir. They're SSC ships."

"I found you Carter, you bastard! Helm, set course for...," Nico was about to order, but one of his officers quickly interrupted him.

"Wait sir, there's something else out there. It's some sort of an anomaly. I have it on the visible spectrum from our telescopes."

Nico sighed, exasperated at the delay in his revenge, but with Carter prowling around out there, he could never be too careful.

"Show me," he said.

At maximum resolution, the holoimage was a white blur, no bigger than a few decks of cards.

"It's not reflecting on any of our scans, but it's definitely emitting visible light," the science officer reported.

"The anomalies are not our concern. Set a course for Carter's ships," Nico ordered. He had waited too long for this moment to allow himself to be distracted by anything. His fingers curled, as if in anticipation of wrapping his hands around Carter's throat.

"Course has been set. ETA, two hours," the navigator reported.

"Good. All ships to battle stations. Comms, give me general broadcast, all frequencies and bands."

"Ready on your mark, Admiral."

"Begin transmission," Nico ordered.

* * *

The Fates' Winds

Though it had been twisted and changed by the First Ones' efforts, much of the *Fates' Winds* technology was still operational, and despite what they had done to his body, the First Ones had left Aric's cochlear implant intact, so he was able to receive the message that Nico was broadcasting.

"To all SSC personnel in this system, this is Admiral Vladislav Nico on board the SSC flagship *Ninkovich*. We have arrived in this system to apprehend the traitor Atlas Carter. He is personally responsible for the deaths of thousands of SSC personnel. Anyone who dares to aid, abet, or harbor him will be considered his accomplices and treated accordingly.

"Those of you who stand against us will not survive what's coming. Those who wish to surrender, the time to do so is now."

A sound like whipping chains and the tearing of paper filled Aric's mind. At first he could not place the emotion they were trying to convey, but then a horrifying realization struck him: this was The Ancient's laughter.

"ARIC KEITH, IS THIS NEW ONE THREATENING US?" The Ancient roared through his thoughts.

"I don't know. It sounds like he's going after Captain Carter," Aric responded through his thoughts.

Atlas' Final Approach

After all this time, Aric could still only speculate as to why The Ancient continued to ask him questions, and persisted in demanding answers. It seemed to delight in taunting his human weaknesses, and boasting about the First Ones' infinitely superior existence. Aside from their need for the physical labor he performed aboard what was left of the *Fates' Winds*, there must be some reason they refused to allow him to die. Could the answer be as simple as the possibility that The Ancient needed his companionship?

"THIS ONE WILL FIGHT THE CARTER?" The Ancient demanded.

"That's what he said," Aric answered noncommittally.

"THEN WE WILL JOIN HIM!" The Ancient bellowed.

* * *

The Dauntless

Without a ship to command, Captain Mephista had found herself wandering aimlessly through the fleet's flagship. One of the ship's supply officers had found a hoverchair to allow her the mobility she needed.

She promised herself that she wouldn't visit Atlas, but her path through the ship's corridors always seemed to lead her to the ship's infirmary.

When she rested her hand on Atlas' forehead and brushed back his hair, strands of it fell out and clung to her fingers.

"My god Atlas, what happened to you?" she asked sadly.

The Bwain beside her groaned and stretched, but said nothing. The alien had followed her everywhere she had gone, even staying outside near the doors to her quarters when she tried to sleep, yet the whole time it had been hovering around her, it had said nothing.

"I had another dream about Kaylee," she said quietly. "This one was better. She was just floating in space, and she almost looked happy. I wonder if that's how she felt when you rescued her."

Mephista felt a rueful smile spread across her face. She couldn't imagine that she'd once been a brutal pirate, interested only in herself. Now she was finally realizing that maybe what Kaylee had been telling her was that she'd been searching too long for what she already had.

Suddenly, alarms blared throughout the ship. Mephista looked up, but there were no holoscreens to be found. She had to rely on the audio she received through the captains' command channel.

"I count thirty, say again, three-zero ships," Pandith's voice called through the communications channel.

"Captain, they're setting a course right for us. What are your orders?" Bryon called from his shuttle. "Signature matches the *Ninkovich*, Admiral Nico's flagship. A number of carriers and fighters as well."

"Incoming transmission, sir. My apologies, but I think you'll want to hear this," Danielle called from her station.

Mephista closed her eyes and listened to Nico's arrogant taunting. The man's ignorance turned her stomach, and she longed to reach out and end his scourge once and for all. She visualized the fleet as Decival would have arrayed it to reach the First Ones. Outnumbered, with Nico's fleet so close and his strongest ships far from the threat, Decival had limited options. He'd have to either execute a retreat that would leave all of the shuttles, as well as the gravity drive behind as little more than a bunch of sitting ducks, or he'd have to somehow find a way to stand and fight. Unfortunately, their strongest weapon in a fight was lying comatose beside her.

She wrapped her hand around Atlas' cold fingers. The Bwain beside her preened and fluttered its feathers, then raised its head in interest.

"Please come back to me," Mephista begged, but the form before her remained still and motionless, trapped somewhere between consciousness and death.

* * *

The Ninkovich

Admiral Nico wanted to reach through his holoscreens and grab the pathetic remains of Carter's fleet with his bare hands. Not a single ship had surrendered, or even radioed back. They were in a terrible formation for a fleet battle, so whoever was leading them was most likely an inexperienced officer. Most likely it was some mutineer scum whose mind and loyalties had been poisoned by Carter. Speaking of the traitorous captain, the alien ship was nowhere to be found, and it was starting to make him a bit suspicious.

"Is it some sort of a trick?" he snarled at his navigation officer.

"I'm not sure, sir. Without knowing the capabilities of the Bwain ship, it's hard for me to say where it could possibly be."

"You've seen its capabilities in action, have you not?" Nico asked.

"Of course, Admiral."

"Then answer my question."

"I don't think there's anything suspicious going on here. They're pulling their shuttles back and tightening their formation considerably, so my best guess is that we caught 'em as they were preparing for some other threat. The formation they were in made no sense. The ships were almost isolated from each other."

"What would they be doing with the shuttles?" Nico asked.

"They could have been using 'em as decoys...or mines maybe?" the weapons officer responded.

The tactic would have fit well enough with Carter's tactics of deception, but then why pull them back?

"It looks like the shuttles are reversing course and trying to dock with the cruisers, sir."

"What are you up to, Atlas Carter?" Nico asked himself as he narrowed his eyes at the holoscreen.

"Comms, what's our status? Why haven't they contacted us? They must have received the message," Nico asked as he glanced around at his communications officer.

"Unknown, sir."

"Admiral, I have a report on the anomaly," another crewman said.

"Not now. How long until we're in weapons range of their first ships?" Nico asked, dismissing the officers' interruption as he continued to focus on the ragtag fleet displayed on the bridge's holoscreens.

"Magna-cannons are charged, sir. We're in range, but at this distance they'd be able to maneuver fast enough to avoid them."

"Lasers?" Nico asked as he continued down his mental checklist.

"Two minutes to effective range."

Nico forced himself to breathe deeply and calm down. He needed a clear head to try and analyze the situation. He had more ships than Carter, in a better formation. Though the alien ship was missing, he could at least deal with Carter's band of traitors.

"Bring Phuri to the bridge. I want him to see what's about to happen," Nico said, smiling to himself. Now was his chance to show the slick manipulator who truly held the power.

"Yes, Admiral."

"Full induction. Don't let their shuttles get away," he ordered.

"Sir, at our current speed, we'll be able to launch our firing solutions in about thirty seconds."

"Fire as soon as we're in range," Nico ordered calmly, but inside, his heart raced with the thrill of the hunt.

"Sir, I think you should see this report from the anomaly," the officer urged again.

"We're about to engage in battle here. I'm sure whatever it is can wait," Nico responded irritably.

"No, it can't, sir."

The holoscreen to Nico's left changed, showing the anomaly at the highest resolution the ship was capable of producing. What Nico saw on the display looked like a swarm of insects peeling off into the void of space. The computer-created view zoomed out, further and further, until the true picture of what was about to happen became clear.

"They're coming for us," Nico uttered with a stunned look as the images before him now commanded his full attention.

"Firing," his weapons officer called.

* * *

The Dauntless

"Try to disable their ships if you can," Decival ordered.

"Yes, sir," the weapons officer stationed beside Danielle acknowledged. "Ready to fire when you give the order."

"Not yet," Decival said.

"But Captain, they're firing on us."

"Remember how Captain Carter treated us," Decival cautioned. "We wouldn't be here if he hadn't shown restraint. Those sailors don't know what they're doing, and we need to try and convince them that what they're doing is wrong."

"But we need to talk to them then," his communications officer said.

"Not yet. You don't know Admiral Nico like I do. Him seeing me on the other side would just make him angrier," Decival said as he quickly scanned the images before him.

"All shuttles docked, Captain," Bryon Purcell's voice announced over the comms channel.

"Lieutenant Hoff, begin evasive maneuvers," Decival ordered calmly. He didn't need to glance in Danielle's direction to know she was already fast at work.

Thousands of bright red streaks appeared on her monitors, showing the path of every projectile. Nico's ships had launched missiles and magna-cannons toward the heart of Decival's fleet as soon as they'd come within range. It was a textbook tactic. The magna-cannon projectiles would travel more quickly, forcing the fleet to maneuver out of their way and into the path of the missiles.

Space was vast though, and Danielle had fought many battles in its blackness. She darkened the tracking for all projectiles not predicted for impact, then began cycling through new courses that would put her targeted ships out of harm's way. In less than five seconds, she had her solution ready, and transmitted it to the fleet.

"Assuming new formation. Stand by to fire missile countermeasures," she called.

Her plan was to break the fleet into a wide arc that would give each ship thousands of kilometers to maneuver behind an interlocking grid of countermeasures. She had to be careful, because with Nico's advantage in numbers he could bring two or three ships' worth of firepower to bear against each of hers, quickly depleting her fleet's countermeasures unless they could remain in range to support each other. Right now she was just maneuvering to buy time, which was the best she could do under Decival's constraints.

"Captain, how long are we gonna hold off?" she asked.

"As long as necessary, Ms. Hoff," Decival answered. Despite the incoming fire from Nico's magna-cannons, he was prepared to bide his time until the moment was precisely right.

"Countermeasures ready. Firing now," the weapons officer called.

On Danielle's holoscreens, bright blossoms of radiation bloomed like fireworks in front of the fleet. The countermeasures were designed to scramble the missile electronics, while also sending micrometeorites into the approaching weapons, knocking them off course, though they could do little against super-dense magna-cannon projectiles hurled at comet-like speed.

"First volley approaching," Danielle reported.

"All hands, brace for impact!" Decival ordered, as he tightened his grip on the railing near his command station.

Magna-cannon projectiles were designed to do damage with kinetic force, so without the ability to steer themselves, they were easily avoided.

"He's firing magnas in random cycles, interspersed with missiles and lasers," Danielle reported. "The pattern's gonna be hard to predict."

"Laser fire incoming," the weapons officer called. "Deploying countermeasures."

Thousands more signatures filled Danielle's displays. Nico's ships were larger and more powerful than Decival's, and they were gaining on the fleet. Every kilometer that Nico closed between their respective fleets reduced the amount of time that Danielle had to calculate solutions.

"Countermeasures at seventy percent capacity, sir," the weapons officer called.

On Danielle's holodisplay, Nico's lasers scattered against the mirrored glass the fleet had released, but a few of the beams broke through, painting ships in the fleet with a bright blue spear.

"I have damage reports," another officer called. "The *Brindle* and the *Mastiff* have been hit. Damage is minor. They're both maintaining readiness."

"Assuming new formation," Danielle called. Decival's ships were farther apart than she'd like with so many ships to counter. Unless they somehow reduced Nico's firepower, it was only a matter of time before they took significant casualties.

"Captain, I'm running out of options," Danielle said as her fingers continued to fly across her controls, searching desperately for solutions that didn't exist.

"Ms. Hoff, we're going to need to revert to local control," Decival said.

"Copy sir," she answered. "On your mark."

"Attention all ships, this is Decival. We're returning to local navigational control. Good luck."

"Captain, can we fire back at these bastards yet?" one of the other captains asked.

From the corner of her eye Danielle saw Decival's jaw tighten. Like her, he knew that it was only a matter of time, but how were they going to stop Nico unless they fired back?

"Open a channel to the *Ninkovich*," Decival ordered.

* * *

The Ninkovich

"I'm not interested in your anomaly reports!" Nico growled to his science officer. "We'll deal with aliens after we finish Carter's fleet. Weapons, keep firing! Break them into smaller groups and finish them off."

"Still no sign of the Bwain ship," his navigation officer reported.

"You set this formation to ensure that no vulnerabilities existed against Carter's capabilities," Phuri noted at his elbow. "Are you sure that's wise?"

"A hit, sir! Critical damage to the *Laurel*."

Nico smiled as the holoscreen showed a bloom of debris shearing from the smaller vessel. A magna-cannon projectile had struck its bow and tore through its upper decks.

"Excellent shot," Nico said as he turned to Phuri. "It looks like Carter's fled, but I see your point. We'll remain in formation on present course. Helm, what is our current strength and damage level?"

"Admiral, they still haven't fired on us," his weapons officer said.

"What?" Nico asked.

"Sir, they're just maneuvering out there. They haven't fired on us at all."

"I don't understand," Nico said as his dark brows drew into a scowl.

"I have a transmission coming in, Admiral," his communications officer called. "It's from the *Dauntless*."

"Put it on the main holos."

Captain Decival's thin face appeared before him on the bridge. Decival had been one of his most loyal captains, and Nico had been sure that he would have been the one to take down Carter, so it was a shock to see him on the opposite end of the transmission.

"Admiral Nico," Decival greeted him without emotion.

"I must say, I expected more from you, Captain," Nico sneered.

"Sir, you've entered into a situation that you don't understand. I know you don't want to hear or believe this, but Carter has been right all along."

"No man that aligns himself with alien scum is right, including you," Nico replied.

"Remember what they taught us in the SSC academy? Hell, you taught me this yourself. The enemy of my enemy is my friend. It's always been a universal truth, but my friendship will only last until I have no other choice but to resist your attack."

"Get to the point, Decival," Nico said as he waved an impatient hand.

"I will defend my ships if you force me too, but I will not surrender until you agree to stand down and let us show you what's happening in this system."

"Admiral...," his weapons officer called.

Nico drummed his fingers on his command chair as he processed the situation. Was Decival playing him for a fool a second time? Could Carter have cowed Decival into obedience, and now Decival saw this encounter as his way out, or was it yet another of the bastard's tricks to lull him into a false sense of security?

"You may want to listen," Phuri said from his side. "We know what Carter and Falconi said about the anomaly. There may be something to it."

"Admiral, we're under attack!" his weapons officer said.

"What?" Nico growled as he angrily swiped away Decival's face with his haptics and replaced the image with a tactical display.

Red flares of damage and attacks were stabbing into his fleet on all sides.

"Admiral, I show six vectors," his navigation officer said.

"Where are they coming from?" Nico bellowed.

"I don't know, sir," his weapons officer said. "They weren't here just a second ago."

"Initiate countermeasures," Nico ordered. "And Decival...the next time I see you, it will be at your hanging after your court-martial."

* * *

The Dauntless

"My god they're fast!" Decival's science officer gasped.

A group of First Ones was streaking toward Nico's fleet at unimaginable speeds. They moved so quickly that Decival's holodisplay wasn't able to track them in a straight line, and could show them only as white targets skipping across the screen.

"Admiral, you have to get out of the system! You can't fight those things!" Decival practically shouted at him.

"He's blocked our transmission, Captain," the communications officer reported.

"Sir, Nico's lead elements are still firing against us," Danielle called from her station.

Decival had seconds only to make his decision. He watched the threat vectors continue to blossom more and more heavily against his own ships while his anger rose.

"Attention, all ships in the fleet. The First Ones have returned. Deploy all shuttles. Shuttle pilots, you are to attempt the engage the First Ones as you see fit. Main craft, wait to take action until Nico's fleet ceases fire." Decival's orders had barely been transmitted before the entire fleet was scrambling in a frenzy of activity.

"The shuttles will be sitting ducks, sir!" his weapons officer cried.

"Comms," Decival barked, "Get the *Ninkovich* back."

"Yes, sir," the officer acknowledged. "Broadcasting now."

"Admiral, cease fire and we can help you! The shuttles we are launching have weapons that can hurt those things," Decival called over the communications channel.

On the holoscreen, he watched as thousands of his fellow officers in Nico's fleet were consumed by the aliens, but the admiral held his formation steady, and kept pouring fire into Decival's countermeasures.

"Damn it Nico, we have weapons that can defeat them if you let us!" Decival shouted angrily, as if doing so might somehow break through Nico's stubbornness.

"Sir, the shuttles are deploying, but they're taking heavy fire. We're losing dozens of them," Danielle reported with a quick glance over her shoulder.

Decival could only watch as his worst fear came true: the First Ones were back, and his entire fleet was in mortal danger.

* * *

Bryon Purcell had just docked his shuttle in the *Dauntless'* bay when Decival's order crackled through his implant. Cursing, he punched his holocontrols, lifted the shuttle back off the deck, and spun it toward the open bay doors. The Bwain beside him started flashing panicked reds and pinks as they slid around the cabin.

"I'm sorry little buddies, but duty calls." Bryon said to them as he pushed the craft to full throttle.

The space outside the *Dauntless* was a nightmare. Bryon's suit HUD overlaid the threat analysis of incoming munitions and likely courses on his faceplate, showing him a tortuous, shifting path through the battle toward the First Ones that was constantly changing as the fleets countered each other's positions.

"This is impossible," he muttered.

A wall of countermeasures was just barely protecting Decival's fleet, but on the other side, but Nico's ships were still pounding away at their defenses, all in spite of the fact that the First Ones were streaking toward the admiral's ships at unimaginable speeds.

"Do we have any idea how many of those things there are?" Bryon asked.

"It looks like a dozen, or maybe two," one of the other shuttle pilots called.

"Danielle, where are the rest of 'em at?" he asked.

"I don't know. I'm scanning everywhere I can, even toward the obelisk, but I can't seem to locate 'em," she answered.

"Well, we're gonna have to get whichever ones we can for right now. We'll worry about the rest after," Bryon said as he pushed his craft toward the edge of the fleet's countermeasures. To the naked eye, they looked like a small star field, or a cloud of dust, yet when Nico's lasers struck the floating mirrors, they bloomed into starbursts of fireworks before dying like a fire's embers in the void of space. Small explosions littered the area in front of him as the missile countermeasures detonated against Nico's munitions.

"We're all gonna be slaughtered out here!" one of the pilots called over the comms channel. Whether he had forgotten he was transmitting to his fellow pilots, or was just overwhelmed by the hopelessness of their situation, he expressed the unspoken thoughts of many of shuttle crew at that particular moment.

"Hang on Bryon, I'm uploading a course to you now," Danielle said. "I'm gonna route you on either side of the battle."

"Ok, but this better work, or we're all gonna be toast out here," Bryon said as he swung his shuttle wide. "If I end up dead because of this, then you owe me a date."

In spite of the joke, he was terrified. Shuttles were meant for transporting passengers or cargo, not for engaging in battle. Their hulls had little armor, they carried no countermeasures, and the only offensive weapon Bryon had was the alien weapon that was mounted to the nose of his craft.

"Bryon, just...please be careful, ok?" Danielle whispered in his ear as his shuttle cleared the countermeasures.

"Oh, you know me. Safety first," he quipped.

The holoscreens showed two of Decival's ships struck with smaller damage. On Nico's side, the First Ones had already laid waste to nearly a quarter of his fleet, and yet he kept firing at Decival.

"Jeez, Nico must be insane," he said to the Bwain.

"Bryon, look out! He's pivoting toward you!" Danielle shouted suddenly over the comms channel.

Bryon mashed his inducers to full thrust, but there was little else he could do. In Nico's paranoid mind, he no doubt thought the shuttles were some kind of offensive attack, despite Decival's warning. To his horror, Bryon saw lasers and missiles lash out at his ragged shuttle wing. Craft all around him bloomed and smoked with depressurizations.

"This is shuttle 3496 to the *Ninkovich*," Bryon yelled. "Nico, you son-of-a-bitch, we're trying to help you! We're the only ones who can stop those things, so stop trying to kill us you bastard!"

As expected, no response from Nico or anyone else in his fleet was forthcoming.

"Time to target, ten minutes," Bryon reported as craft all around him were swept from existence by Nico's stupidity.

"What are we gonna do?" one of the other pilots called out anxiously. "He's killing us!"

"Everyone, execute evasive maneuvers and just try to hold on," Bryon said as he watched a new volley of missiles streak toward his beleaguered shuttles.

*　*　*

"Captain, you will report! What is your status?" Nico shouted.

On his holoscreen, one of the disgusting white creatures was crawling like an octopus through the hull of the *Hellfire*. The ship was foundering, and Nico couldn't believe that the computer's holographic interpretation of the trillions of data points it was receiving was correct. There was no known weapon that could do this, no intelligence that would have prepared him.

"This is what Carter found," Phuri breathed next to him.

"What's our status?" Nico bellowed.

"Sir, formation and firing solutions holding. We are still engaging Carter's fleet," his weapons officer reported.

"Sir, I've received several communications from Captain Decival. He's asking us to cease hostilities. He claims to be able to fight those things,"

Atlas' Final Approach

Nico's communications officer called from his station on the bridge.

"I don't believe him," Nico muttered like a petulant child who was unwilling to concede.

"Sir, Decival's fleet has launched what appear to be all of their shuttles. The craft are taking heavy losses, but they appear to be trying to rendezvous with the other aliens."

A third of Nico's fleet was flashing yellow for damaged or red for out of action. The creatures attacking him were like gibbering nightmares, consuming everything in their path.

"This shouldn't be happening!" Nico shouted, still unable to take in how utterly unprepared he had been for the ferocious devastation before him.

"Admiral, it's my recommendation that we withdraw back to Earth," Jansen said. "That would be the prudent choice."

"This is not the time for pride," Phuri added. Nico glared at the smaller man, furious at Phuri's fearful sniveling.

"I am the admiral of the Sol Space Command," Nico bellowed. "I am the president of the Galactic Senate. I am the strongest man in this universe. I will not be denied!"

"Your orders, sir?" his weapons officer asked shakily.

"Target everyone! Kill them all!" Nico screamed into the chaos.

*　*　*

The Dauntless

"Sir, they've begun to maneuver away from the First Ones, but they're still firing at us," Danielle called over her shoulder.

"That idiot is trying to kill us all!" Decival fumed. "Ms. Hoff, get us into a shielding position. We need to give our shuttles cover so we can help him."

"I'm on it," she said as her fingers worked the controls furiously.

She punched in a navigation solution that brought the *Dauntless* and the other ships so that they were facing Nico's formation broadside. That way, their slow-moving shuttles would benefit from the fleet's protection. The *Dauntless'* chaff and antimissile munitions filled the space around them, taking the brunt of Nico's volley while she watched the first of the shuttles curl far out and around the conflict.

"Countermeasures at forty percent!" the weapons officer called.

Danielle brought the ship a few hundred kilometers farther back and lower, so that a series of magna-cannon shells passed harmlessly above them.

"Shuttles are five minutes to targets, sir," Danielle noted with a steady voice.

"Countermeasures at 20 percent!"

The ship shook under the impact of a laser strike that had pierced their defenses.

"We have a small hull breach on aft deck eight. Minor damage," someone called.

"Nico, you bastard. You can't keep doing this, or you're gonna kill us all," Decival muttered. Apparently not even shouting, would get Nico to listen to reason at this point.

On the holos, Nico was still directing the majority of his fury at Decival's ships. It was all the Admiral knew how to do. He would spew his rage and hatred, and keep fighting regardless of the fact that it would get him and his entire fleet killed.

"Countermeasures exhausted!"

"Shuttles two minutes from targets. We're getting dangerously close to the First Ones," Danielle noted.

"All ships, get your Bwain ready. We'll do what we can," Decival ordered the shuttle pilots.

There was little that Danielle could do now other than to watch and see how it all played out. She couldn't adjust course when the goal was to shield the shuttle deployment from Nico's fire. Nico's missiles and lasers chewed their way through the clouds of countermeasures, and there was nothing that anyone could do to stop it.

Then her heart punched into her throat as a series of magna-cannon shells streaked through the debris and tore into the ship's spine.

"We have massive damage amidships. Batteries Tango and higher are offline," the environmental officer called.

"Reactor? Thrust?" Decival asked tersely.

"Responsive. Shuttles are engaging," Danielle answered after a quick check of her holoscreen.

"Get us out of here, Ms. Hoff," he ordered, but the order came too late. A nuclear armed missile slipped through the countermeasures and struck the main induction bank at the bottom of the cruiser. The explosion lifted the crew from the deck and dropped them again, knocking many to their knees.

"Decompression forward, decks three and up," someone called.

"Get us out of here!" Decival yelled.

"Sir, I'm at fifteen percent thrust, and there's another volley on the way!" the weapon's officer cried as another impact rocked the craft.

"Mayday! Mayday!" Decival's voice rang through the communications system, if only for the benefit of the devices that would continue to record the battle. After all, who would be able to respond to their distress call?

There was nothing else for Danielle to do but close her eyes and pray.

* * *

Mephista could follow the battle through her implant, but she knew that the more important struggle lay in whatever was happening behind Atlas' closed eyes. Carter had grown more and more agitated throughout the battle, his limbs surging up from the bed and his lips parting as if he were murmuring arguments. But he still hadn't woken, and Mephista could tell that Decival was running out of time.

"Do you know what's happening, Atlas? Wherever you are, can you see?" she asked.

Sweat shone on his face. His head snapped from side to side.

"You know, before I met you I would have given anything to be anywhere else. To leave my own body."

His hand spasmed in hers. His palm was alternately chilly and clammy.

"You showed me that there was another way. That the small things made the biggest difference."

The ship lurched, and her hoverchair tried to drift away from Atlas' side. She grabbed a rail at the bedside and pulled herself close once more. The Bwain who'd remained with her fluttered its wings and let out a crackling cough.

"I've always thought that you might be worried about what you had to do, to protect all of us, and to make the sacrifices that you've had to make. I know what happened to your wife. I know why you were sent to the Sword Belt, but I also know that we can count on you, and that you won't let us down."

Atlas' body convulsed as if he was trying to sit up, but his eyes stayed closed.

Squawking, the Bwain waddled to her side. Then the bird-thing did something she'd never seen. It rested its head on Carter's chest, raised its stubbed arms and placed its wings and hands near his heart. The effect was of an awkward hug, and somehow she had the feeling that the creature was saying goodbye. Before she could stop herself, she was patting the rough skin of the creature's head.

"I saw Kaylee...you know, after...," Mephista continued. "I think she was trying to tell me something. She was trying to tell me that it's not too late. It's never too late, so before this goes any farther, I just want to say that...I love you Atlas. I really love you."

The *Tranquility* lurched violently upward. From years in command, Mephista recognized the feeling of a massive impact. The physics of the weaponry would throw the ship upward, and depressurization would magnify the effect.

With her attention on the damage reports that were flooding into her ear, it took Mephista a long moment to realize what was happening. She looked down at her hand and saw that he was squeezing it with all the strength that remained in his ravaged body. He turned his head to her, and his eyes were filled with both love and concern.

"It's not over yet," he said.

Chapter Six

Lunar orbit

When Lana Delgato finally finished telling her story of her pursuit of Capra Falconi, her interaction with Phuri Vongsa, and Pandith's confirmation of the altered broadcasts, the intelligence detachment captain ran his hand up the back of his scalp. His eyes flicked to his subordinates, who had stood expressionless the entire time.

"So, do you see now?" she asked. "Are you gonna tell me what's goin' on out there?"

While she'd been talking, the soldiers had been tapping their hands to their helmets and subvocalizing between each other. From the pilot's reaction, Lana knew something had happened outside the shuttle, but she couldn't see anything from where she'd been bound to her acceleration couch.

"Canaveral is asking us to confirm their orders, Sergeant," the pilot called from the flight deck.

The red-haired non-com was still considering Lana. His expressionless stare made her wonder if anything she'd said had mattered after all.

"Get us into boarding position," he ordered.

"What's happening?" Lana asked. "What's out there?"

"We're gonna find out if what you're telling us is true or not," the sergeant said. He then resealed his helmet, swung his rifle down from his shoulder, and turned back for the airlock as his men readied themselves beside him.

The shuttle twisted around, pushing Lana against her restraints. She had no idea which direction they were moving, and tried to get her bearings by finding the moon outside her porthole. Instead of the pockmarked lunar surface, she gasped at what she saw.

What looked like an entire fleet of mangled SSC ships had appeared in Lunar orbit. It was as if some giant creature had come and punched holes in the most powerful vessels humanity knew how to construct.

Lana's mind started racing, praying that she wasn't correct about the fleet that had appeared, trying to think of everything Pandith had told her about the other aliens in the Sword Belt. Then she played the only card she had left:

"You know what happened to those ships! I told you what it was! It's not the Bwain or anything else. Let me go and I'll help you, I promise!" Lana pleaded.

The sergeant glanced at her, then triggered his helmet's speaker.

"Let her watch," he said.

Deceleration pushed against Lana's chest as the pilot drew them close to the derelict fleet. A dim clank vibrated through the shuttle, and the craft's airlock seal flashed green before the sergeant and his squad darted through the airlock.

One of the remaining soldiers tapped a holocontrol, and a grid of six different views appeared against the shuttle's forward wall. It took Lana a moment to realize that she was looking through the helmet cameras of the team as they spun right and then left to cover the other ship's entry compartment. The vessel's lights were flickering, and it was difficult to make out any other figures, or the extent of the damage on the other ship.

"Clear," the sergeant's voice crackled through the radio.

"Atmosphere's been thinned out. Oxygen is down to forty percent. Ship's power levels are fluctuating rapidly," another voice reported.

"No crew or communications. Let's get to the bridge," the sergeant said.

On the holos, the marines hopscotched their way from the entry compartment into a larger access corridor. They then turned to the right and jogged through a cramped tunnel. Lana wondered how they could know exactly where they were going, until she realized they had the ship's schematics in their database and were viewing them on the HUDs in their helmets. It *was* an SSC ship after all.

"You know this ship," she said. "You know I'm right!"

"We don't know anything. Now stay quiet," one of the soldiers guarding her said.

"Still no contacts," the sergeant's voice said through the comms channel.

"Sir, I'm picking up a transmission," the shuttle pilot called.

"Hold on," the sergeant said. The detachment had come to a hatch that was flickering with warnings. "Looks like we've got power loss and depressurization up ahead. Ramirez!"

One of the other soldiers stepped forward and drew a small cutting torch from her utility belt. The brilliant plasma sliced easily through the metal, and the soldier began working methodically to cut a circular hole through the damaged hatch. A rush of atmosphere whistled through the hole she was cutting, buffeting her as she continued her work.

A few minutes later, she had completed the task enough the atmosphere rushing to vent into space bent and blew out the damaged hatch.

Lana gasped at the sight before the soldiers.

The entire compartment on the other side, along with the decks above and below it, had been melted and fused, and crew members' bodies floated lifelessly in the debris. Gray strips of skin had peeled away from their bodies, and their faces were locked in mummified stares.

"I don't know how they could have made a jump like this," one of the soldiers said.

"That's what we're gonna find out," the sergeant answered. "Inducers on. We'll take a shortcut."

Flashes around the joints of each marine indicated where their suit-borne propulsion systems triggered. The soldiers flew up several decks, angling for another airlock that indicated its healthy status with a green light.

"Sergeant!" a voice called in shock just as the soldiers reached the landing.

The soldiers quickly spun around and shouldered their rifles.

Floating toward them was a clutch of small, bird-shaped monsters. The creatures were winged, with frigid feathers spread at awkward angles. Their skin looked to have once been composed of leathery scales, but they were just as cold and dead as the humans.

"Bwain," the sergeant said. "It's all right. They're dead, just like the others. Come on, let's get that hatch open."

"We don't wanna depressurize the other side sir," one of the others called. "There might be survivors."

"Copy. Use the bubble," the sergeant instructed.

One of the other soldiers pulled out what looked like spider steel in a thin webbing, and began fixing the material around the airlock using electric charges from his suit. The steel mesh expanded, and the soldiers stepped under the fabric as the soldier worked it into the shape of a bubble. A few more welds, and he had created a temporary seal to keep atmosphere from escaping.

"Seal is good, Sergeant," he reported as he stepped back to examine his work.

"Sir, the transmission?" the shuttle pilot reminded the sergeant.

"I said wait on that," the man answered. Lana could hear the tension in his voice. Involuntarily, she was rooting for her captors now. If they perished, she knew that somehow Nico and Phuri would blame whatever happened on her. More importantly, these soldiers could help her find the truth.

"Weapons ready," the sergeant ordered.

The other soldiers leveled their rifles at whatever they expected to come across the other side.

"Unseal the airlock."

"Sir, you need to hear this message!" the pilot's voice said urgently. "I'm sorry, but I'm gonna go ahead and play it."

"This is Ensign Julie Ford, in command of this...fleet. The people aboard these ships are civilians. They're refugees from the colony planet Gertie in the Sword Belt. The entire system has been destroyed by a threat far greater than the Bwain. There's another species of aliens out there that are capable of consuming entire stars and planets. We, along with the Bwain and Captain Carter, have found a way to fight them, but we need your help. Please treat these people with respect. We mean you no harm."

On the holoscreen in front of Lana, hundreds of terrified faces looked back at the marines facing them. The people were dirty, terrified, and they raised their hands in desperate surrender.

Slowly, the soldiers lowered their weapons. In the grainy footage, Lana could see tears of joy streaking down the passengers' faces. She could only imagine what they'd been through.

More importantly, they could tell the truth about what was happening out there, and their arrival was only the beginning.

* * *

The last thing that Julie Ford had expected after she'd sent her broadcast was to be led from the damaged *Reichstag* at gunpoint, but that's exactly what the intelligence detachment who had boarded her ship were doing. Their sergeant had asked her to don an EVO suit and come with him, and his tone had made it clear that she had little choice.

"What about the rest of us?" Kilver had asked the soldiers.

"Do they have food? Water?" the sergeant asked Julie.

"For a few days. We need to get them to Earth. If you could just...," she started to say, but he quickly interrupted her.

"Canaveral will tell us what to do. Now, let's go."

"What exactly are your orders?" Julie asked as they worked their way back through the wounded guts of the *Reichstag*.

"Investigate the ships, and return any gathered intelligence to Canaveral," the sergeant answered. "We did, and we found you, so you're coming with us."

"Is that it?" she asked, dumbfounded. "Haven't you been listening to anything that Captain Carter has been saying?"

The soldiers gave no response, other than to nudge her forward through the exterior airlock and into their shuttle. There was another woman, apparently a second prisoner, shackled to one of the jump seats. Five more soldiers greeted her at gunpoint.

Fed up, Julie ripped off her helmet as soon as the airlock cycled green.

"Listen, I'm on your side," she pleaded. "Ensign Julie Ford, serial number 39275-9, in service on the *Fates' Winds*. Well, what used to be the *Fates' Winds*."

"What ship did you say?" the sergeant asked as he pulled off his own helmet. His eyes were cautious, and piercingly intelligent. They reminded her of someone whom she couldn't quite place.

"The *Fates' Winds*," Julie repeated. "I was...well, I am a member of Captain Carter's crew. He's working with Captain Decival, and Decival sent me here. I'm authorized to speak on both of their behalf."

"I don't need you to speak to me. We'll see what you have to say at Canaveral," the man said.

Julie swallowed and marshaled her courage. There would have been a time when she would have cowered before a man like this, but she'd found her own strength on the edge of the galaxy. She'd conquered her addiction to weight-loss medication, and found her center amid the chaos of the evacuations and the battles. Her friends were counting on her to make sure the civilians from Gertie were safe and that she could stop the SSC from attacking the refugee fleet, and that's exactly what she intended to do, no matter what.

"Then you don't need me to go with you either," she retorted as she grabbed her helmet. She sealed it back over her head and strode to the airlock, but the sergeant pulled her back. Two other soldiers lifted her helmet and took it from her.

"Look, you need to understand something. We're at war. Atlas Carter is considered a war criminal, and a traitor to his species. He is most recently responsible for the deaths of more than two thousand SSC personal in a battle outside of Pluto. Two of his crew, Dashan Pandith and Aaron Granger are considered to be in commission of high treason as well," the sergeant said, glaring at Julie as if he was daring her to try another move.

"Our primary mission is to locate Carter's agents in order to find the rest of the alien and human ships with him so that they can be destroyed. It doesn't matter what message you carry, or what you think you know. My orders are all that matters here."

Julie simply nodded, feeling her old lack of confidence creep back. There was no sense in arguing with the man, and she let them unseal her EVO suit, but then the other prisoner spoke up.

"Did those people look like a threat to you?" the woman asked. "You saw the shape that they were in."

The other prisoner was wearing jeans and a blouse, which seemed ridiculously out of place. Julie wanted to know more of the woman's story, but for now she could only nod her thanks while the sergeant glared at her angrily. There was a slight shift in his expression though. From spending so much time with Danny Xiao, she'd learned to recognize when a man was struggling against himself.

"Open up the comms channel," the sergeant ordered.

"Sergeant?" one of the soldiers asked in shock.

"Just do it."

"Yes, Sergeant," another soldier said. The woman keyed in a code on the holocontrols, and after a brief pause the screen cleared and was replaced with a man's face. The officer bore no rank insignia on his uniform, but Julie knew that he would be a high-level member of the intelligence service. His eyes widened in surprise at the view before him for just a brief moment before an expression of annoyance filled his face.

"Granger, what is the meaning of this?" the man demanded.

It was Julie's turn to be surprised. The sergeant had red hair with a last name of Granger. Could he be related to the Granger that she knew?

"Sir, we've boarded one of the damaged ships, as ordered," the sergeant answered. "The craft are known ships from Captain Decival's fleet. We can confirm the damage is extensive, caused by some unknown weaponry. The ships are carrying survivors. Colonists from the Sword Belt, and an Ensign Ford who claims to have been a member of Captain Carter's crew."

"Verified, Sergeant. She checks out," one of the other soldiers offered.

"Your orders were to return to Canaveral immediately. Why are you breaking protocol?" the intelligence officer asked.

"Sir, I have a request. The people on these ships don't have a lot of food, and they're scared, sir. Is it possible to offload 'em back on Earth?" the sergeant asked, and then he paused to allow the man on his screen time to think.

A malevolent frown clouded the face of the man on the holoscreen.

"We are at war, Granger. Do you know how many traps Carter has placed for us in the past few weeks?"

"He gave you every opportunity for peace! I was the one transmitting those messages. I know what he and Nico said!" Julie exclaimed.

"Oh, did you now?" the officer said, his eyes narrowing for a moment before he refocused on Sergeant Granger. "Then you picked the right asset, Sergeant. You accessed the navigation logs from the ships?"

"Yes sir, I did."

"Then carry out your orders."

The holoscreen flicked dark as the officer terminated the connection, and Sergeant Granger turned to face her.

"What does that mean?" Julie demanded. "We're just gonna leave 'em there? To what? To die?"

"I'm carrying out my mission," the sergeant said.

"What about all these people?" Julie's voice was rising now as she became more and more exasperated by his intransigence.

"That's not my problem to solve. They'll remain on the ships until the SSC decides what to do with 'em. Set course for Canaveral," the sergeant ordered.

"You don't know what you're doing! I can tell you exactly what's going on! Whatever Nico's telling you, it's not the truth!" Julie practically shouted as her throat tightened from the panic that was rising within her. How could she convince this man that what she was saying was the truth? She *had* to find a way to make him listen.

"You're the second person to tell me that today, and maybe none of us do, but we have our orders and we have to follow 'em," he replied stiffly.

Julie could feel the ship rumble to life, ready to begin its journey back to Earth, and whatever awaited her when they arrived at Cape Canaveral. Her mind was working a million miles an hour, trying to figure out some way to convince the sergeant, but in the end she realized that it was most likely a lost cause. He was too intent on following orders to listen to reason. It was obvious that he was having some doubts about the situation, but if those doubts weren't strong enough to persuade him to see the truth of the situation, then it didn't really matter one way or the other.

* * *

The Sword Belt

Atlas Carter tore off his restraints and stood. Beside him Mephista was caught between a startled gasp and a smile.

"Atlas," she cried. "There's so much happening."

"I know," he said as he turned to the Bwain beside her.

"You know what to do," he said to the creature. The alien nodded, closed its eyes and clacked its beak together as Atlas turned for the infirmary's door.

"You're on the *Dauntless*," Mephista called after him. "We've been hit. Decival thinks the ship is critical."

"Yeah, I heard," he said. Alarms flashed in the corridor, and though his body was weakened to the point of exhaustion, he pushed himself into a run. There was so little time left.

"How did you know? Were you awake that whole time?" Mephista called after him as she did her best to follow.

He glanced back and smiled when he saw her hovering just behind him in her chair.

"Not exactly. There's not enough time to tell you everything. Right now I just need to find an EVO suit, and then I need to get to the shuttle bay."

*   *   *

"Should we abandon ship, sir?" Decival's adjutant asked.

"I think we have the damage contained, sir. We took a pretty big hit but we're still able to navigate," his engineer reported.

"I can confirm. The inducers are back up to sixty percent thrust, and holding," Danielle reported.

"But what about the fleet? Decival asked.

Danielle's fingers flashed over her holocontrols to pull up the overall picture of the battle. Decival's ships were battered but functioning. Her evasive solutions had helped them avoid the brunt of Nico's wrath so far, but they were in serious trouble.

"Countermeasures are at maybe twenty percent effectiveness at best, and the shuttles are in bad shape," she reported.

"What about the First Ones?" Decival asked.

"They're...oh my god," Danielle said as an image of the battle flashed onto the screen before her.

Nearly half of Nico's fleet had been consumed. His ships were panicking now, trying to run in all directions, while the *Ninkovich* and a core group of the flagship's escorts continued to pour on fire at the *Dauntless*.

"That stupid bastard's gonna kill himself just to get to us," Decival said.

"Should I open a comms channel?" the communication officer asked.

"I'm showing an unknown signature in Shuttle Bay 12, sir."

"There's no point in opening a comms channel. The man's clearly lost his mind," Decival replied to his communications officer. "As for the signature...," he started to say, but Danielle quickly interjected.

"Captain! There's a new signature in the middle of Nico's fleet!" Danielle shouted. She felt a sudden feeling of relief and elation as she stared at the display, because for the first time since this battle began, it seemed as though they might actually have a chance of surviving the encounter.

"It's the *Bwainhome,* sir! It's back!" she added breathlessly.

*   *   *

"Express squid cleanup, at your service!" Bryon Purcell howled into his intercom. Nico's ships had turned their attention to the *Bwainhome,* clearing a path for Purcell's remaining shuttles to focus on the First Ones. The Bwain beside him leaned forward as the dimensional cannon mounted to the nose of Bryon's shuttle glowed and released a pink streamer of plasma. The projectile struck a First One that had seized the stern of one of the frigates in the back of its misshapen carapace, dissolving the thing into pieces. There were maybe two dozen of the creatures, and the fleet finally had a chance now that Carter was back in action.

Bright lightning streaks filled his vision. For a moment, he thought his shuttle had been struck, but then he realized that the *Bwainhome* itself had joined the fight against the First Ones. It was lashing out with thick bands of plasma, disintegrating First Ones as if they'd never existed.

"Let's send these bastards back where they came from!" Bryon called. "Pour it on, everyone. Hit 'em with everything we got!"

*　*　*

The Ninkovich

The marines guarding Shuttle Bay 27 onboard the *Ninkovich* had an important job when the ship was on battle footing. Bay 27 was the closest to the bridge, and as Admiral Nico himself had instructed them, any attempted boarding actions by Carter or the Bwain would likely target bay 27 as their point of entry. As a result, they had drilled endlessly to repel boarders.

When the ship had entered battle, they'd donned their combat EVO gear in under 30 seconds, and sprinted to their positions facing the shuttle bay's massive doors. They'd anchored themselves to the deck with their magnetic boots in order to remain in place while the *Ninkovich* conducted its evasive maneuvers, and they constantly checked the status of the gear that hardened them against radiation, impact damage, and any other weapon known to humanity.

What they had never prepared for was the sudden appearance of a craft that looked almost like a deep black spider with a series of webbing around it. The thing was maybe eight meters across, and when it suddenly appeared before them, it was already inside the bay and skidding toward their position. The Bwain shuttle crashed into the barricades the marines had erected for cover, knocked barriers and soldiers aside, and slammed through the bulkhead at the back of the shuttle bay. Too disoriented to mount a resistance, the marines' sergeant stayed conscious just long enough to see a human in an SSC uniform drop from the inky black craft to the deck. The intruder was a tall man who covered the ground between them so quickly that the sergeant couldn't even raise his plasma rifle before the man's fist crashed down and shattered his faceplate.

His last thought as consciousness fled was that Admiral Nico would have him executed for failing to see an invisible ship.

* * *

As he watched the strange aliens consume Nico's fleet, Phuri realized that he was going to die in the Sword Belt. He'd escaped his end in this godforsaken system once before when he'd tricked Capra Falconi into transporting him to Earth, but now this idiot Nico's fixation on destroying the human ships in front of him had driven him to the point of suicidal madness. Phuri knew that his destiny was not to die in this useless patch of space, but yet he had tied his fate to a brute of a man who could only think about inflicting pain.

"The *Bridger* and *Dreason* are gone, sir," Nico's navigation officer called.

"Maintain course and tactics," Nico responded.

"The shuttles that Decival released are rallying to the Bwain ship, sir."

"Have we gotten a shot at that thing yet?"

"Sir, our vessels on that side of the formation are trying to avoid the other hostiles."

"I don't care!" Nico shouted. "Target the Bwain and fire!"

"Yes, Admiral," the weapons officer said.

"Admiral, this doesn't have to happen!" Phuri said, hoping the sound of a familiar voice would bring the man to his senses. "If we withdraw to Earth, we have more intelligence. We can restock, and analyze the new threat that's out there."

Phuri rocked backward as Nico backhanded him across the jaw. Sinking to a knee, Phuri spat blood from his lips while Nico rose out of his chair and stared down at him with disgust.

"You led us to this," the admiral growled. His eyes were smoldering, and his chest was heaving in anger. "And now you want to run away in our moment of triumph?"

The ship rocked as its evasive maneuvers pushed it out of the way of some external manner of threat.

"Triumph? What do you mean triumph? This is nothing but suicide!" Phuri said unevenly.

"This is war!" Nico shouted. "Fire everything we have at the Bwain ship. I want it taken out of the sky. And switch to nuclear missiles for Decival's fleet. I want that traitor executed."

With Nico distracted, Phuri regained his feet and ran for the airlock. His plan was to find the closest escape pod and take his chances with Decival's fleet. It was clear that Captain Carter hadn't been lying about the weaponry that Cazador so desperately coveted. What remained of Decival's shuttles were having an effect on the First Ones, and Phuri hoped that at least he'd find some form of sanity with Carter.

A hand seized the back of Phuri's collar, lifted him from the deck, and slammed him down beside the admiral's station. Nico's eyes were alight with rage, and consumed with bloodlust. The man had lost all control.

"We came here for Carter's head, and I am going to claim it whether it costs you your life, or the lives of every last sailor in this fleet," Nico hissed through clenched teeth.

"That won't be necessary," a deep voice said from the airlock.

Phuri tilted his head up to see the intruder. There, standing on the bridge of the *Ninkovich*, was Captain Atlas Carter.

"Impossible," Nico said, clearly sobered by this unexpected intrusion. He released his grip on Phuri and stood slowly to his full height.

Carter looked worn, almost unhealthy. He was slightly hunched, as if a combination of old age and pain had caught up with him. Phuri was shocked at the difference between this man and the one who had toppled Sickyl Tannin, but he had no time to process what might have happened to him.

"Well? What are you all doing?" Nico cried to his bridge crew. "Seize him!"

The marines on either side of the airlock were struggling to draw their weapons, but they looked as if some invisible force was fighting against them.

"I've come to ask for your surrender Nico, but if you touch me, I will tell every Bwain here to execute you," Carter said threateningly. He stared Nico directly in the eye, and never flinched in the slightest as he spoke.

"Your threats are over, Carter. There aren't any Bwain here," Nico scoffed.

As Phuri watched, the walls around them shimmered, and three dozen of the creatures suddenly appeared in a ring around the bridge. They'd been somehow camouflaged, and though the marines and officers on deck were armed, they were clearly outnumbered.

Carter held up his hands, trying to urge restraint.

"This can all end right now. I'm not here to kill anyone," Carter said in a calm voice.

"Then what are you here for, Carter? To give our minds over to these things? To turn us into your slaves?" Nico fumed, his nostrils flaring with anger. Carter just eyed him steadily.

"I'm here to stop you from making a mistake that will get you killed. Those other aliens you're fighting can't be stopped with any weapon you have, and if you keep fighting against Decival, you'll destroy the only weapons we have that can stop them. I'm asking you to surrender. It's the only way."

"You reek of desperation, and only the strong are worthy of rule!" Nico sneered at the sickly man standing before him.

The Admiral drew a hunting knife from under his belt and sprang forward. The Bwain surrounding the bridge were too far away from Carter to help, and Carter seemed too weak to be able to resist effectively.

Phuri reached into his vest pocket and drew his plasma pistol. Carter had raised his arms in a boxer's defense, but instead of warding off a knife strike, he ended up catching Nico's body as the admiral staggered into him. Carter looked down at the hole smoking from Nico's severed spine as the admiral's knife clanged to the deck. Two of the bridge crew seized Phuri and tore the plasma pistol from his grasp.

"I hope you'll believe me, Captain, that I share your understanding of threats both foreign and domestic," Phuri said as the crew members checked to make sure he had no other weapons on him and posed no further threat. "And if nothing else, I'd very much prefer not to die in this godforsaken system."

* * *

The Fates' Winds

The Ancient had sent only a handful of First Ones to attack the fleet. Aric was puzzled, because in every other attack the creatures had used their full strength.

"YES, ARIC KEITH. IT IS CALLED A 'DECOY' IN YOUR LANGUAGE," The Ancient bellowed into his thoughts.

To his horror, Aric saw that the hideous aliens were disappearing all around him, streaking toward unknown destinations.

"Whatever you're doing, it won't work," Aric said. His defiance and faith in Captain Carter was all that remained to him, and he clung to that idea with a fierce intensity.

"YOU WANT TO DIE, BUT YOU WILL BE THE LAST OF OUR SLAVES STANDING. ONCE WE HAVE CONSUMED YOUR EARTH AND YOUR PEOPLE, I WILL RETURN TO TELL YOU OF THEM!" The Ancient roared in the tearing paper sound again

Aric tried desperately to force his body to move even a finger's breadth, to push the reactor to critical mass, or trigger the inducers to break his orbit, but it was impossible. Just as before, he could move only in service of the First Ones.

"I'll kill all of you myself!" Aric screamed through his thoughts. *"I'll send you back to nothing!"*

After his struggles faded, it took Aric a long time to realize that the space around him had darkened, and he was only screaming to himself.

* * *

The Ninkovich

Carter let Admiral Nico's body drop to the deck. Smoke from the dead man's boiled chest drifted into the still air of the flagship's bridge. The crewman who'd seized Phuri alternated between staring at the Bwain and Carter, whom they weren't quite sure they'd surrendered to. The Bwain were shifting to face them with strange double-barreled weapons, while on the holoscreens their ship was lashing out at the new aliens to protect the humans.

"Captain? We may need an explanation on what you intend to...," Phuri stammered, but Carter cut him off without a glance in his direction.

"Who's in command here?" Carter demanded.

"I am," a female officer declared as she stepped forward, "Captain Linda Jansen."

"Jansen, I can stop those things, but you need to stand down. There will be time to explain when everything's over," Carter stated succinctly, and the SSC officer could see the earnestness in his eyes.

Phuri had been on board long enough to know that Jansen was a more level-headed foil to Nico, and that she would likely go along with Carter, but Carter interested him more. If Phuri didn't know better, he'd say that Carter was sick, possibly cancerous. If that were the case, then maybe Phuri's desperate gamble to assassinate Nico would pay off even more handsomely than he'd anticipated.

"Sir, the command is yours, but if you take any hostile action toward this fleet, it will be my duty to stop you," Captain Jansen informed him. Carter, a fellow SSC captain himself, knew exactly what her duty would entail. She made the snap decision to accept the risk of surrendering to this strange man before her, as their survival seemed to be far more likely under this man's calm experience than it was under Nico and his all-consuming madness.

"I've been trying to save all of you from the beginning," Carter said, shaking his head slightly. "Comms, general broadcast, please."

"Go ahead...sir," the comms officer said.

"This is Atlas Carter to all SSC craft. I am on board the *Ninkovich* and in command with Captain Jansen as my second. Admiral Nico is dead. If you want to survive the First Ones, you will follow my orders exactly," he said. There was absolute silence on the bridge.

"Weapons, cease fire immediately. Human weaponry only makes the First Ones stronger. Direct all excess power to propulsion. Navigation, loosen your formation and plot course to circle behind the *Dauntless* and Decival's fleet," Carter said, throwing out his orders in rapid succession.

"But sir, that would expose our defenses," Jansen started, but then she realized she wasn't in a position to protest at the moment.

"We have weapons that can fight those things, and you don't. We *are* your defenses. On my mark, execute," Carter said as he turned back to the holoscreen images before him.

For a moment, the bridge crew simply stared. In a matter of a few minutes they'd gone from being Carter's mortal enemies to serving under him, and their hesitation was understandable. It was clear to Phuri what made Carter such a formidable opponent. The man had no need for Nico's theatrics or power games. He was simply a professional, driven by a sense of duty and selflessness that compelled others to follow him. In truth, those qualities nauseated Phuri, but they could prove useful to him in standing up to Cazador.

"The longer you wait, the more sailors will die," Carter barked. "Now execute!"

The crew spun into action as their shock wore off. On the holoscreens, Nico's remaining ships circled behind the *Bwainhome* and made way for the relative safety of the other human fleet. The massive Bwain ship lifted toward the area of space that Nico's fleet was vacating. The First Ones were locked in death rolls with the wounded ships, but pink jets of some kind of plasma lashed out from the alien ship and struck the creatures, tearing them apart and turning them inside out in harsh red flames that quickly cooled to a black nothingness.

In a matter of minutes, Carter was destroying the things that had cleaved through Nico's fleet without any resistance.

"Carter to Decival. Hostilities with the SSC have ended. Target the First Ones at will."

"Captain, it's a turkey shoot!" an excited voice cut through on the command frequency. "You showed up just in time!"

The comms officer glanced at Carter in shock. Nico would never have allowed an interjection of that kind, but Carter only wore an exhausted smile.

"Go get 'em, Mr. Purcell," Carter said, then added, "Pandith, what's your status?"

"This is Granger, sir. Pandith is busy piloting us. We didn't want to risk getting the *Gravity Drive* hit in the fighting, but we're en route now."

"Hold off on engaging, Mr. Granger," Carter ordered. "We're gonna need to be ready to fight again soon. Mr. Xiao, how's the fleet holding up?"

"We took a beating, sir. The *Dauntless* is in the worst shape, but we've got ten battle-ready cruisers."

"And the shuttles?"

"Not good, Captain," Decival said. "In spite of Mr. Purcell's enthusiasm, we've got less than a hundred remaining."

"Damn it," Carter grumbled as he cast an accusing glance at Nico's body.

"They're retreating!" the nav officer called.

On the holos, Phuri saw the horrifying white creatures pulling away from the human fleet and hurtling into space at unimaginable speed. Already, the possibilities were assembling in his head. With Carter at the head of this fleet, returning triumphantly to Earth, Cazador would have no choice but to step aside. Perhaps, even, Carter would make war on the *Narcos* as he must have been dreaming about in his days lost in the Sword Belt. Yes, he would give every appearance of contriteness. He would become Carter's ally in the same way that he had with Nico. With Cazador out of the way, he'd put together his case for Galactic President.

"You've done well, Captain. May I suggest we discuss the situation back on Earth," Phuri began, but Carter waved him aside.

"Earth can wait," Carter said. The man's eyes were locked on the withdrawing forms disappearing from the holoscreens. "Our fight isn't finished here."

Chapter Seven

Earth Orbit

When Julie Ford had joined the *Fates' Winds* crew immediately upon graduating from the SSC Academy, it had been a shock to encounter the crew's sullen hostility. She had always been self-conscious and shy, and when she'd had difficulty fitting in with the other more experienced crew members, she had latched onto Danny Xiao's bitter loneliness as a survival mechanism of sorts. Captain Carter had built a confidence in her as he'd shown the entire crew how to live up to their duty, and his expectations. She was no longer afraid to make decisions, or to stand up for herself. When she agreed to go back to Earth with the civilians, she imagined that she'd be able to help the entire fleet. The last thing she'd expected was to return to Earth as a prisoner, and she felt as if she was letting both her captain, and herself down.

"You have a choice," she said to the sergeant. "You could at least send a messenger to the Sword Belt."

"I don't have to do anything other than take you to Canaveral for questioning," he said firmly. He'd refused to even look at either of his captives, but Julie couldn't give up.

"The First Ones could come here at any moment," she said. "They can travel faster than light. You would be utterly defenseless. Kilver on the *Reichstag* can build weapons for you."

"And what if that's exactly what Captain Carter wants? What if it's a trap?" the sergeant asked.

"You saw the condition of those ships. Tell me what human weapon would have done that?" Julie demanded, trying desperately to get him to listen to the truth he was so blindly ignoring.

Atlas' Final Approach

The sergeant tilted his head just slightly toward them

"Or what Bwain weapon," he answered.

Julie gave up, exasperated. From where she sat she could just see through to the pilot's station and the blue disk of Earth was swelling in front of them. The planet was now home to fifty billion people, and all of them were at risk because she couldn't make this hardass see reason. Captain Carter had sent her because she was their communications ensign, and the one thing that she had done well, she was now failing at miserably. As long as she could talk though, she would.

"I know a Granger," she said, trying a different tack. "He was the *Fates' Winds* science officer. Any relation?"

The sergeant's jaw muscle tightened. Outside the shuttle windows, flames replaced the blue disk of Earth's oxygen as the shuttle dipped into the atmosphere for its re-entry.

"Red hair, Scottish name. You must be related," Julie persisted.

Shaking in his seat from the turbulence, the sergeant still said nothing.

"He's the smartest one of us in the crew. He figured out how to track the Bwain. If he wouldn't have known about Majorana radiation, they would have surprised us and taken the Sword Belt."

"Oh, seriously? You know Granger?" the other prisoner asked, astonished. "You served with him?"

"I did. Well, I still do. Did you know him?" Julie asked, looking rather surprised.

The woman laughed, a deep chuckle that drew the attention of the soldiers.

"That's how I got involved in this whole mess. I'm a reporter. I was just working on a story on Majorana radiation and I was trying to reach the *Fates' Winds* science officer."

"That's enough!" the sergeant growled.

For a moment, Julie stayed silent. The roar outside the hull filled her ears, and her stomach was curdling as the shuttle forced its way toward the surface.

"Your father has a temper too," Julie continued. "He just never mentioned he has a son."

"He doesn't, and you can save your stories," the sergeant replied curtly. "My orders are to take you to Canaveral, and that's where you're going. You can say as much or as little as you want, it makes no difference."

"Correction, sir," the pilot called back to the cabin. "We've been rerouted to Johannesburg."

For a moment, Julie thought she saw the sergeant's eyes widen. He gave them a grudging frown, whether of respect or consideration she couldn't tell.

"Apparently you've just been moved up the priority list," he said.

*   *   *

Johannesburg

Questions burned in Lana Delgato's mind as the shuttle streaked over Africa's ruddy plains. She watched Johannesburg's white buildings and brown streets grow larger and larger through the window, trying to formulate some kind of plan to get the truth to the people. If she could find a spare moment to talk to her fellow prisoner, she would understand so much more about what was happening. Julie Ford had been in the Sword Belt, and had first-hand knowledge of everything that she wanted to know. It was infuriating to not be able to ask her questions.

What angered Lana even more deeply, was the lack of curiosity among her captors. The soldiers might as well have been robots for all the interest or compassion they showed. When the shuttle slowed and settled onto a landing pad in the presidential compound, they hefted her and Julie without a word and marched them to an elevator that led underground to a dim gray corridor. Then they marched through the concrete passage for nearly ten minutes until they reached at an unmarked door that slid open when the sergeant placed his palm on the hand scanner.

The sergeant's soldiers pushed Julie inside first, and then Lana. When she turned, she found plasma rifles trained on her chest.

"What are you gonna do to us?" Lana asked.

"Step back," the sergeant ordered.

"You wouldn't take us all this way to kill us," Lana said. "Just what do you intend to do with us?"

"You're guests of President Nico," the captain said. "He'll decide what to do with you."

"If Nico went after Captain Carter, then he's probably dead by now," Julie said as the soldiers backed through the entryway.

Sergeant Granger stood in the doorway, his face impassive as ever. He tapped the control to close the door, then pressed it again just as it reached halfway closed.

"Think about the people you're trying to protect when they ask you to cooperate, and it won't be so bad," Granger advised, and then the door sealed itself shut.

They'd been jailed in what could almost be compared to a luxury hotel room. Lana stood in a comfortably appointed foyer that held a sitting area, several holoscreens, and a reception bar. A short hallway led to a set of bedrooms and a lavatory that were sumptuously appointed in marble and dark hardwoods.

"So this is how the enemies of the president are kept," Lana said.

"Will you help me with this?" Julie asked.

Turning back to the foyer, Lana found Julie kneeling underneath the large holomonitor along the wall. The ensign was running her fingers against the edges of the plate underneath the projectors. When she reached the edges, she dug her fingertips into the seal to try and pry away the plate that protected the system's components.

"What are you doing?" Lana asked.

"We need to warn everyone we can about the First Ones," Julie said. "We don't have time, and no one in Nico's government is gonna listen to anything we have to say, so I'm gonna try to broadcast from this station. Oh, there we go," she said as the cover plate popped open.

Lana smiled, realizing that she might have found a kindred spirit. The decorative plate that they'd removed revealed another metal plate held in place by four flat-head screws. She dug her thumbnails into the screw heads and twisted. It was slow work, twisting and shearing her thumbnail, but eventually the screws turned and the covering loosened enough for them to remove it.

"Are you ready?" Julie asked. "On three. One ... two ... three!"

Together they lifted the heavy plate and set it aside.

"Oh no...," Julie murmured with disappointment.

Behind the plate, there was just a set of wires that ran into the concrete wall. There were no controls, or even any further screws to try and penetrate more deeply.

"I'm afraid you'll find that you're quite secure in here," a voice said beside them.

Startled, Lana and Julie bolted upright to face the intruder.

The man standing in the doorway in front of Granger's soldiers was hideously disfigured. A mass of scar tissue ran from his hairline, down one side of his face, and disappeared beneath his pale white suit. His good eye glared with a hard malevolence, while his dead right eye was gauzed, nearly lidless.

"You're Belizean?" Lana asked in shock.

"Yes, and you are...?"

"Spanish," she answered.

"Ahhh, such a beautiful culture," the man responded pleasantly.

"Why are we being held?" Julie asked.

His face flicked with annoyance at his socializing being cut short.

"Well, you're here because you both possess information that could affect the safety and security of my citizens, and I'd like to hear that information, before anyone makes any rash decisions."

"What do you mean *your* citizens?" Lana asked. "I thought Admiral Nico was the Galactic President?"

The man made a great show of affecting sadness.

"Well, this isn't public knowledge, but a covert messenger recently returned from the admiral's fleet. Nico was unfortunately killed during the fighting with Captain Carter, so in this difficult period, I've volunteered to run the government until a new election can be held."

"And who are you?" Lana asked.

The man's smile was a crooked monstrosity, conveying warmth in the same way a knife felt hot when plunged into your stomach.

"Allow me to introduce myself. My name is Felipe Cazador," he said formally. "I believe you've already met several of my associates in Madrid and Florida before you so rashly fled their protection."

Lana swallowed. It was the hunter. After all this time, he'd finally found her. Things were much more serious than she could have ever imagined.

"We're not gonna answer your questions until you tell me what happened to Captain Carter," Julie said.

"Julie!" Lana hissed.

Cazador turned to face Julie, the smile never leaving his face.

"No doubt you've heard rumors about me?"

Julie shook her head. She honestly had no idea who he was.

"No? Well, it's nothing really, but you should know that I'm a businessman first and foremost, so what I propose is an exchange of information. I will answer your questions, if you answer mine. Would you consider that fair?"

Julie considered the man before her for a moment, then nodded.

"Ask," she said.

"The First Ones you spoke of, the aliens that Carter has been warning us of, they can travel faster than the speed of light?"

"Yes."

"And you have weapons to defeat them?"

"The Bwain developed the weapons. Their ship helped us manufacture the ones we're using, and it grew its own as well."

Cazador snorted, spreading his hands.

"You don't really expect me to believe that weapons so powerful that they could destroy a creature like you describe simply grow out of nothingness right when you happen to have a need for them, do you?"

"The Bwain are telepathic, and so is their ship. Captain Carter's able to talk to 'em...to make 'em do whatever he wants."

"Ahhh, so that's why he says they're not a threat then. It's because he controls them." Cazador noted.

"Yeah. They call him the Bwainslayer. He's their leader now," she added.

Lana expected Cazador to keep asking questions, but instead he frowned and began to stroke the rough stubble of his scarred face as he considered everything she'd just told him.

"Tell me, how did he gain the ability to communicate with them?" he asked after a few moments.

"There's a link between the Bwain and the ship," Julie said as she folded her arms across her chest. "It's called the Endless Knot. He touched it, and then after that he was able to communicate with them."

"Oh, I see. So once he did that, he was able to make powerful weapons spring from his mind that bested three SSC fleets?"

"No, that's not exactly what happened. What he did was..."

"OF COURSE THAT'S NOT WHAT HAPPENED!" Cazador roared. Both women stepped back, startled at the man's sudden ferocity.

"Weapons don't just grow out of thin air!" Cazador cried. "Carter isn't a leader. He's nothing but a weakling, easily predictable and defeated, and you expect me to believe these lies about him?"

"Well how the hell else do you think he defeated those fleets? Why would I lie about that?" Julie shot back.

"Yes, that is the question now, isn't it?" Cazador asked as he narrowed his good eye and considered her for a moment.

"We have questions too," Lana interjected.

"I'm sorry, but I am afraid this interview is over. We can reconvene when you both come to realize that it's in your best interest to give me the truth instead of bunch of ridiculous lies," Cazador said, glaring hard at them both for a moment before he spun around angrily and left the room. The door sealed behind him, and Julie stared down at the useless panels she'd removed. She was trapped underground, stuck with a madman who refused to believe the truth, and couldn't see any clear path of escape. The whole situation seemed absolutely hopeless.

* * *

The Ninkovich

Atlas Carter looked out over the officers, crew, and Bwain assembled in the flagship's mess hall. Some were on holoscreens, others had come in person, but he knew that each one of them wanted to know what was next. He'd been in the Sword Belt for less than three months, and it already felt like a lifetime. Although, he thought with a wry inner smile that didn't reach his face, his definition of what a lifetime entailed had changed significantly as of late.

Mephista had joined him in person, as had Danny, Bryon, Pandith, and Granger. Hal Yellowknife was just walking into the hall, while Captain Jansen and her senior officers filled most of the chairs. Danielle had joined them in person as well, while Captain Decival stayed behind to coordinate repairs on the crippled *Dauntless*. The Bwain chattered on the edges of the gathering, some of them picking at the lockers and cabinets that lined the walls. While the aliens indulged their natural curiosity, the humans had greater concerns. Not only had they just been fighting each other, but every single sailor on the *Ninkovich* had been Nico's most loyal. If Atlas wanted their support, it had to start here. It had to start with them following him to war.

"Let's get started," Atlas said. The ship's intercom system picked up and amplified his voice, sending his words to every sailor in the fleet. The room stilled, waiting for his vision.

"You've all seen what we're up against out here," he started. "I'm not going to address anything you might have heard from Nico or the other leadership back on Earth about the current situation. The only thing that matters right now is survival. Not just for us, but for every single lifeform in this dimension."

He was pacing in front of the room now, trying to work off the weakness he felt in his legs. Occasionally, the Bwain's view of him flashed into his own mind. He'd once carried a fighter's weight. It was a shield of muscle that would ward off any punishment, but his body had thinned considerably, and the longer he spent in the Endless Knot, the more his very essence winnowed away. There was a price for such power, and he'd willingly made the decision to pay that price.

"Some of you probably want to go back to Earth. We've been out here for months now, fighting every single day to survive. We've seen a lot of our friends and fellow crew members die, sometimes because of each other."

Dissatisfied rumbling came from the *Ninkovich's* crew. They bristled at being called the aggressors, but they needed to understand the situation clearly if they were going to follow him, so he had to be honest with them.

"Others of you have spent your entire careers fighting the Bwain, but whether you like it or not, these aliens you once considered your enemy are now our best chance at stopping the First Ones. We don't know when those things will strike or where they'll be next, but we do know that they won't stop until we've killed every last one of them. Just driving them out of this dimension and back to wherever they came from isn't enough. They'll just come back again someday. We have to make our stand, and put an end to the threat once and for all, before it's too late."

"So, I've called you all together today to tell you that we need to strike at their heart. I want to move against the obelisk immediately with the resources that we have here. At this point, pursuing any other course of action would be unconscionable."

He paused for a moment to allow them to ask questions if they so desired. Captain Jansen was the first to raise her hand.

"How do you expect us to fight those things?" she asked.

"You need the weapons that Hal here can make for you, and then you need the Bwain to operate them for you," Carter said, and then he nodded toward the next officer who had a question.

"Do you really expect us to give weapons to the Bwain?"

"The Bwain saved all of your lives a few hours ago. Until anyone on your science team can figure out how to trigger dimensional weapons with your minds, that's the way it's gonna have to be," Carter replied.

"What about you?" another officer asked. "Can't you do it?"

"I can, but I can't do it alone. That's why I'm asking all of you for your help. This is quite probably our one and only chance to put an end to these things and to keep 'em from ever coming back, but we need to strike now," he said.

"How soon is *now*, Captain?" Bryon Purcell asked with a grin on his face. He couldn't help but feel a renewed sense of relief and hope, knowing that Captain Carter was with them once again.

"We've got two days," he replied quietly.

Chaos erupted in the room. Atlas had known that this was going to be the hardest part, but he had little choice. It would be difficult for him to last even that long, but if he was gone, then he had no idea what would happen to the Bwain in his absence.

He waved his hands for silence, and then waited for a moment longer to let the reality of the situation sink in.

"If you'd rather run from this, then say so. Raise your hand right now, and we'll have a ship make the jump that takes you all back to Earth."

Fighting against the exhaustion just to keep himself upright, he scanned the audience for hands. When he saw that there were none, he nodded.

"Okay," he said, "let's get to work."

* * *

Mephista pushed her hoverchair forward as the meeting broke, aiming to cut Atlas off at the mess hall's exit. He reached the hatch first, but she followed close behind into the hallway.

"So you're unconscious for three days, wake up just in time to save the fleet, and you think that you can get away without an explanation?"

He turned and offered her a pained smile. His shoulders seemed to have stooped since his speech, and he looked as if he'd aged into his sixties in a few months.

"I knew you'd be the first one to corner me," he said.

They turned a corner to a lift. Atlas pressed the bridge button, held the door for her, and then they rose up toward the top deck of the ship.

"Atlas, what's going on? Two days isn't nearly enough time. And something's different about you. You need to go to the infirmary." Mephista said, her thoughts tumbling out in a jumble. There was so much she needed to know.

Atlas closed his eyes for a moment to gather his thoughts.

"Things are different now," he said quietly. "The *Bwainhome* is changing. It's changing me."

"It's changing you? How? Why?"

"I don't want to talk about whys of it right now, but if we're gonna use it to fight the First Ones, then we've only got two days until...," he said, but then he paused to take a breath before letting it out in a heavy sigh.

"Until what?"

"Until I don't know if I can control it anymore."

"Is that what it was doing to you? Did it take control of you?" she asked with a concerned look.

"No, not exactly. I think, if anything, I became more like it," he said as he reached up and rubbed his tired eyes.

"You became more like a ship?"

"It's not just a ship. It's a living thing. It used to be a First One, and it wants my help," he explained.

Taken aback by his revelation, she wasn't really sure what to say. He'd always put others first for as long as she'd known him, but now...what was he trying to say?

"Are you saying you're gonna go with it?" she asked. "Where?"

The look of pain he gave her nearly broke her heart. She could see the same despair and exhaustion that she'd found in her own face after the Bwain had taken her legs; the weariness that never wanted to see another life lost.

"I'm saying I don't think I have a choice," he said as the lift opened. A pair of marines on the bridge snapped to attention.

"There's always a choice," she said. To her surprise, Atlas actually smiled.

"I remember when I had to convince *you* of that. Listen, I'm gonna need you to take command of the fleet."

Too much was happening too fast for her to process. It was hard to imagine Atlas Carter as having a weakness. It was even more difficult to consider the possibility that he'd be leaving her soon, and that this might be the last time she ever saw him in person.

"You want me to command the fleet? I don't know if I can," she protested. This was all so much to take in.

"I heard everything you said in the infirmary. You're stronger now than I am, and I need you to stay that way," he said. She stared into his face, as if she was somehow expecting to wake up and find out that this was all just some sort of a cruel nightmare, but alas, it was not to be. As she stood there staring into his eyes, all she saw was sadness, and emotional scars that had never healed. It broke her inside to see him like this, but she had to be strong for him now, just as he'd asked. It was all she could do, and the least that she owed him.

Chapter Eight

The Constantinople

"The gravity drive works, but as a weapon it has some design flaws. Namely, things like maneuverability, accuracy, etc...," Pandith explained.

"That's not what I'm asking you," Carter said with a tired sigh. "I need to know about range and spread of the gravitons."

The men were circling the experimental shuttle, studying the ring of gravity thrusters that were bolted to its stern.

"We've got good data from the students' experiments," Granger said as he checked his holoscreen. "The range is technically infinite, because to our knowledge, nothing stops a graviton. If you wanna know the effective range against the First Ones though, there's really only one way to tell. Why? What are you thinking?"

"I want to be able to keep any more of those things from coming out of the obelisk," Carter said. "If we can lock down their ability to generate more of themselves, then I'll be able to close the portal."

"And how do you intend to do that?" Pandith asked, cocking his eyebrow questioningly.

Carter leaned against a stack of crates near the shuttle bay and sighed. He seemed as if his body was hurting him. It was as if the pressure of command was aging him more rapidly than Pandith could have expected, and what made matters worse is that he still hadn't shared what had happened during the time that he'd been unconscious.

"How? Heh...isn't it obvious? I'm gonna to fly the *Bwainhome* into it," he said.

"You're gonna...but that would... Sir, I don't understand." Pandith finally managed.

"The *Bwainhome* is a First One. You and Granger discovered that when we did our first survey of that ship. You've seen it changing, growing. As such, it knows how to seal the obelisk," Carter said matter-of-factly.

"But what'll happen to you?" Granger asked, even though he was pretty sure he already knew the answer.

Carter was silent for so long that Pandith thought he might have fallen asleep. He stood up from where he'd been examining one of the engines, and turned to find a mixture of both sadness and relief on his captain's face.

"I don't know. I can control the ship remotely now, but I don't know what'll happen if the link to the Bwainsong is cut," Carter said as his eyes drooped tiredly.

"Is that what happened to you before?" Pandith asked.

"No," Carter said. Both of them waited for the captain to elaborate, but he said nothing more.

"You know...we could refashion one of the Majorana cowls we made to keep the Bwainsong out of our heads on the *Fates' Winds*. It might come in handy," Granger suggested.

Carter started, as if he'd drifted off with his eyes open.

"No, I don't think I'll need one of those this time Mr. Granger. I'm sorry, I'm gonna have to try to get some sleep," Carter said as he squinted and pinched the bridge of his nose.

"I think you need it, sir," Pandith said. "We'll be ready in the morning."

"Thanks...to both of you," Carter said with a slight nod before he turned and left the shuttle bay.

When the hatch had sealed behind him, Granger glanced over at Pandith.

"What do you think he was tellin' us just now?" the science officer asked.

"I don't know, but to me it felt like he was sayin' goodbye," Pandith said with a sadness in his eyes as he stared at the hatch that his captain had just passed through.

* * *

Hal handed the last armful of the Bwain weaponry to an eager sailor, and the young crewman jogged up the shuttle ramp with the mixture of glass and coral tubing.

"How much more is there?" one of the other crewman from the *Ninkovich* asked.

"Two more. Though for an old man like me, it'll feel more like four," Hal said.

Hal, Danny, and the SSC personnel were gathering the dimensional weapons that Hal's factories had been printing from the various ships in the fleet. Though many of his factories had been onboard ships that had been damaged or destroyed, they'd been operating continually up to this point, and had created a surplus of weapons that would ensure that every operational cruiser out there would be able to defend itself.

"Hey, stop gawking. We got work to do," Hal said as he slapped the sailor on the back. The crewman and technicians stopped frequently to stare at the alien ship's interior, and Hal had to continually remind himself that he'd been the exact same way when he first came aboard. Duty called however, and they had little time for sightseeing.

"Do you think you'll be able to get all of these delivered?" Hal asked after peeking into the shuttle's stuffed hold.

"If we're lucky," Danny said.

"We've been lucky so far. That is, if you can call any of this luck," Hal said as he hunched his shoulders for a quick stretch.

"Well, if it hadn't been for you and your factories...," Danny said with an appreciative grin. He realized now just how much he had come to appreciate working with Hal.

"You saved me plenty of times on Gertie. It's nothing," Hal said, returning Danny's smile.

Danny took one last look into the hold, and then they both headed over to join the other workers at the factories. One of the sailors was handling the weapons as if they were glass. Hal took the icicle shape from the man's hand and threw it on the deck. The material bounced, making a dull chiming sound.

"I dunno what they're made of, but you don't have to worry about breaking 'em, so grab as many as you can. We're runnin' outta time," Hal said. They needed to move things along if the fleet was going to complete its preparations.

"You know, it's funny to think how much we've all changed in just the past few months," Danny commented as he joined in the loading.

"What do you mean?" Hal asked without looking up.

"I mean, personally...but also in all the stuff we've learned. Like, who ever thought much about other dimensions and dimension travel before all this, or about aliens that could consume whole star systems? Who ever thought about how the Bwain communicate with each other? Yet

Pandith and Granger have already started piecing together just how they do it."

"Yeah, but what about it? I'm not following you," Hal replied.

"It's just...I can't help thinking about how different we all are now, and how much bigger our whole outlook on the universe has gotten. And also...how different things will be after it's all over."

"We're all gonna be heroes," Hal said with a light chuckle as he scooped up a group of weapons that looked like tubeworms and lifted them into the arms of a waiting crewman.

"That's not what I mean."

"Yeah, I know kid. Back on Gertie I used to fill myself full of booze and then just sit for hours staring up at the stars. It was so quiet out there...you got a sense of just how small you really are. I mean, you think about whether anything you do matters, and then you get into a situation like this, and you realize that it does. It absolutely does."

With the carts loaded, they crossed back over the strangely worn, almost living deck of the *Bwainhome* to the shuttles.

"You know, I spent a lot of time wondering what I could have done differently with my sister," Danny mused quietly. "If I'd been standing in a different spot when the Bwain had attacked, or if I'd reacted faster. What I realized is that you can never go back. Captain Carter showed me that. I was living in the past out here, and that's how Tannin manipulated me for so long. I would have sold out my ship to keep my sister alive, but she had pretty much died years ago, and I was still holding on to some ridiculous hope that I could save her somehow."

"You think we're all pretty much dead out here?" he asked.

"No, I don't actually. I wonder where the sudden optimism came from?" Danny asked with a hint of a grin.

"It comes from knowing that we've got a man with a plan," Hal said with a grin of his own. "Now, we need to get our asses in gear. If we don't get these loaded up in the next hour, that man with a plan is gonna be really upset with us."

* * *

"Now *this* I could get used to," Bryon commented as he looked on in awe.

"We brought these on board in case Carter tried to use the same tactic that he did against us near Pluto," Captain Jansen said.

"What'd he do to you there?" Bryon asked.

"He used the Bwain fighters for close-in work. They were able to disable our systems incredibly accurately. These were going to be our counter-response."

Bryon circled the fighter, smiling as he ducked under its flat v-shaped hull. The craft resembled a ten-meter-wide boomerang, with a slim cockpit rising from its center and a cluster of weapons pods spread on either wing. He ran his hand over the hull, then pulled back in surprise.

"Inducers?" he asked.

"Almost the entire hull is made of them," Jansen said. "You'll go faster than anything out there aside from a messenger ship."

"Maybe we'll even catch a First One or two, huh boys?" he said.

The Bwain that had joined him jostled each other to examine the fighter. The aliens were grasping at his pants with their talons and nipping at his elbows, restless to get on their way. The aliens had more than proved their courage to him, giving their lives to power the strange weapons that Hal's factories had produced. Now, he and the hundreds of other shuttles would carry even more of them to their deaths in what he hoped would be the final battle against the First Ones.

One of Hal's assistants stepped away from the nose of the craft. The woman had sealed the modified version of the alien weapons to the fighter's nose right in front of the cockpit. The weaponry somehow knew to fuse itself to the hull, and Bryon couldn't help but be impressed.

"Double-barreled," Bryon said appreciatively. "I like it!"

The tech smiled, then patted Bryon on the back as the weapons officer trotted up the gangplank.

"I had a lot of friends that died on the *Dauntless*," the sailor said. Bryon stopped and looked at her thoughtfully.

"We all did," he said with an uncharacteristic seriousness. "Believe me, we're gonna make 'em pay for every last one of 'em."

* * *

The Ninkovich

Atlas Carter had one last task remaining before he left for the *Bwainhome* and the fleet could depart. The preparations were laid, the officers were briefed, and the weapons had been distributed. The only thing that remained now was a final loose end.

He saluted the marines on either side of the brig's entrance, and then stepped inside Phuri's cell. The small man was sitting on his bunk, waiting.

"Please, come in," Phuri said with a smile. "The accommodations aren't as good as the colonial palace, but...you know. One does what one can."

Carter immediately cut him off. He had neither the time nor the patience to deal with the conniving little man.

"I hear you wanted to see me, so talk. I don't have a lot of time."

Phuri blinked at his abruptness, and quickly recalibrated.

"I've heard that you're planning on flying the *Bwainhome* into that obelisk out there, and that it might be deleterious to your health," Phuri began again.

"How do you know that?" Carter asked.

"You're not hiding the Bwain's effects on you very well," Phuri stated flatly. "Even Nico recognized that I can still be of some use on this ship."

"All right, yeah...that's our plan. So what? It's the only way we can save the Earth, and every other living thing out there."

"May I submit that you would not be doing so by sacrificing yourself?" Phuri offered.

"If you can't see that the First Ones are a threat, then you're even more ignorant than Tannin was. Goodbye Phuri," Carter said as he turned to leave.

"Of course I know they're a threat. I've seen what they can do, but have you seen what Cazador's done back on Earth?" Phuri asked, and then he quietly studied Carter's haggard face to see his reaction.

Carter froze. The mention of the man's name was like a lightning strike to his soul. He felt an anger and disgust well up in him that had lain dormant since before he'd been exiled to the Sword Belt.

"What did you say?" he asked through clenched teeth as he turned and faced Phuri.

"Felipe Cazador. I believe you were acquainted with him many years ago?" Phuri said causally, as if they were just two buddies sharing a drink after a hard day's work.

"And what about him?" Carter asked. He was struggling to keep his voice under control, but Phuri noted the muscles clenching in the man's jaw.

"He's how we overthrew Kidewange. He's how we sold the people on fear of you and the Bwain until they were ready for the coup," Phuri stated simply.

"Cazador died in Belize City. I saw it. I was there."

"Tannin had always been involved with the smugglers and the trafficking. We shipped drugs to dozens of systems and made a lot of senators very rich, but when they asked for more and more of our profit, we rebelled. That's when they sent us to the Sword Belt."

"When I escaped back to Earth, I went to Belize City," Phuri continued, his voice gaining in confidence. "I looked up some old contacts, but they were gone. Every one of them had disappeared amid rumors of brutal murders. Some were boiled alive, while others were dissolved in barrels of acid. I made some inquiries as to who'd been killing them all, and every contact I could find said that it was Cazador. I searched for him, but eventually I just gave up. At least I'd managed to get away from Gertie, so I figured I'd try to get back to some semblance of a normal life away from that godforsaken purgatory. However, when I boarded my shuttle with the intent of going back home to Indonesia, there was one other man on the shuttle with me. He was seriously disfigured. Half of his face horribly burned, and he's missing one of his eyes. When he looked at me and smiled, I knew this was the man that so many others had spoken of," Phuri said, and then he paused for a moment. He knew he had Carter on the hook now, and he wouldn't be able to resist finding out more about his old nemesis.

"What did he offer you?" Carter asked finally.

"In exchange for money to fund the coup, he would be left alone to run his cartel as he saw fit. All we needed was the funding, and for a time he was content with the arrangement," Phuri explained.

"You don't deal with Cazador. He'll always demand more and more, regardless of what the original deal was," Carter said, staring at Phuri with renewed contempt. "That man has been responsible for so much death and destruction."

"And that man is in the Presidential Tower in Johannesburg as we speak," Phuri hissed. "I've made my share of mistakes, and I know you detest me for the things I've done, but you are the only one who can rectify this situation. Nico is dead because I gave him that chance, but he was too brutish to see it. You, Captain...you are the planet's only hope of getting rid of that animal, before it's too late."

Atlas couldn't speak. His throat was choked, and he felt as if he were torn in two.

If Cazador was alive, then Aída could be as well, but he had a duty to all of humanity even before his duty to himself.

"To Earth, then?" Phuri asked with an oily smile.

Carter was already leaving the cell and ignored Phuri's question. He needed to think. He needed space. He needed, once more, to lose himself.

*   *   *

The Ninkovich

"Ma'am, Captain Carter has departed and is en route to the *Bwainhome*," Captain Jansen reported.

"He's...already?" Mephista asked.

"Yes, ma'am."

"Comms, get me a private channel to the shuttle. I'll take it in my quarters," Mephista ordered.

"Yes, ma'am."

Mephista felt as if her mind were in a fog. She pushed her hoverchair through the airlock down the corridor to her quarters and slipped into the temporary cabin that had been assigned to her. When she was ready, she tapped the flashing holocontrol.

"Your channel is live, ma'am," the comms officer notified her before closing the channel.

"You left without saying goodbye?" Mephista asked without preamble. For a moment, there was no response. Then she heard a deep sigh. "Are you all right? Are you there?"

The holoscreen flickered, and Atlas' face appeared. The pallor he'd had when she'd last seen him had changed; his face was flushed, and his breathing seemed too rapid.

"Will you please just talk to me?" she asked.

"I don't know what to do, Elise," he said.

"About what? Did something change?"

"I was ready. I was ready to go, and now...," he said, and then trailed off without finishing the thought.

Mephista's heart fluttered. Was he reconsidering? She'd certainly hoped that he'd change his mind, but she didn't know why he seemed conflicted all of a sudden.

"Atlas, you need to level with me, right now," she said firmly. His eyes suddenly focused, and his face softened.

"Do you remember when we first met?"

"Of course," she said.

"We were both ready to die, weren't we?"

"You don't need to bring that up. We've both changed," Mephista said.

"I'd made peace with it. I was ready to die because I was alone, but now..."

"Atlas, what are you saying?"

"I can't close the obelisk. I'm not ready."

"What do you mean? What should I tell the fleet?"

"The operation goes as planned. We're gonna kill every First One we find, but after we finish with that, I have to go back to Earth."

"We're all going to Earth, Atlas. That's the plan."

"But we can't. Not until the obelisk is closed."

"Why? What's left for you there?" she asked.

"My wife. I'm sorry Elise, but I have to know if she's still alive or not."

*　*　*

Mephista returned to the bridge with a heavy heart, unsure of exactly what was happening with Atlas. As always though, she hid her pain behind the calm order of command.

"Attention fleet," she transmitted. "This is Captain Mephista onboard the *Ninkovich*. I will be flag for this engagement."

She paused to let the announcement reach the SSC personnel spread out in the ungainly fleet. They still had twelve ships from Decival's original fleet, plus fourteen from Nico's. Every ship was fueled with antimatter, fully armed with Hal's weapons, and had a compliment of Nico's fighters as well.

"You all know the plan," she continued. "The *Gravity Drive* will fly point with the *Bwainhome* behind it and the fighters on either side. We're gonna track down every single First One and destroy them. It's time to send 'em back to whatever hell they came from. Nav officers, execute solution now."

She tapped off the holocontrol to end the transmission. For a moment she thought she had some static in her cochlear implant, but then she realized that it wasn't static at all. The bridge crew was applauding. She blushed, then raised a hand to acknowledge them all. The sailors and officers around her had seen their friends and fellow crewmates die, and they were ready for revenge. It'd been a long time since it'd felt this good to captain a ship, and looking around at all the eager faces around her only served to strengthen her resolve.

"See ya on the other side," Mephista said to the Bwain beside her.

* * *

The Bwainhome

As soon as Atlas slipped into the Bwainsong, he felt his confusion and despair start to build. The Bwainsong acted like an amplifier, with millions of minds sharing in and reflecting back whatever emotions he was feeling until the feedback he felt from it screamed through his mind.

"I've given you everything I have. I need more time, Carter said to the voices that called to him relentlessly.

The ship surrounding him was a giant pumping heart, a fist the size of a moon, and he would take it to destroy those who'd ended so many other lives. In exchange for harnessing its powers, the ship had asked for him to end its own life as well, and he'd been willing to do so until he'd learned that Aída might still be alive.

"Time is pain," the ship said. In its voice, he heard the despair of an abandoned creature pushed beyond its limits.

"But I have to know," he said. Somewhere, deep within the Bwainsong, Carter felt the ship's frustration as a vast impatience.

"We spent a millennia knowing. There is nothing more to know," the ship responded with an agonized moan.

"Please," Atlas said, knowing the Bwainsong could sense his agony and desperation as well.

Then for a time he heard nothing. He floated in nothingness, watching the fleet, growing ever closer to the obelisk, but something was wrong. The tension he felt in the ship grew nearly unbearable.

"They are not here," the Bwainhome said.

"What?" he asked, confused by the statement. He focused on what the ship showed him, and saw that the space around the obelisk was empty.

"What happened? Where did they go?" Carter called into the void.

"Captain?" a weak voice whispered to him. *"Captain, is that you?"*

Chapter Nine

The Fates' Winds

Danny felt waves of emotion surge over him as he drew his shuttle closer to the wreckage of his former ship. The corvette had been a scout vessel, designed for a maximum twelve-person crew, but after becoming so used to the massive battle cruisers and the *Bwainhome,* it was a shock to him just how small his former home had been.

"I can't believe we did so much in such a small ship," he said to Captain Carter.

In the battle against the Bwain when they'd first entered the Sword Belt, Carter and his crew had held off the aliens' entire fleet with a battery of mirror-strengthened lasers, but the corvette's repaired laser had malfunctioned, rupturing the starboard side of the hull, and the unopposed *Bwainhome* had struck a crippling blow against the *Fates' Winds* that had exposed the ship's bridge and engineering compartments to space.

"Someone else has been doing more after we left," the captain said.

As Danny's telescopes swept the ship, the First Ones' transformations were evident everywhere. A white crust the consistency of coral had begun growing from the jagged carbyne, and parts of the ship were webbed with a strange crystalline lattice.

"What do you think the First Ones are trying to do here?" Danny asked.

"The ship's reactor is still active. If the First Ones need to consume energy in order to sustain themselves against gravity, they might have kept the ship intact in order to use its radiation," Granger said as he strained to see the images.

"Show me the stern," Carter said.

"Captain, I don't think…," Danny started to protest, but the captain interrupted him.

"Mr. Xiao, I need to see engineering."

Danny chewed at his lip. He and Aric Keith had never gotten along when Aric had been elevated from the *Fates' Winds'* engineer to acting captain. Aric had even gone so far as to court-martial him, and though at the time he'd been furious about what Aric had done, the truth was that he'd deserved his punishment for being a double-agent for Sickyl Tannin. Carter had rescued him from the penal planet, but it had been Aric Keith who'd shown Danny just how wrong he was. Whoever, or whatever had contacted Captain Carter when the fleet had reached the obelisk couldn't be Aric Keith. The engineer had died saving the rest of his crew, and Danny wasn't sure if he could handle whatever discovery they were about to make.

The hull facing the obelisk was intact amidships. Danny's telescopes tracked along the glistening carbyne steel until they reached the first opening.

"That's the shuttle bay. The doors never closed," Granger noted as a sudden shudder shook his body. Just seeing the *Fates' Winds* in this condition brought back the memories of what they'd all endured together.

"Aft of the bay doors, Mr. Xiao. Show me that breach near engineering," Carter instructed.

"Yes sir," Danny said as he shifted the view.

Here the hull had been ruptured by a Bwain weapon. The carbyne steel was punched inward, leaving a jagged hole hung with more of the gossamer webbing.

"The ship should be dark," Danny said.

"But it's not. Why?" Granger asked no one in particular.

"Because someone's maintaining it," Carter said as he raised his hand and pointed at the display. "There."

Danny swallowed, then zoomed in on the shuffling shadow passing back and forth in front of the dim light from the reactor's controls.

"It can't be him," Danny whispered.

The figure stopped. It still wore the rags of an EVO suit that Aric must have worn when he'd evacuated the crew after the Bwain attack. Danny hadn't been on the ship at the time. He'd been with Hal down on Gertie leading the resistance. He and Aric had had their differences, but he never would have wished this fate on anyone.

The thing looking back at them had once been Aric Keith, but the *Fates' Winds* engineer had died on the ship and become something else. Where his skin was exposed, it pulsed with a weird worming glow. The creature's eyes were frozen shards, and his lips were torn and peeled back, revealing his teeth and jaw bone.

"Help me," a robotic voice rasped through the speakers.

"Captain, he's exposed to the vacuum," Danny said, unable to pull his gaze from the horrible sight before him.

"What we are looking at can't be Aric Keith," Granger said. "The First Ones kept him alive for a purpose. We have to look at him like that, sir. Whatever he says, we can't trust him."

"Please. I'm begging you."

Danny glanced at Captain Carter. The man looked ill in the pale light that shone from the obelisk, but his face was hard, almost angry.

"What do we do, sir?" Danny asked.

"The same thing I'd do for any of you," Carter answered solemnly.

* * *

"Captain, I don't know if I can do this," Hal said as he faced the shuttle's airlock.

"You didn't think you could stop drinking either, but you did," the Captain's voice said from behind him.

Hal was trying to force his breathing back to a steady rhythm while the airlock door flashed red and slipped open. He'd never done a spacewalk before, had never been this close to nothingness. The sight of the obelisk's massive fissure in front of him was terrifying. White lightning curled at the formation's edges, as if at any moment a storm would erupt into the empty space where the Sword Belt had once been.

The fact that the obelisk wasn't even the worst thing he would see on his first spacewalk was not improving his mood.

"Remember, just look where you want to go. Your inducers will do the rest," Carter's voice sounded in his cochlear implant.

"But how do they...whoa!" Hal exclaimed as the tiny quantum thrusters built into the joints of his suit kicked on and pushed him out of the shuttle. He was hanging in nothingness, his breath coming faster and faster, until something bumped his side.

"I've got you tethered," Granger said through the suit's intercom. "You won't need to worry about getting loose."

"I'm not sure I want to follow you," Hal said.

"We have to do what we can," the captain said in a steady voice.

Hal felt Granger pull against him, and then a gentle push as his inducers kicked on. Danny was coordinating Hal's movements from the shuttle. He was only along for the ride, at least for now. That would change when they reached the *Fates' Winds*.

The ship was a mangled mess, with gaping holes torn in its hull that sizzled with a strange whiteness like the residue of the First Ones.

"The nanobot activity is concentrated within Aric. That's why we needed you to come," Granger explained.

"I still don't know what you think I can do. I don't even know if I can access SSC nanobots," Hal said with a frown.

"Maybe you can give him some peace," Carter said quietly, though Hal heard him loud and clear through the implant.

In the blackness of space, it was hard to get a sense of his target's size, so as the *Fates' Winds* loomed over him, Hal's stomach began to churn. He wondered what would happen if he vomited in the suit, and if it was possible to drown in your own vomit in one of these things.

As he was passed through a tear in the hull. His boots magnetized and locked him onto the frozen deck where he found himself staring face to face with a once-human monster.

"Jesus!" Hal exclaimed in horror.

The thing before him was a zombie, its flesh rebuilt in the way a child would draw a human. The thing's right shoulder was swollen and grotesque looking, while his left seemed to be more or less normal looking. At least, as far as he could make out through the shreds of its EVO suit. One of its eyelids still blinked over the frozen ruin of its socket.

"I don't think I can do this."

"It's all right," the thing's voice said in Hal's helmet. *"I won't hurt you."*

"I'm...sorry. I've just never seen," Hal stammered in shock.

"Come on now Hal, just focus," Carter said encouragingly.

"Okay...okay, right," Hal said as he tried to calm himself. He took a deep breath to steady his jangled nerves, and then returned to the matter at hand. "All right, let's see here. Initiating programming handshake."

When he focused on the readouts scrolling down the electroglass of his helmet's visor, Hal found that it wasn't all that different from what he was used to in his engineering job. The coding had been modified from what he would have used to program the microscopic robots in his factories, but it wasn't all that dissimilar.

"It looks like the language is mostly intact," Hal said.

Nanobots swarmed the hulls of every SSC ship, patching small holes in the vessels' hulls made by space debris and the harsh environment. Normally, he would have seen an orderly accounting of the number of bots that were currently active, the number that were inactive, the volume of material transmitted, the heaviest area of repair, and everything else that was pertinent to their operation, but what he was looking at now was nothing of the sort. Flickers of human communication protocols still showed up on his display, but the vast majority of the nanobots were simply gone.

"I know they're in there Captain, but I don't know if I can talk to 'em," Hal reported.

"Keep trying, Hal," Carter said.

"Please," the thing in front of him asked, and then it reached out and touched his arm.

"Gahhh!" Hal whooped as he stumbled backward.

"I'm sorry," Aric said as he withdrew his hand.

"It's uhhh...it's okay," Hal said nervously. "I'll figure it out. We'll get you all fixed up, and back to Earth before ya know it."

"Earth won't exist."

"What?" Carter asked. It wasn't that he hadn't heard, but that he was stunned by the implication.

Hal's readouts were flickering. Whatever the First Ones had done to the nanobots, he wouldn't be able to hold the connection for long.

"Earth will be gone. The First Ones tricked you. They lured you here while they went to Earth," the thing that used to be Aric Keith said. His head dipped a bit as he spoke, and trips of hair and scalp floated from him.

"Oh my god," Granger gasped.

"Aric we...I'm sorry. We need to get back to the ship," Carter said with extreme urgency in his voice.

"It's all right. I don't deserve any better," Aric said. Hal gave him an apologetic and regretful look, and then he turned and began the long spacewalk back to the ship.

* * *

Atlas' Final Approach

The Constantinople

"How much antimatter do we have?" Atlas asked her.

"Enough for every ship to return to Earth," Mephista said.

They were all crowded into the cabin of Mephista's new ship. The *Constantinople's* previous captain had been lost in the First Ones' attack, and she was still breaking in a new crew with the help of Danielle Hoff.

"They're already on their way to Earth," Carter said.

"But what if Granger was right? How do you know that we can trust him?" Danielle asked.

"We don't, which is why we need to keep the fleet back here along with the gravity drive," Carter said.

"Captain, how are you gonna fight the First Ones without the fleet?" Bryon asked.

"The *Bwainhome* can hold its own," Pandith offered.

"No, it can't," Carter said flatly.

"What do you mean?" Mephista asked.

"Julie's ships would have reached the solar system by now. Her orders were to send back a messenger if things went well," Carter said. His statement hung heavily in the air. The fact that there'd been no messenger meant that things hadn't gone well at all.

The room was quiet for a moment. Everyone remembered being forced to fight their fellow service members on more than one occasion. It had taken a terrible roll on all of them.

"If I show up there with the *Bwainhome*, it'll be total war. That's why I'm gonna take the *Ninkovich*," Carter explained.

"Sir? I don't understand," Decival said with a questioning look.

"They'll be expecting Nico's ship, so we should be safe when we enter the system. That'll buy us enough time for Nico's flagship crew to explain things. Once they do, the SSC will have no choice but to stand down."

"Yeah, unless they blame it on Bwain mind control or somethin' like that," Bryon said.

"We'll just have to expect the worse, and hope for the best. That's all we can do," Carter said. "Now, we need to put things into motion. We don't have much time."

* * *

While he waited for a shuttle to take him to the *Ninkovich*, Atlas found an empty stateroom and sat alone with his thoughts. He was worried that he was going to Earth for the wrong reasons, that Aric could be trapping him, or even worse, that he was going for the right reasons, but everyone who depended on him would pay the price.

If Cazador was alive, then Aída might be too. He thought he'd put his former wife from his mind and moved on. Back on Earth, while he'd lain in the brig waiting to learn his fate for what Cazador had forced him to do, the thought of revenge had never entered his mind. The man who had disgraced him was dead, and the only thing that had been left for him to do after being assigned to the Sword Belt was to fling himself into oblivion, so he could join his dear Aída in the next life.

Now, after everything that had happened, he'd finally found hope where previously, there was none to be found, and it wasn't just him. The *Bwainhome* had hope, Aric had hope, and even the Bwain had found hope. He just needed to make sure he didn't let them all down.

Sighing, he retrieved a ream of electropaper from a drawer and began sketching with a stylus. It was a pastime he'd picked up in Belize. There were no jobs, no opportunity, and while others had turned to the cock fights or drugs for entertainment, he'd spent his time learning how to sketch. There was something liberating in letting his hand travel without any attachment to his mind as he created the patterns and curves in an almost automatic way, adding shading here, and blurring shadows there. It was like therapy for him. For the first time in months he'd been able to focus on something other than the fighting, and it felt good.

He didn't know how long he had been drawing Aída when he looked up and found Mephista floating in the cabin's doorway.

"May I come in?" she asked.

"Of course. It's your ship," he said with a tired smile.

"She was very beautiful," Mephista said as she drifted closer to him, and then stopped herself by placing a hand on his shoulder.

Flushing, Atlas pushed away the electropaper.

"Will you talk to me now?" she asked quietly. "There's no one else here."

Mephista's face was lined with the scars of her past and the weight of her command, but there was beauty there as well that all the pain and misery hadn't been able to erase.

"I have to go back to Earth. I have to confront him," he said as he studied the sketch before him. "If we bring the whole fleet along though, we'll be slaughtered. It's as simple as that."

"Yeah, I know that. I was just wondering what happened when you were unconscious all that time. Decival's doctors are dying to know, and I gotta admit, I'm curious too."

"You're sure takin' this a lot better than the last time I had to leave," he said as he glanced over at her.

"Well, this time you told me first. You didn't just disappear all of a sudden."

She was trying to be lighthearted about things, but it was difficult. He'd had been withdrawing into himself ever since he'd started sinking more and more deeply into the Bwainsong, and she didn't understand why.

"Listen, I want to go over the plan, and the chain of command in case one of us is incapacitated," he said, avoiding a response.

Mephista slipped off her hover chair to nestle beside him. He reached his arm around her and pulled her slight body to his chest.

"Which one of us is planning on not coming back this time?" she asked.

"The *Bwainhome*," he said. "It's...I mean, every time I use it...every time I'm with it, it takes a piece of me. It needs me."

"And what do you need, Atlas?" she asked gently.

"I don't know anymore. I'm just so tired," he said as he leaned his head back and closed his eyes. Mephista reached up and brushed his hair back gently.

"I know," she said quietly. "I can see it in your face. You look twenty years older."

"You know, when the time comes, I might have to go with it if we're going to have any chance of stopping these things once and for all."

"Well, whatever happens, if you need us, you know we'll come running," she said. "I hope you know how loyal everyone is to you."

"I do," he said with a weak nod. "I just hope I don't let 'em down before this whole thing is over."

"None of us are ever alone out here, Atlas. You just need to remember that," she said as she reached up and brushed away a tear. He gave her a gentle squeeze, and then leaned his head back once again with his eyes closed.

Chapter Ten

Earth

"All right, let's start again with an easier question," Cazador said, eyeing Julie with his good eye. "How do the Bwain communicate with Carter?"

He'd breezed into their quarters just after Sergeant Granger had brought them a breakfast of oat porridge. Julie had been telling Lana what Captain Carter had really been like, how he'd kept a difficult crew intact and given them confidence in themselves on board the *Fates' Winds*, but then, suddenly, the disfigured man had reappeared.

"It's telepathic, like I told you."

"And how does he prevent his mind from being taken over by them? There's been many reports of them doing that in the past."

"Oh, well Granger made us Faraday cowls that we could wear, but we don't need 'em anymore. The Bwain aren't hostile."

"Well, that's reassuring. Now, the weapons we discussed. Tell me all about them."

"I told you before. The ship created 'em. Some it grew, and others it created by interacting with the printing stations," Julie answered truthfully.

"You will work with our armorists here. You will show them what you know," Cazador said.

"But I don't know anything!" Julie protested. "Why the hell would I know about how any of of that stuff worked? I already told you. I was in charge of communications!"

"Yes, you did mention that," Cazador said as he unbuttoned his jacket. He slipped the coat from his shoulders and draped it over a chair. The man was powerfully built, with thick shoulders and a tense, precise way of moving.

"You know, we have drugs that are well suited for this sort of thing," he said as he rolled back his silk cuffs. "And of course...various tools that have proven to be quite effective."

"What the hell do you think you're doing?" Lana demanded. Cazador's good eye flicked up, crinkling in amusement.

"But...I have always preferred my hands," he said as he continued to smile in a grotesque imitation of humor that belied his intentions.

He moved so quickly that Julie barely registered what was happening. Lana tried to block the thick man, but he tossed her aside with a vicious strength. The reporter crashed into the sofa, flipped over, and struck her head against a coffee table. Then Cazador came for Julie.

"Help!" she cried as she scrambled back against the wall. It was a useless thing to do, but she had no other choice. Cazador was just too fast and too strong. She evaded his grasp twice, but the third time she caught her foot on an armchair. The *Narco* seized her shoulder and drove his fist into her stomach.

The pain was agonizing, and created a wave of nausea that flowed through her. She tried to breathe, but could only manage a croak as her lungs collapsed.

"To absorb a body shot, you exhale and flex your stomach at the same time. Now, look at me!" he said. His voice was calm, almost as if he were lecturing a class of neophyte boxers at the gymnasium.

Julie was doubled over and couldn't move, so he grabbed her by the hair pulled her head back, and jammed his stubbled chin against her throat.

"You *will* look at me when I talk to you. Is that understood?"

"Yes," Julie gasped. Her windpipe was spasming, and she felt a hard vacuum in her stomach.

"Now, let's try this again. Tell me how the weapons are made," he demanded.

"I already told you how. The ship did it," Julie gasped, trying to catch her breath from the pain roiling in her abdomen.

"By interfacing with the human factories? Factories like the ones I have?"

"They're...no. I don't know."

"Well, yes...perhaps you don't," Cazador said. He held her there for a moment longer, and then he released her.

Shuddering, Julie tried to stand, but too late she saw movement out of the corner of her eye as his fist slammed against her jaw like a rock. She fell against the wall, her muscles limp, and her vision blurred.

"This must have been what it was like to be absorbed by the First Ones," she thought dully as she lost consciousness.

* * *

When Lana regained consciousness, her head was pounding. She couldn't understand what the two blurs were in front of her until they moved, and she realized that she'd been staring at a pair of boots.

"The reporter's awake, Sergeant," a voice said.

She tried to sit up, but pain ripped through the left side of her face.

"Probably a concussion," one of the other soldiers commented.

"He's a monster!" Lana tried to say, but her lips and tongue weren't working right, and it came out as a mumble. She tried to pull her arms under her and lift herself from the carpet, but she was still too weak. Instead, a set of hands helped her to sit up. A bright light shone in her eyes, and she raised a hand to block the glow.

"You'll be all right," Sergeant Granger assured her.

"Where's Julie?" Lana asked.

"I'm here Lana," the ensign called from across the room. The woman's voice sounded different, thicker.

Lana squinted, trying to focus, but when her vision finally settled, she gasped.

The left side of Julie's face was a mass of purple bruising. Dried blood trickled from a split lip, and the ensign had a swollen black eye as well.

"Did he do that? Was that Cazador?" Lana asked. Julie nodded, wincing in pain.

"This is the man you put in charge? This is the man that Admiral Nico would have chosen in his absence?" Lana asked Granger.

"That's enough," the sergeant said.

Lana shook her head, trying to clear the hair from her face and the cobwebs from her mind.

"You have to know that this is wrong. You have to see!" Lana pleaded.

"We see a lot of things, and most of them don't matter," Granger replied without emotion.

"They don't matter because you don't make them matter! That man is nothing but a thug! He's a damn *Narco*, and you take orders from him. He tells you to starve those people on the ships, and you do it. He tells you to fix up Julie and I so he can beat us again, and you do it. You're just his subservient little lap dog," Lana spat in disgust.

The sergeant drew closer until his chin was inches from her face. His eyes were wide, and she felt the tension in him.

"I'm gonna give you five seconds to calm down, or I *will* sedate you. If I have to do that, then you won't be able to help your friend, and neither of you are gonna be any closer to gettin' outta here. Do I make myself clear?" the sergeant growled.

It took everything that Lana had hold her tongue. Her blood was boiling, and yet it seemed as if, in a way, the sergeant was trying to tell her something. She nodded, wincing at the pain the movement brought as the door opened behind her. Granger stood up and saluted. Lana couldn't turn her head, but she knew who had entered the room.

Cazador squatted in front of her, dabbing at his knuckles with a red-streaked towel.

"Do you think you might be ready to cooperate now?" he asked.

Lana said nothing.

"I asked you a question," Cazador said with deadly calm.

"It doesn't matter what you do. A man like you would have the truth and continue the beating whoever gave it to him, because that's who you are," Lana mumbled through the fog that seemed to move through her head.

Cazador smiled as he reached behind Lana and stroked her hair.

"I've always liked the fire of the Spanish women. I'll enjoy putting it out," he said. Lana gave an involuntary shudder, repulsed by his touch.

"Mr. President," a voice called from the corridor.

"I told you not to interrupt me," he snapped impatiently.

"Apologies sir, but a ship just arrived in orbit. It's Captain Carter. He's on the *Ninkovich* with Phuri. They say they want to talk."

* * *

The Ninkovich

Captain Carter stood at the ship's forward observation window, staring down at the blue and green swirls of the planet far below. Clouds whisked across the surface, shadowing whole continents as they reached out to the sea. It was daytime in the western hemisphere, and he could make out the Yucatan in the middle of Central America. He traced it with his eyes until he reached the approximate location of Belize City. The last time he'd seen this view, he'd been going into exile, and had no hope of ever seeing the Earth again. Now that he'd arrived, memories of the past had begun to stir within him.

If Aída was alive, what would he say to her? How would he find the strength to close the obelisk, and where were the First Ones if they weren't here?

"I'm sure there are no hard feelings," Phuri said from behind him.

Carter turned and glared at the small man.

"How many people have died so you could feel important?" Carter asked.

Phuri pursed his lips and stared at the deck in embarrassment.

"Power means different things to each of us. I know you, if anyone, can understand that," he said, trying to sound contrite and agreeable.

"Yes, but I wonder if you do," Carter responded with a sigh.

"Captain, we're getting a response," the comms officer said.

"Put it on the main holos."

The face of an officer he didn't recognize appeared. The man looked vaguely Slavic, with narrowed eyes and a clenched face.

"I am Captain Nadurov, acting chief of the SSC in Admiral Nico's absence," the man announced importantly. "What is the meaning of your arrival? Where is Admiral Nico?"

"We'll talk when the president joins us," Carter said firmly. "Where's Kidewange?"

"Admiral Nico has replaced Nelson Kidewange," Nadurov said. "I am the civil and military representative on this call."

"That's not my understanding. I understand from Mr. Vongsa that you do in fact have a civilian authority in the Presidential Tower. I would very much like to speak with him as well before this conversation goes any further," Carter said. He wasn't going to deal with anyone who didn't have the authority to act.

Nadurov offered a precise nod.

"I will confirm our response," he said, and the holoscreen darkened.

"Well, you've certainly stirred things up," Phuri said with a wry smile.

"I won't do Nico's posturing," Carter said. "I'm here to talk to Cazador, and that's it."

"That's your plan?" Phuri asked. "You're going to *talk* to him?"

"You already know how smart he is. I need to see his face. I need to understand what he wants." Carter said as he continued to stare at the dark holoscreen before them.

"I told you that already. He wants the weapons," Phuri said.

"Well, there's something I want too," Carter admitted, but he would not discuss his plan with a man who had proven himself to be so completely untrustworthy. His loyalties changed like the wind with every hint of self-serving opportunity.

The holoscreen flickered to life once more, and Nadurov's icy face stared back at them in three dimensions.

"The government's representative will be joining us momentarily," Nadurov said. "He was in another meeting, but I am authorized to discuss things with you until he arrives."

"Well then, the tactical situation is extremely simple," Atlas said. "There are hostile aliens in the universe more powerful than anything we've encountered before, and certainly far more powerful than the Bwain. Every man and woman on the crew of this ship is loyal to the SSC and this planet, and they've seen what those creatures can do first hand."

"We have heard these lies before," Nadurov replied, trying to sound bored and uninterested.

"Comms, transmit the file package," Carter said, and then he turned back to the holoscreen. "I'm sending you the *Ninkovich's* full, raw science logs of the First Ones. There has been no tampering. You know that these aren't lies. You saw what Capra Falconi has seen, what the survivors of Decival's fleet witnessed, what..."

"Those survivors are in quarantine."

"What?" Carter asked, dumbfounded. "We sent them here so that they'd be safe."

"And how did we know that was your intention? How were we to be sure that there were no Bwain hidden among the survivors?"

"What did you do to them? Where's Ensign Ford?" Carter demanded.

"As I told you, they are in quarantine. You may speak to Ensign Ford when we allow you this privilege."

"File package transmitted," his comms officer confirmed.

"Did you bring me a present, Captain?" a new voice asked.

Carter had been preparing himself for this moment ever since Phuri told him that Cazador was still alive, but seeing his face again after so long was still a shock.

Cazador was breathing heavily, as if he'd just come from exerting himself. The right side of his face was filled with waxy scar tissue, and yet Carter could still remember what he'd looked like before the fall of Belize City. His friend had always worn the same half-smile before a fight that he showed now.

"These things are coming for Earth, Cazador. I can't say when, I can't say how, and you have no way to defend yourself against them. I can help you, but you need to put aside this vendetta against me and the Bwain, and you need to surrender yourself to me."

Atlas' Final Approach

Cazador's lips twisted into a grimace.

"I recall once saying something similar to you, and that didn't work out well for you, did it? Let me speak with Admiral Nico."

"Nico's dead," Carter said.

Atlas had expected more of a reaction, but neither of the men on the holoscreen flinched, even in the slightest.

"Well then, in the unfortunate event of a sitting Galactic President's death, we go to Protocol Delta," Cazador said.

"What does that mean?" Carter asked.

"You've been gone a long time, Atlas. We have a new Galactic Constitution, and according to that document, in the event of a loss of the head of the government during a period of martial law, power is returned to the designated representative of one of Earth's continental blocks. Fortunately for me, Central America happens to be on the rotation," he said with a serpent-like grin.

"I don't care about your power games, Cazador. I don't care about any of this. Every second we're standing here brings those things closer."

"That's a shame, Atlas. Your biggest weakness was always that you didn't understand the bigger picture. You were always too focused on landing a punch...on working your opponent into a corner. You could never tell when that's exactly what they wanted you to do."

Carter stared at Cazador's smug face, trying to force down his anger.

"You surrender yourself to me, and I'll keep these things from reaching you," Carter said directly into the holoscreen. Cazador simply laughed, but Nadurov seemed confused. The officer tried to say something, but his transmission suddenly disappeared, leaving Cazador's ruined face to fill the entire screen.

"No, Atlas. See, you overestimate your leverage. Let me give you my terms. You, along with Phuri Vongsa, will surrender to me here on Earth. You give me these weapons of yours that your Ensign Ford has been telling me about, and in exchange for your cooperation, I'll let your refugees live."

Carter squeezed his eyes shut. Once more, he'd underestimated Cazador's amorality. He'd thought Cazador would recognize the danger to the entire planet and concede, but he'd forgotten that the man thought only of himself and his goals, and would stop at nothing to achieve them. If the world burned, Cazador wouldn't care, as long as he ruled the mountain of ash.

"I swear Cazador, one day I'm gonna send you straight to Hell with my bare hands," Atlas growled through gritted teeth.

"You'll come down to Johannesburg on a single shuttle," Cazador said. "No tricks, and none of your Bwain friends with you, or every one of the colonists you sent me dies."

"And then what?" Carter asked with scorn. "You'll just release them?"

"Then we'll talk about these magical weapons that your Ensign Ford tells me you have control of, and we'll relive old times. Perhaps we'll even discuss family life."

"Is Aída alive? You bastard, tell me what happened to her!" Carter yelled at the holoimage before him.

"You have five minutes to decide, or I give the order to destroy your colonists' ships. I strongly suggest you hurry," Cazador said as he leaned forward and closed the comms channel.

Chapter Eleven

The Constantinople

"The First Ones aren't anywhere near Earth orbit. I don't know where they are, but they're not here. Not yet anyway," the Bwain squawked to Mephista in its best approximation of Carter's voice.

"Send the *Bwainhome* to search for 'em," Mephista suggested.

"I can't!" the creature squawked. "If I do, he'll kill the hostages."

"What about one of the SSC ships?"

"He'll have all the serial numbers. I've already told him about the fleets. I showed up on the *Ninkovich,* for God's sake!" Carter argued.

"But you can't just surrender to that animal!" she cried.

The creature picked at the feathers under one of its wings for a moment, and then refocused.

"I'm not surrendering," it said. "I can still talk to you and the *Bwainhome*, and it'll save thousands of lives."

"I don't like it, Atlas. You can't trust him."

"I'll contact you as soon as I can," he said, and then the Bwain suddenly relaxed and started preening itself.

"What do we do now, ma'am?" Danielle asked.

"Now...we wait," Mephista said with a frown.

* * *

Johannesburg

"What's that sound?" Phuri asked.

When the *Ninkovich*'s shuttle had first touched down on the presidential compound's interior landing pads, Carter thought that the trembling he felt through the seat was the idling of the craft's engines, but the pilot had powered down and was standing before her two passengers. Whatever the rumbling was, it was coming from outside.

"We've arrived, Captain," the woman said.

"Yeah, thank you," he acknowledged.

He unlatched his restraints and stood in the small cabin. As instructed, he and Phuri had come alone. A small mirror was bolted to the bulkhead just beside the airlock, and Atlas stooped to consider his uniform. He'd had to borrow the SSC's dress blues from the *Ninkovich*'s science officer, and the uniform was slightly short on him. The ship's supply officer had pressed the captain's insignia onto his epaulets, and Atlas had requested the fashioning of several new insignia for his chest. The first was a black star medal, signifying the victory over the Bwain. The next was an image of a collapsing planet portraying the saving of Gertie's colonists, and finally, one that looked like a spear through a white squid, which symbolized the battle against the First Ones that still had not reached its conclusion.

He faced the hatch, sighed, and nodded to the pilot to unseal the bulkhead.

"Sir, are you certain?" the pilot asked. "We can't guarantee your safety."

"You're not the first to tell me that. Go ahead," he said.

Atlas' Final Approach

The pilot nodded, and then opened the hatch.

As soon as the hatch finished opening, he and Phuri stepped out into a dizzying scene. The causeway that led from the landing pad to the Presidential Tower was lined with marines at stiff attention. Below the elevated platform, what must have been hundreds of thousands of citizens roared and bellowed at him. The sound of their anger was a physical force, a punch to the chest so loud that his ears couldn't register it.

Ten meters away from the pad, Cazador stood smiling, and two others that Carter didn't know flanked him on each side. One was a shorter, heavier man with dark hair, and the other was a taller, more serious-faced man. These would be his enforcers. They were the kind of thugs who had always lurked in the shadows of Belize City, smoking their cigarettes in the corners of the gym while they kept an eye out for the fighters who showed courage, so they could recruit them into their gangs.

"My friend, I didn't think you'd come!" Cazador shouted.

"Release the refugees," Atlas replied tersely.

Cazador nodded. Marines who'd been hidden on either side of the shuttle hatch seized Carter and Phuri's arms, pulled them backward, and sealed their wrists in a set of spider cuffs.

"Your reflexes are slow," Cazador said.

"The ships," Atlas responded, refusing to be baited into meaningless banter with his former friend.

"Of course," Cazador answered with a leer. "The refugees will be offloaded to Luna station. There will need to be some processing time, but they'll be given the chance to resettle at another colony, or go through a repatriation process to return to Earth."

"Thank you," Atlas said, then added, "I'd expected more of a fight."

"Well, so did I, but I'm not a monster like these Bwain of yours," Cazador said. The taunting remark was intended for those who were listening, making sure they all realized this was the man who'd chosen an alien species over the human race.

"They aren't...," he started to say, but then from behind he felt someone slipping a wire mesh over his head. Before he realized what was happening, he heard the crackle of an electric charge, and the spider steel snugged itself against his scalp.

Suddenly, the mental buzzing of the Bwainsong stopped. Atlas was alone in his own mind for the first time in weeks. Cazador looked back, smiling as they began to walk.

"Just a little insurance," he said. "We need to make sure you don't have any nightmares or anything that would cause the monsters to come running to your rescue."

* * *

Cazador led Carter and Phuri into the tower, and then up to a large room filled with holobroadcasting equipment, and a swarm of aides and functionaries that were milling about. Two of them jogged toward Carter with an orange prisoner's jumpsuit in hand. The marines surrounding him held up their rifles as the attendants cut away Carter's uniform.

"You're out of shape my friend. It pains me to look at you," Cazador commented. "Now, get dressed."

One of the marines undid Carter's spider cuffs, but when the captain made no move to clothe himself, the orderlies drew up the cheap fabric around him and zipped up the front. They stepped away, and the marines replaced his cuffs.

"Is this really necessary?" he asked.

"I can't have the public seeing a traitor in a uniform," Cazador said. "Put Phuri next to him."

"Now, Cazador...what about our agreement?" Phuri asked, concern edging his voice.

"Agreement? What agreement? There is no longer any agreement between us," he said. "I'm Earth's law now, and I have no more use for the likes of you."

Phuri paled, swallowed, and let the aides shove him into place on the dais, where a group of marines in battle gear flanked them on both sides. The lights rose on the holocameras. They would be broadcast in full 3-D, as opposed to the normal computer-interpolated formats. Cazador wanted his audience experience the broadcast with all possible realism.

"Oh," Cazador said as he tapped his jaw. "There's just one more thing."

He turned with blinding speed, unleashing a right hook against Carter's eye. Carter's boxing training took over. He tried to lean back and roll his face away from the punch, but the marines behind him held his head and forced him into the punch. Cazador's knuckles hit Carter's cheek and eye socket with the force of a brick.

The nominal president stepped away, shaking his hand, and Carter felt blood rushing to his injured face. In a few minutes, his eye and cheek would be swollen, making him look just battered enough on the holocameras for the people to feel satisfied.

"Bare-knuckle, just like the old days," Cazador said, smiling to himself. He then turned to the cameral, raised his hands, and began speaking.

"People of Earth, and all of the outlying settlements, today is a great day.

The SSC has brought the traitor Atlas Carter to justice, along with his coconspirator, Phuri Vongsa. These two men are guilty of sympathizing with the Bwain to invade our planets and colonies, to take over our minds, and to bend us to their twisted vision of what humanity future should be."

"Sadly, Admiral Nico gave his own life to capture these two traitors, and for that, I ask that you bow your heads in remembrance," Cazador said as he closed his eyes and placed his hand over his heart, presenting the picture of an official in mourning.

Carter's heart pounded as Cazador folded his hands. Twice now, he'd miscalculated the man completely. Without a connection to the Bwain, he had no way to call for help, and if the First Ones suddenly appeared in the system, he would have no way at all to fight them. Cazador had known exactly how to neutralize his greatest advantage, but how?

Cazador's head rose, and the lights gleamed on his mangled face.

"Now, I know many of you are angry, but it is only right and just that we give Atlas Carter a fair and honest trial. My administration will be one of openness and transparency as we lead humanity into a new era of peace and prosperity. But first, a warning."

Cazador turned and pulled a plasma pistol from his waist. He leveled the weapon at his prisoners and pulled the trigger.

Carter had learned long ago never to close his eyes in a fight, and so he watched as the bolt of ionized energy struck Phuri's chest and burrowed into the man's heart. The marines behind the dais caught Phuri, lowering him to the ground as his feet kicked. The wounded man rolled on his side, grasped Carter's pant leg and stared up with pained eyes.

"Help me," Phuri gasped, but it was too late. The man who had caused so much harm to so many people stilled against Carter's boots.

"It won't be nearly as easy for you," Cazador whispered to Atlas before turning back to the microphone.

"Those who oppose progress, who seek to stab others in the back, will be dealt with harshly. Thank you for your time."

*   *   *

"I'm surprised you don't have more questions for me," Cazador said as he walked at the head of a squad of marines leading Carter through the bowels of the Presidential Tower.

Atlas knew he wanted to hear him beg for his wife, or to plead for the ability to help the planet. It was how Cazador had always been...taunting and cruel, right down to his very core.

Atlas refused to give in to the desperation building within him. What was happening in the universe was bigger than any grievances between himself and Cazador. He needed to convince Cazador how dangerous the First Ones were.

"You're gonna be the last president this planet ever has if you don't listen to me," Carter said.

"By the way, it was Ensign Ford who gave me the idea for the cowl. Quite ingenious, really. Our science team was very impressed. She also told me about your dimensional weapons," he said as he reached around and patted the back of Atlas' head. "They spring from your mind, eh? The Bwain build you whatever you want?"

"It doesn't work like that. I'll tell you everything, anything your scientists want to know, but you have to let my ships come to Earth."

"Tell me about these aliens, the First Ones," Cazador said, ignoring his remarks.

The party turned a corner into a corridor that appeared like a cross between a prison and hotel. Guards stood at each doorway, while orderlies pushed carts with food and drinks along the walls.

"They're from another dimension," Carter said. "They were the first sentient life to develop in the universe. Eventually, when they discovered the ability to travel between dimensions, they left our physical universe. Now they're back, but in order to sustain their physical forms and resist gravity, they have to keep consuming matter. We finally figured out that gravity can be used to kill 'em. That's why we took the gravity drive, but we only have the one prototype. The Bwain's dimensional weapons are more focused."

"And they're coming here to destroy us, that's what you're telling me?" Cazador asked.

Atlas' group passed a door guarded by another detachment of marines. A red-haired sergeant who looked familiar to him glared at him as he passed. The air in the tower was hostile.

"The First Ones captured one of my crew and tortured him. He gave them the location of the Earth. I know they're coming, and there's nothing that any SSC ship, or anyone else in the solar system can do to stop them."

The leading marines stopped at an open door. Inside could have been a resort suite, with a marble floor and an ornate fountain sprinkling water up from the mouths of two dolphins.

"This is basically the same story your ensign gave me, but she was less forthcoming about the weapons." Cazador said as he paused momentarily to admire the surroundings, almost as if he were seeing them for the first time.

"What do the weapons matter? Didn't you listen to anything that I said?"

"You have access to weapons that you can create with your mind, and you also control the Bwain with your mind. For a boxer, you seem to have become quite intelligent," Cazador noted. He was smiling now as he ushered his prisoner into what was to become nothing more than a fancy cell. "I'd like you to use that brilliant mind of yours to think about how you can give me control of these weapons. Once you've done that, then we'll talk further. Until then, enjoy your new accommodations."

* * *

Lana dabbed at the crusted blood around Julie's lips. Cazador had most likely broken several of Julie's ribs. The ensign's face was a swollen wreck, and she could barely turn her head.

"We need to get the hell outta here," Lana said. Julie grimaced, trying to turn her head to scan the room.

"Look for...anything... we can use as a weapon," Julie gasped, gritting her teeth against the pain. "We have to surprise 'em."

Lana nodded and began studying their quarters. A bureau along the living area's wall was empty, but the legs might do as a club. In the bathroom, there were two plastic tumblers. The bedroom had a few wooden hangers in its empty closet.

She dumped these items on the coffee table in front of where Julie sat, but she wasn't convinced.

"None of these are gonna help us against the guards," she said.

"It's not the guards we need to kill, it's Cazador," Julie said in a strained voice. She reached for one of the wooden hangars and turned it over in her hands, and then she set the plastic tumbler on the floor, raised her boot, and stomped on it. Plastic pieces scattered in every direction, and Lana helped her gather them up.

* * *

Shuttle Tiderian
In orbit around the obelisk

"You're two meters off, Bryon," Danny said from his shuttle pilot's seat. He was holding station outside the *Danube*, one of the cruisers in Nico's fleet. He was providing support for Bryon Purcell and the other engineering teams who were retrofitting the last of Hal's dimensional weapons onto the ship's hull. While they waited for Captain Carter, Mephista had ordered every ship to be armed as best as they could, and Danny was guiding Bryon in positioning the weapon so that it could achieve the maximum field of fire.

Bryon's inducers at the joints of his EVO suit fired briefly, nudging him more toward the ship's spine.

"And...hold," Danny called.

"Got it," Bryon answered. He tossed down an electromagnetic ring that cleared the hull-repairing nanobots from the area, triggered his boot magnets, and drew himself to the surface.

"I don't know if I'll ever get used to this," Bryon said.

Aside from the slight golden glow and the silver ripples from the obelisk's strange light, most of the ship existed in gray shadow.

"I know. You don't realize how empty space is until you're out there in the emptiness," Danny answered.

"It's not just that. I'm talkin' about us...all the old crew. Aric's...well, whatever he's become. Kaylee's gone, Threed's gone, Julie's back on Earth, and now the Captain's gone too."

Danny stayed silent, unsure what to say. In truth, he'd been worrying about Julie ever since she'd failed to report back to them, and Bryon, who normally was so enthusiastic about everything, had finally put his finger on what had been bothering him.

"Yeah well, we started somethin' out here, and we're not gonna get to finish it," Danny said.

"That's exactly it," Bryon said. He was kneeling on the hull now, working on the Bwain weapon. "I just…I guess I just wanted to say thanks, to the captain, and to all of you guys."

Danny zoomed in his telescope, watching Bryon work out the positioning of the weapon on the hull. It looked like a set of purple stalactites that ended in bulbous spheres, but despite their strange appearance, the weapons worked.

"Correct to twenty-two degrees," Danny said.

"Copy," Bryon said as he twisted the strange weapon slightly clockwise.

"You know, I was a huge jerk to all you guys back on the *Fates' Winds*, but I was even worse to Julie," Danny continued reflectively.

"She cared about you. I know you didn't see it," Bryon said.

"I saw it. She was the only one I helped, out of all of you. Those weight loss drugs were addictive, but she wanted 'em so bad, I just couldn't say no. I just wish I could go back and change things. I'd have never given her those damn pills in the first place. I'd have told her she was beautiful, just the way she was. You know, anything to keep her from takin' those damn things," Danny said, sighing at the memory of the man he used to be.

"Well, at least she managed to turn it around and get off of 'em. That's all that matters really. At least she eventually got off of 'em and got herself clean. She did it all by herself too. Took a lot of strength on her part to get through it, but she did it," Bryon reminded him.

"She never told me that," Danny said.

"Pandith wanted to help her, but she wanted to do it herself. I think it helped her. You know…made her stronger," Bryon said. "Sealing the weapon now."

A brief glow popped under the weapon where it fixed itself to the *Danube*'s hull. Bryon pulled on the spheres, but the weapon didn't budge.

"Seal complete," he confirmed. "I'm detaching and coming back to you."

As Danny watched, Bryon released his boot magnets and kicked himself away from the hull. The spider steel barrier he'd set up released with him, and he gathered it into a loop as he twisted and triggered his inducers toward Danny's shuttle.

"Does it feel right to you?" Danny asked. His eyes were on the obelisk, but his mind was on the Earth. "I mean, just staying out here, waiting like this?"

"Now you know that any good weapons officer wants to be in a fight at all times, so I'm gonna have to say no, but I'm not sure what we can really do about it. We're under orders," Bryon noted as he approached the shuttle.

"Yeah well, maybe it's time we changed those orders," Danny said.

* * *

The Bwainhome

Mephista was touring the *Bwainhome* with Granger and Hal, going over the things that Hal had reported. Wide passages that had once been a dim purple, now throbbed with a bright orange. The Bwain that scuttled through them showed a wider variety of pigmentation. Their eyes were clear, and their feathers seemed more kempt. It appeared that the creatures were doing a better job of grooming themselves for some reason.

"Is it just me, or do they look bigger to you?" she asked as she floated along in her hoverchair.

"They've certainly gotten fatter," Hal agreed. "The ship's been feeding 'em again."

"Pandith saw evidence of this back when we first met up with the First Ones. The Bwain led him to a feeding station," Granger added as he stooped to examine new developments in an area that had previously seemed inactive.

"It's gettin' ready for something, isn't it Hal?" she asked as they turned into a larger passageway that headed down toward the main shuttle bay where Mephista had entered.

"The captain believed that the *Bwainhome* itself was alive, and that it might have been one of the First Ones that stayed behind," Granger explained.

"The thought of it makes my skin crawl," Hal said.

"But if it is, then why would it be on our side?" Mephista asked.

"I think it's because of the captain. When he entered the Knot, he became a part of the ship."

"And now the ship's recovering," Mephista said as she eyed a group of Bwain that were fluttering and squawking among themselves. The aliens seemed more relaxed than ever. "That has to be a good sign for Atlas, doesn't it?"

"I'd like to think so, but there's no way to know," Granger said.

The *Bwainhome*'s shuttle bay was a massive rounded hangar, and Mephista was surprised to see another shuttle parked beside hers. Danny and Bryon were leaning against its hull, waiting. They snapped to attention when she neared, and she returned their salute.

"Is everything all right with the retrofitting?" she asked.

"Yes, ma'am, but that's not why we're here," Bryon said..

"Permission to speak freely, ma'am?" Danny asked.

"Of course."

"We need to go to Earth. Waiting here like this...it's...," Danny said, but then he hesitated, not quite sure how to put into words the feelings of restlessness that pulled at him.

"It just feels like this is what the First Ones want," Bryon finished for him.

"On what evidence are you basing that conclusion?" Granger asked.

"It's...I dunno. I don't really have any evidence, but we've been here for a week now, just sittin' here waiting. It feels like something's wrong. The captain would have been in touch by now if things were ok."

Mephista sighed. Morale was starting to flag across the fleet as the crews agonized over the fate of what might be happening back home. More than a few times, she herself had fought off the urge to issue the order to return. She'd been worrying though that she was being influenced by her feelings for Atlas, more than her sense of command.

"Captain Carter ordered us to remain on station until he could contact us," she reminded them. "We've received no word through the Bwain or any other channels..."

"That's just it, ma'am. There's been no word for a week now. It used to be daily," Bryon said.

"It just feels wrong. It doesn't feel like him," Danny added.

"Be that as it may...," she started, but she was interrupted when a sudden howling rose from the Bwain. The humans spun, seeing one of the creatures flashing pink and white in agitation a few dozen meters from them. The pigmentation spread from first several, and then hundreds of the creatures as they fell to the ground, writhing and snapping at themselves, and at each other. It was as if they were all dying simultaneously, or being attacked.

"What's happening? What's going on?" Mephista asked helplessly as she watched the invisible chaos ripple through the Bwain.

Chapter Twelve

SSC Kuiper Belt Research Facility
In orbit around Pluto

Declan Rowe's shifts had become much busier since Atlas Carter had entered the solar system. The ten-man crew on Kuiper Belt Station was in charge of keeping the shipping lanes clear of the occasional asteroid, comets, or other bodies that swirled at the edge of space beyond the solar system. When the *Bwainhome* had appeared and Admiral Nico had led his fleet to encounter the alien craft, all hell had broken loose.

Declan had watched in awe as Carter's ship had appeared in seemingly dozens of places at once, slipping in and out of visible space so quickly the ship appeared as if were in some sort of a strobe effect. Everywhere it appeared, it had struck at Admiral Nico's fleet with deadly precision. The battle had raged for barely twenty minutes, but when it had ended, sixteen ships in Nico's fleet had been incapacitated and a massive debris field filled the shipping lanes that had formerly been so pristine.

His job would have been hard enough monitoring and directing the fleet of probes that was cleaning up the debris while the remaining SSC ships conducted their repairs, but the arrival of SSC intelligence complicated things significantly.

"I need access to the recordings from probe serial numbers 1587 through 1600," Lieutenant Schmidt said. The slender officer filled the small command deck of the station with a quiet intensity. Declan had never worked with someone from intelligence before, and he was nervous about it, but eager to make a good impression nonetheless.

"You should have access to all master footage. If you've been in the core..."

"I need you to find it for me," Schmidt said. "You're familiar with what I'm looking for. You know the probes. I can't be expected to comb through all that data by myself."

"But that's your job," Declan wanted to say. The two-man intelligence team hadn't disclosed their mission, but he surmised that they were trying to study the *Bwainhome*'s propulsion method and offensive capabilities.

He'd already sat beside Schmidt while the officer pored over endless different angles of the battle, noting the time signatures, how quickly the alien ship had disappeared and reappeared, and how its fighters flashed in and out of existence.

"I'll get it to you right after I finish this next round of operations," Declan sighed.

On the holoscreens, a swarm of nearly one-hundred probes were blinking orange, waiting for their next assignments. The probes were little more than electromagnets and grapples with inducers attached to them. Their job was to attach themselves to the battle's debris and redirect the material out of the shipping lanes. It was a tedious process, but Declan took the job seriously. If a ship got hulled by a piece of debris, people could die, and it would be his fault.

He began tapping out various debris zones for the probes, and then identified safe vectors for the debris disposal. He'd only been at it for a few minutes when Schmidt stepped in front of him.

"Rowe, my orders are coming directly from the president," he said. "The Bwain threat is a priority, and I'd prefer not to have to report you for insubordination."

"Which president is that again?" Rowe asked.

He couldn't resist the dig, particularly since Schmidt seemed to have been born devoid of manners. If he was honest with himself, something about the whole narrative of Kidewange's departure, Nico's rise, Nico's death, and now this Cazador character struck him as being a bit off somehow.

"I serve the office, not the man," Rowe said flatly.

With a heavy sigh, Rowe called up the recordings from the requested probes, split their views on the holoscreens so the computer would display a composite picture, and then began replaying the footage. There again was the Bwain ship darting through the fleet, striking with an incredible precision. When he'd first begun the debris cleanup, he had worried part of what he would be doing might entail sending dead sailors' bodies out into the void, but he'd learned from his superior that casualties had been surprisingly light.

"Don't you think it's a little bit strange? I mean, Nico and Cazador both say that this guy Carter is such a huge threat, but you see what that ship can do. He could have torn the whole fleet apart, but he didn't. He was holding back or somethin', like he didn't want to fight 'em, but Nico claimed he was some kind of an animal," he commented as he paused to make sure the correct images were loading on the holoscreen before him. He was taking some small pleasure in the fact that he was purposely working at a snail's pace, which he knew irritated the impatient and self-important officer to no end.

"That's enough, Rowe. I'll make my own conclusions. You can go back to garbage duty," the lieutenant said, dismissing him rudely.

Declan flushed for a moment, and then he proceeded to shunt Schmidt's display to a smaller monitor before he left to resume his duties. Something was strange though. Half of his orange-lit probes had disappeared, and in their place were strangely shifting white shapes that looked something like jellyfish.

Frowning, he adjusted the telescope's resolution to give himself a better image.

"I've had about enough of your little games, Rowe. You and I need to have a talk," Schmidt snarled as he squinted at the smaller monitor and then angrily compared it to the larger screen at Rowe's work station.

"Yeah well, we've got bigger problems right about now," Declan said as he pointed to the screen where the First Ones were streaking through the Kuiper Belt, leaving a trail of empty space in their wake.

* * *

The Ancient felt those around him growing stronger. Each of them were still diminished from what they had been before they'd left this physical universe so long ago, but they were satiating their hunger in the ice and asteroid fields that surrounded the small system that Aric had directed him to. The system was rather unremarkable in the grand scheme of the universe. It was nothing more than a small volume of matter in a less dense part of the universe that he would not have otherwise targeted. After Aric and Carter's insolence however, The Ancient had decided that a show of force must be made if they were to cow these humans.

The First Ones were the culmination of existence, the ultimate expression of life. It had been they who had evolved first in the physical universe, and brought the light of intelligence to the creatures they'd enslaved. It had been they who had mastered the transition between dimensions, and it was they who would teach these pathetically limited human beings that occupied the third planet from this system's sun how to properly serve a new master.

But first, they would feast.

It had taken many of this system's days to revolve around the outer orbit of its sun, filling themselves with the icy matter that could help them heal their wounds. Now they were ready to once again strike out against the humans.

"ATLAS CARTER'S HOME IS NEAR!" The Ancient roared to his brethren, and he felt their anger flow back to him. Carter had sent many of their kind back to the empty dimensions, where they howled in fury at the loss of their physical forms. The Ancient would bring the lost back through the obelisk again soon, but first he needed to strengthen himself.

"We will consume him first," one of the First Ones answered.

"No, it shall be us," another answered.

In the space before him, a chitinous spike shot out against the flank of a First One that had taken on the appearance of a hermit crab. Both flashed red, damaging each other. The beings halted their advance, rising to face each other while the brethren around them watched the spectacle. The crab coughed a ball of antimatter, spitting it toward its rival, but The Ancient reached out one of its dozens of tendrils and clutched the projectile in what might be considered its hand, and destroyed it utterly.

"ENOUGH!" The Ancient roared. *"WE HAVE COME TO DESTROY THE EARTH. THE CARTER IS ON THE EARTH. THAT IS OUR ENEMY. NOW, SO GO FORTH AND CONSUME!"*

The swarm hung still for a moment, shuddering in the agony of their hunger and rage.

"They are bringing ships against us," one of the group warned.

The Ancient shifted its focus, studying the small human craft that had often seemed so formidable when Carter was in command of them. This time however, it saw no evidence of Carter, nor did it sense any of the dimensional rift weapons that the humans had used against them. If it had been capable of smiling, The Ancient's hungry grin would have split its face wide open.

"THEY ARE WEAK!" he roared. *"WE WILL DEVOUR THEM!"*

* * *

Kuiper Belt Station

"We need to get outta here!" Declan exclaimed.

"These observations...they're important. Are you transmitting to Earth?" Schmidt asked, trying to control the tremor in his voice.

Declan slammed the communications controls, then stood up from his station. The creatures that were headed toward the dry-docked fleet were the stuff of nightmares. Wriggling and juddering where they should have been still, they looked like Dr. Moreau's failed experiments at melding animal parts together. The wounded ships that stuttered toward them in a ragged battle line had no chance at all of survival.

A heavy volley of magna-cannons launched toward the creatures, but instead of causing any damage, the projectiles seemed to slow down as they approached, and then disappeared entirely as they came in contact with the skin of the creatures.

"Station alarm!" Declan called. The computer reacted, and the station's siren roared to life. Lights flashed red, and on the decks below, his fellow crew members tumbled out of their bunks, manning what few, pathetic weapons the stations possessed while they awaited further instructions from the observation deck.

On the holoscreen, missiles surged toward the oncoming creatures.

"Jesus, they're only fifteen-thousand kilometers away!" Declan cried.

"Their speed is incredible," Schmidt murmured, unable to tear his eyes away from the images that were flashing across the various screens. "I've never seen anything like it."

"Rowe, what's going on out there?" the lieutenant called. His voice was a bit hoarse since he'd just woken up, and he sounded worried.

"Sir, we've got new alien signatures. They're engaging the damaged fleet. The ships are firing, but...," he said, but then he fell silent and point at the main screen.

On the holoscreen, the creatures absorbed the missile fire as if nothing had happened. They were less than a thousand kilometers from the ships.

"Our weapons are having no effect on 'em at all," Declan finished for him.

Schmidt, ever loyal to the office of the president, was muttering observations into the transmission. Declan on the other hand was inching his way back toward the station's lift. The escape pods were on the deck below, and he had no intention of waiting around to see what the nightmarish creatures would do to the station once they finished with the damaged fleet. On the holoscreen, the ships spread further apart and began engaging with both laser fire and whatever manner of close-quarter weaponry they still had available, but nothing they tried was having any effect at all on the enemy.

Then, in one horrifying instant, the creatures reached the ships. Their claws and tentacles sunk through the hulls as if the thick carbyne steel were made of nothing but air.

"Oh my god!" Declan exclaimed in horror.

"What's our status?" the lieutenant asked.

"We need to abandon station!" he squawked. "Abandon station!"

"Rowe, what are you doing?" Schmidt furiously called to him, but the intelligence officer never saw the massive creatures streaking toward the station.

Declan's last sight was of an unearthly whiteness growing closer and closer until it filled the tunnel through which he was fleeing, washed over him, and crackled across his skin.

* * *

Earth

Alone in his cell, Atlas Carter felt the weariness wash over him. The life essence he'd sacrificed in joining with the *Bwainhome* made every movement feel heavier. His joints ached with every move, and his body felt decades older.

His wrists were still bound, but without the marines watching him he lifted his hands to his head and felt the cowl that Cazador had put over him. The metal bands had dug painfully into his flesh, but he might be able to work his fingernails under the strips. He tried digging at one of the threads that crossed his temple, ignoring the scratching pain and the blood that dripped down his wrist. But as he scraped at the flesh underneath the band, the spider steel only tightened. His head felt as if it was locked in a vise, and he had to abandon his efforts.

"If there's one thing that I've realized, it's that Cazador's tortures are even more devious than the man himself," a voice said from beside him.

Carter stood in surprise, fighting off the light-headedness that came from the cowl's pressure.

"President Kidewange?" he asked, unable to conceal his astonishment at seeing the man standing before him.

The former head of the Galactic Senate nodded, and offered a thin smile. The man's regal forehead and wide, intelligent eyes were instantly recognizable, and he wore a wrinkled suit that seemed to be the only clothes he had.

"I'd offer you a drink, Captain Carter, but the hospitality of the president's office isn't what it used to be."

"You know who I am?" he asked, still trying to grasp the fact that he was sharing a prison cell with the former president of Sol's system and extended colonies.

"Of course I'd know what the chief threat to Earth would look like, although I must say, you look much the worse for wear than I would have expected. Here, let me take a look at that," he said as he reached out and turned Carter's head to either side. "I'm afraid that's not going anywhere, which probably means that neither are we."

"I thought he'd have killed you," Carter said.

"Ha!" Kidewange laughed without humor. "He gets more pleasure in telling me everything he's doing to ruin the galaxy. I think that he keeps me alive because he needs someone to brag to. Although, now that he has you, my usefulness might be over."

"You talk about me?" Carter asked.

"Oh, all the time. He's been obsessed with you and those mental weapons your ensign told him about."

"Julie's here? She's alive?"

"Well, as of a few days ago she was. Whether she's still alive now or not, I don't know, but Cazador wants those weapons more than anything."

"He doesn't understand. They won't do him any good without the Bwain. They won't work on human ships."

"So then, give him the weapons," President Kidewange suggested. "What other choice is there?"

Carter stood and paced back and forth in the quarters he shared with the deposed president. His head ached, and he felt oddly lost and alone without the buzz of the Bwainsong around him.

"Never mind the fact that I can't create the weapons without the *Bwainhome*, or that the Bwain control them. If I give him the weapons, do you think he'll keep his word?" Carter asked dryly.

"You know him better than I do, but I would say no," the president said with a grim smile.

"I thought coming here would be the easiest way to get rid of him. I never thought he'd be this clever. He's always been one step ahead of me, ever since we were kids," Carter said with a heavy sigh as the childhood memories washed over him.

"Never judge yourself on the past. The mistakes we make are only in hindsight, and we have to deal with the present," Kidewange said gently.

For a moment Atlas stared at the president as the gears of his mind started to turn.

"The present. That's it! That's the key! Cazador has to know about the Bwain controlling the weapons, and needing the *Bwainhome* to create 'em. He'll need 'em here to make the weapons for him, and he can't get 'em here without me," Carter reasoned, a glimmer of hope shining in his eyes.

"You can't seriously be considering bringing those things to Earth?" Kidewange asked incredulously. "The SSC will destroy 'em as soon as they enter the system."

Carter scratched at the stubble on his face. Would this be the way he could reconnect with the *Bwainhome*?

"It might be our only hope."

"You know, when Admiral Nico and my advisors were all advocating for me to take your head, I urged caution. The reason I'm here with you now is that I didn't think bloodshed was the answer. Any path that relies on violence, is one that is ultimately doomed." Kidewange said. He studied the man before him with interest. He'd heard so many things about Atlas Carter, but now that the rogue captain was finally here before him, he found it hard to reconcile the contrasts. Clearly, he was a man who was worried about the survival of Earth and its people, and not the traitorous monster that he'd been led to believe.

Carter sat back down on the couch and continued to think. He didn't see any other way to defeat Cazador. If there was another path, it wasn't apparent to him in his current state of mind.

A few moments later, he looked up as the cell door opened. The man who entered was one of the Belizean bodyguards that accompanied Cazador throughout the tower. He tossed a bundle onto the floor at Carter's feet.

"The president requests the honor of your company in his training ring," the man said.

"The training ring? What does that mean?" Kidewange asked.

Atlas knew quite well what it meant, and he felt every weakness in his battered body as he reached down for the bag that the man had thrown. Inside was a pair of cracked boxing gloves that reeked of long-ago sweat and violence from another part of the world.

He glared at the smirking thug as he rose to his full height.

"Tell the president I accept," he said.

* * *

Kieran Granger hadn't followed his exacting father into the navy and used his family's curiosity to join the naval intelligence service in order to be ignorant. He had looked into the rumors surrounding the recent transitions of power, and had tried to find out what he could about Cazador in the days since the man had risen to prominence on Earth, but all he truly needed to learn about the acting president came from the smile that Cazador wore on his face after leaving Julie and Lana's cell.

"Do you know why I prefer the hands?" Cazador asked him as he toweled the blood from his knuckles, and then flipped over the cloth and mopped his sweating face.

"No, sir," Granger answered.

"For empathy. One should never forget what it feels like to cause pain," Cazador said, as if the answer should be obvious. He then tossed his rag on the floor and walked away down the corridor.

"Haven't you gotten what you need from them?" Granger asked.

"Not yet. Carter trained his crew very well, but you may want to check on the ensign. Keep her alive for me," Cazador said as an afterthought.

Sergeant Granger fought to keep the disgust from his face as he watched Cazador disappear down the corridor. The man enjoyed brutality in all its forms, and more and more Granger thought of the terrified faces of those he'd left behind in lunar orbit. The women in the cell behind him had been trying to do the right thing, and this was the consequence.

"Sarge? The president's orders?" the private on duty with him asked.

"Right," Granger answered. Private Ramirez had only recently been assigned to his squad, and he barely knew her. It wasn't uncommon for intelligence units to rotate personnel in order to ensure that loyalty remained absolute, but he'd given the private no reason to doubt him as of yet, so the plan that formed in his mind might just work.

"Stay in the hallway," he told her. Then he thumbed open the door and stepped into the dark room.

It was late at night, and the women had turned off the lights. When the private closed the door behind him, Granger flicked on his helmet flashlight. For what he was going to do, speed and discretion was best. He stepped over ruined furniture and splatters of blood, then passed through the hallway and stopped at the first bedroom where Ensign Ford was sleeping. He saw her twisted under the covers, and tapped on the doorjamb.

"Ensign. Ensign Ford," he whispered, but the woman didn't wake up. He coughed and stepped closer, trying not to startle her.

"Ms. Ford, wake up," he said.

Suddenly a set of arms twisted against his neck, while someone else kicked at his knees. Granger toppled backward, but rather than put his arms out to break his fall he threw his weight against whoever was holding him from behind and tried to draw his pistol at the same time. The person at his legs was scrabbling for his holster, but he kicked her away and then drew his pistol. As he did, a sharp blade dug against his throat.

"Drop it," Julie said.

He lowered the pistol to the floor, and Lana quickly seized it away from him. Her hand shook as she held it on him, and she hadn't unlocked the safety. He was no longer these women's enemy, and he wouldn't try to resist.

"What are you doing here?" Julie asked. Her face was a swollen mess in the beam of his flashlight. Her words slurred from swollen lips, and he could feel her strength weakening already.

"I came to tell you that Captain Carter is here in the tower," he said, then added, "and that I want to help you rescue him."

"What? Why should we trust you?" Lana demanded.

"Because Aaron Granger is my father," he said.

"I tried that line earlier," Julie reminded him.

"The *Narcos* took the families of everyone in the intelligence service. They told us that if we didn't stay in line and follow orders, that we'd never see 'em again," Kieran said quietly.

"I'm sorry, but you have to understand. I feel the same way about my crew," Julie said.

"I do understand," he said.

"Now, what do we do?" Lana asked as she lowered the gun and handed it back to him.

* * *

"What is this about?" Carter asked. One of Cazador's henchman was wrapping tape around his knuckles, while the other held a plasma rifle pointed at his chest.

"You and I have unfinished business," Cazador said. The *Narco* faced him across a square patch of concrete in an empty hangar. Four pylons had been set at the corners and laced with cabling to form a rough boxing ring. Cazador himself had stripped off his shirt, exposing the burn scars that swept down his left flank to his waist. As the man twisted in his warm-ups, the burned skin stretched and wrinkled as if it would tear at any moment.

"I'll give you the weapons, but the Bwain have to use them. You have to bring them here," Carter said, ignoring the men guarding him.

"You still think I am stupid? All those years ago in Belize, me telling you to go to the academy, to study hard. You thought it was because I couldn't do those things?" Cazador asked, squinting at him malevolently.

As Cazador's assistant finished wrapping his hands, he involuntarily flexed his fingers. In his exhaustion, he knew there was no way he'd be able to put up any kind of fight, but he could still take punishment. He'd endure whatever Cazador decided to throw at him in order to make his plan work.

"I thought you were my brother," he said accusingly as Cazador's henchman shoved the gloves on his hands, laced them up, and then pounded them together for him. The padding inside was rotten and crumbling, but that was what Cazador wanted, so all he could do was play along.

"If you want the weapons, that's what you have to do," Carter said as he stared at his former mentor with quiet resolve.

"Now why would I allow you to make demands?" Cazador asked. He was circling Atlas now, spinning his arms to loosen up. "You want to bring those creatures here. Maybe you want to bring them in by the millions so they can kill me, eh? No my friend...whatever you do, you do it on your own, without your alien friends."

"That's how you've always been, isn't it?" Carter said.

Cazador's smile faltered.

"I told you to make no attachments. They only make you weak."

"That was power to you? Taking my wife?" he asked.

"This isn't about power. This is about settling a score," Cazador said through scarred lips.

Cazador stepped into a jab. Carter raised his arms and shuffled aside. He had so little stamina left that he could waste none on offense. In fact, there was no point to the fight at all. The only plan he could come up with would be to give in to whatever Cazador wanted, lull him into a false sense of security, and try and make him believe that the Bwain were not a threat.

The *Narco* came forward once more, throwing two hard jabs. A fighter's instinct was to harden his shell by exhaling and flexing the abdomen at the same time, but Carter held his breath, kept his hands low, and absorbed the blow.

Cazador frowned, then swung a hard right hook into his kidney. The pain was a sharp shock, and Carter lowered his arms, grimacing in pain. He stood stock still on dead legs, his arms at his sides.

"Fight me!" Cazador challenged.

A quick flurry of punches knocked Atlas' head from side to side. He staggered backward, trying to clear it.

"Fight me!" Cazador yelled again.

"Why? Didn't I already give you what you wanted?" Atlas asked, refusing to give in to the unrestrained anger.

Fury filled Cazador's face.

"You won't trick me," he said as he opened up on his opponent's body. The muscled *Narco* landed shots against Carter's ribs and sides with savage force, but he took the pain and controlled it as stoically as he could until Cazador abruptly stopped.

"I thought you'd already learned that you accomplish nothing with surrender," Cazador said, breathing hard from his exertion. "If you don't fight me, I'll make sure that darling wife Aída *really* dies this time."

Atlas' gloves slowly lowered. Cazador's words had been those he'd hoped not to hear, but now that he knew Aída was still alive, his fury began to build.

He charged forward, all hope of negotiating with Cazador forgotten. This was the score the *Narco* meant, and he was going to settle it with a vengeance.

*   *   *

Julie limped after Sergeant Granger and Lana to the door of her cell. Her fractured ribs tore painfully at her side, and her right eye was swollen nearly shut, but she forced herself to grit her teeth and keep going. Any minute the First Ones would reach Earth, and if Captain Carter couldn't use the Bwainsong, Earth would have no hope against the unstoppable destruction by the voracious aliens.

Granger punched a code into the door's holocontrol. The cell door opened, and he sprang forward toward the other guard. Before the soldier even knew what was happening, he'd grabbed her rifle barrel, pulled her inside the cell, and shut the door.

"At ease, Private," Granger said as the woman struggled.

"Sarge, how did they capture you?" she gasped.

"They didn't. I'm taking them out of here. And you're free to join me or stay here. I don't know what your family situation is, if you need me to I'll make up a story about your capture."

"I don't understand," the young soldier said.

"Yes, you do. Look what the president did to this woman," Lana said as she gestured at Julie.

The private flinched when Granger shone his light on Julie's face.

"That could be any of us. Ensign Ford served with my father, and I know my father isn't a traitor. We're gonna find Captain Carter and get him back into space before those aliens come and destroy this planet," he said, studying the woman's face as if he were trying to gauge her loyalty.

Julie felt the private relax and stop struggling.

"I'm with you, Sergeant. I hate those slimy *Narcos* wandering around the tower like they own the damn place. As for my family situation, they have my grandparents, but if there's any way to stop 'em and put an end to this, then I'm with you," she said.

"Good. Now, I need you two to stay here for a little longer," he said as he turned to Lana and Julie.

"That's not much of an escape," Lana commented wryly.

"Just trust me. I'll leave the door open for you," he said as he headed out, jogging down the empty corridor. The private followed him out, and just like that, Lana and Julie were alone.

"Do you really think we can trust him?" Lana asked.

"I don't know if we have a better option," Julie slurred.

The sergeant reappeared a short time later to retrieve them. Julie limped after Lana as quickly as she could, though every step she took was a new experience in pain. Turning the corner, they rushed toward where another man stood beside two crumpled bodies.

"President Kidewange!" Lana exclaimed in utter shock. "Sir, it's an honor to..."

"I don't believe we have much time for pleasantries at the moment," the man whispered.

"Where's Captain Carter?" Julie asked.

"He was supposed to be here," Kieran said.

"That bastard Cazador took him. He wanted to box with him," Kidewange explained.

"Box with him?" Kieran asked. "How the hell are we supposed to find a boxing ring in this tower without getting caught?"

*   *   *

Atlas opened with a series of charging jabs and crosses, trying to work his way inside Cazador's arms so he could strike at the man's face. Cazador leaned back, avoiding the damage, but he kept his hands up to protect himself. He'd been hoping that Cazador's vanity would cause him to leave his body open, and it did. He swung at Cazador's sides, landing a series of hooks against his kidneys. Normally the *Narco's* technique would have been to grapple with him and pull him close, minimizing the effort of defending himself, but here there was no referee, and no rules for them to enforce, so Cazador kicked out at Carter's stomach, knocking him backward.

"Ahhh...there he is. Now that's the man I remember. All the other soldiers in Belize told me you couldn't be turned to our cause. They begged me to kill you as an example to those who resisted, and do you know what I told them?" Cazador asked as he took a few steps back, his feet dancing in constant motion.

While Carter took a moment to catch his breath, memories of fifteen-round grudge matches in the humid Belizean gyms came flooding back to him. With their arms burning, each one's stomach and kidneys battered, their legs limp, and their footwork shot with exhaustion, they'd still be working against each other in the ring. Cazador had always been more brutal and violent than the others, while Carter had been the cerebral fighter, looking for weaknesses in his opponents, and exploiting those weaknesses to his advantage. They each found their own way out of the ghetto. They were polar opposites, but brothers in every way, constantly pushing each other to never give up.

Cazador pounded his gloves together and came forward, alternating jabs and hooks that Carter struggled to block with his weakened conditioning.

"I told them no...he's a good man, and deserves a chance," Cazador continued, as the bloodlust grew stronger and stronger.

Cazador landed a blow against Carter's abdomen, but he was able to harden himself in time. Cazador grimaced, something gone awry in his wrist, and Carter pressed his advantage with hooks targeting Cazador's head. Cazador was forced away, but the *Narco* was in better shape. He ducked under Carter's haymaker and launched an uppercut that struck Carter's jaw and knocked him backward, leaving him momentarily stunned.

"I told you to join the navy. I kept you away from them...and from me, and you never thanked me for that. Not even once!" Cazador shouted, a crazed frenzy twisting his face.

Carter tried to keep his arms up to guard against his opponent's attacks, but he was gasping for air and becoming disoriented. All he could think about was Aída.

"And you thought I did it for you. You thought I did it for you and your wife, but I did it for me. It was always for me!" Cazador screamed as his voice echoed off the walls of the empty hangar.

The *Narco* sent a vicious hook against Carter's solar plexus that rocked his body a second time. Carter dropped to his knees, feeling the shock roll through his legs from the concrete. He raised his hand, trying to ward off further punishment, but Cazador's attention was elsewhere.

"I couldn't bear to watch you die when you could have been something better," Cazador gasped. "And now I simply ask you to do the same. Give me the weapons, with no tricks, and I'll let you live."

"*Señor,*" one of the henchman called urgently. "We must go to the situation room."

"What is it?" Cazador fumed.

"The aliens, they've struck Pluto."

"The Bwain?"

"No, *Señor*...the other ones.

Carter stared through his blurred vision at Cazador.

"Aída," he gasped. "Is she alive?"

"Another time," Cazador said as he turned and walked away, leaving Carter there on his knees, beaten and exhausted.

* * *

"Sir, where are you? It's Ensign Ford. I'm in the tower," Julie whispered through swollen lips.

As they ran through the darkened corridors, Julie was gambling that Captain Carter's cochlear implant was still installed, and she was trying to reach him on the old *Fates' Winds* frequency. Prisoners usually had the devices removed, and she ran the risk of someone in the tower picking up on her transmissions, but it was the only way that she could think of for two soldiers and three very recognizable prisoners with them to try and figure out his location.

The sergeant peeked around a corner, studying the approach. He then pulled back and nodded for them to jog down a different hallway.

"We're gonna need to put you three in another cell. I can't let you be recognized," the sergeant hissed.

"Just give me a little more time," Julie pleaded as she paused for breath. "We'll find him."

"We don't have a little more..."

Suddenly, an alarm's squall pealed through the corridor. Emergency lights lit the prisoners in yellow and oranges.

"They've found us!" the private called.

"No...listen," the sergeant said as he held up his hand for silence.

"All personnel report to duty stations. We have an active alien threat in the Kuiper Belt. They are *not* the Bwain. I repeat, they are *not* the Bwain. All SSC personnel to battle stations."

"What does that mean?" Lana asked.

"It means the First Ones are here. Oh, my god...and we can't find the captain!" Julie gasped.

"Try your message again," Lana urged.

"We don't have time. Come on!" the sergeant said as he motioned the odd group forward.

He pulled Julie into a limping run as fast as her shattered ribs would allow. Groups of marines and functionaries passed them, but in all the confusion, no one even gave them a second glance. Looking back, she saw that Kidewange was keeping his eyes glued to the floor, but sooner or later she knew they'd be recognized. It was a miracle they'd come as far as they had.

"Where are we going? We're not gonna make it very far!" Lana hissed.

"We're gonna get to a shuttle and get the three of you outta here. From there, I don't know," the sergeant answered.

"Not without Captain Carter!" Julie said as she felt a sharp stab of pain in her side.

"We don't know where he is. We can come back for him," he argued as he looked around, trying to formulate an escape route.

"He'd never do that to me," Julie said.

"But we don't have a choice!" he snapped.

"There's always a choice!" she cried. Though it sent knives of pain down her side, she pulled free of his grip and skidded to a stop. He faced her, looking absolutely exasperated while the klaxons blared around them.

"Julie?" Captain Carter's voice gasped weakly in her ear. "Julie, is that you?"

*　*　*

"Squad 421, what's your status?" Sergeant Granger called as he sprinted with Ramirez through the tower's corridors toward the location that the captain had given Julie. There was chaos all around them. In spite of the warnings that both Carter and Julie had been trying to provide, the navy was in no position to respond to this new threat. People were filling the hallways, and panic had taken over the broadcast waves. It took the building's telecom routing computer four long seconds to connect with the sergeant's target.

"Who's requesting?"

"Sergeant Granger, Squad 1020. We've been sent as backup due to the value of your asset," he replied matter-of-factly.

"We're in elevator Four South. The asset is in bad shape," the voice on the other end of the transmission reported.

"Four South, copy," the sergeant acknowledged. "We'll meet you on sub-floor eight."

"Copy," the other guards said.

"We're close, Julie. Just hang tight," he said after he'd switched channels.

He was borderline amazed that their escape hadn't been noticed yet, but now the most difficult part was still to come. They were already in the south wing, and it was just a short jog to a set of elevator banks that were guarded by a squad of marines.

"Are you ready for this?" he asked Ramirez.

The woman met his gaze for a moment, and then nodded.

"Oorah, sir!" she replied with enthusiasm. "It's finally time to do some good around here."

The lift doors slid open, revealing two marines and two of Cazador's thugs standing in a circle around the battered captain. He'd seen his fair share of training accidents and combat wounds during his time in the intelligence service, but even to him Carter looked bad. The man's eyes were swollen nearly shut, and blotched bruises marred his skin. Worse than the beating was his overall physical condition. Metal bands were cutting into his scalp, and he seemed to be trembling and shaking in the guards' arms.

"You're 1020?" one of the marines asked.

"Roger that," the sergeant said as he stepped into the lift beside the guards.

"They thought we needed two more marines?"

"The rest of my squad is outside the asset's quarters. I wanted to see him for myself," the sergeant replied.

The doors slid shut, and the lift started downward once more.

One of Cazador's henchman lifted Carter's head up by the chin and turned his face to Kieran.

"He's no good now, eh? And for so much trouble," the man breathed in heavily accented English. Before he could get out another word however, the sergeant drove his knife through the thug's ribs and knocked the man backward. He fell gasping as he tried desperately to staunch the blood spilling from his chest.

"What the hell are you doin'?" one of the marines cried, but Ramirez had already drawn her plasma pistol and was holding it on the other men.

"We're here to right a wrong," the sergeant said. "Now, everyone...just calmly drop your weapons."

"This is treason," the other marine snarled as he lifted his sidearm and dropped it to the ground."

"What Cazador did is treason. We're under attack because he didn't listen to what this man tried to say," the sergeant answered.

Roaring, the second *Narco* drew a pistol. Granger pushed the marine in front of him out of the way, trying to save the soldier's life. Ramirez didn't have a shot. A sizzling crack heated the elevator, and for a brief moment the sergeant expected to feel a searing hole in his gut, but that didn't happen. Captain Carter had knocked the *Narco* against the wall, and the sergeant quickly seized the opportunity he'd been given. He pounced on the shorter man and drove his knife straight into the *Narco's* throat.

"That's two," Ramirez said as the sergeant stood and cleaned his knife.

"So we're next then?" the marine that the sergeant had been guarding asked. He was trying to hide the fear in his voice, but he was clearly afraid of what he thought was coming next.

"No, you guys were just doin' your job. I'm gonna tie you up and leave you here, but I will need to borrow your uniforms," Granger said with just a hint of a smile.

* * *

"You gotta get this thing off my head," Carter said. "It's the only way I can let the fleet know what's happening. The human ships will take days to get here, but the *Bwainhome* can be here in seconds."

Granger and Ramirez had taken Carter to the storage room where Julie, Lana, and Kidewange had been hiding. The two intelligence officers were examining the lattice embedded in Carter's scalp while Lana and Julie changed into the marines' uniforms. Ramirez slipped out her knife, but Granger pushed her hand away. Instead, he tried the electro-charge in his suit. A spark leaped onto the spider steel, but nothing happened.

"Who set this on you, sir?" he asked. "I think we're gonna have to use their key."

"It was Cazador. We'll have to find another way," Atlas managed through blood-caked lips.

"Sir, how did you get to Earth?" Julie asked as she zipped up her disguise.

"The *Ninkovich*," he said. "They're still in orbit. Can you contact them?" he asked.

"The SSC has been blocking any transmissions, but if you can get us on a shuttle, we can deliver a message in person," Julie said as she looked over at the sergeant.

"Let's do it," he said.

* * *

The Presidential Tower
Situation Room

On the giant holoscreens, Cazador watched the creatures that Carter had tried to warn him about writhe toward the vanguard of the outer solar system's defense fleet. The silver ships were positioned just above the icy blue glow of Neptune. The computer-created vantage point was from behind the human ships, constructed from data received from the ships themselves, the telescopes around Neptune, and other observatories throughout the system. Despite the best technology and processing power in the galaxy, Cazador still had a hard time understanding exactly what he was looking at.

"How long ago was this?" he asked.

"Just under four hours, Mr. President."

"What are they?" Cazador asked, squinting.

"They fit the description of the dimensional beings that Captain Carter mentioned," a science attaché said. "They appear to be so many things at once because they're existing on a number of planes simultaneously."

"But the fleet will take care of them, no?" Cazador asked.

"Sir, they've already destroyed our assets in the Kuiper Belt, and our local fleet has been depleted by Nico's activities in the Sword Belt," one of the other officers said.

Thousands of indicators appeared on the display, showing the fleet's weapons firing. Cazador tracked the radioactive symbols until they reached the disgusting creatures. Nuclear clouds blossomed in sickly green on the display, and the creatures stopped and shuddered for a moment.

"Yes!" Cazador shouted in triumph. "They aren't that tough after all, are they?"

"Mr. President," a voice nearby warned.

Where Cazador expected to see the emptiness of space return, the creatures remained unharmed, as if they'd merely paused to bask in the sun. Then, when the radiation clouds had faded, the things came on even more quickly than before, seeming to swell larger and larger as the fleet battered them to no effect.

"They're bigger than the ships," Cazador said to no one in particular, as he tiled his head to view the images writhing before him.

"Yes, sir. They've grown in size since they first appeared in the Kuiper belt. Considerably," someone else answered.

Cazador watched with a sinking feeling as the creatures met his ships. Vessel after vessel winked out of existence on the screen. One minute a ship would be firing and maneuvering, then in a heartbeat, the things would wrap it in their tentacles and the craft would just disappear, as if it never existed at all.

"What are your orders, sir?" an officer asked.

Cazador had become adept at reading people over the years, and he could sense the disapproval in the naval officer's tone. Worse than the insubordination however, and worse than the sudden uncertainty that he was feeling, was the realization that Carter had been right.

"Bring Carter to me! Now!" Cazador growled.

* * *

The sergeant cracked open the door and peered down the corridor. It was clear for the moment, so he slipped through and disappeared down the hallway. When he came back, he was shaking his head.

"We're two levels below the shuttle bay, but there's a full squad at the elevator. We need to find another way," he reported, as he mentally reviewed the layout of the Presidential Tower.

"What about charging them?" Ramirez asked.

"That's what soldiers always do," Lana said, shaking her head. Then she shouldered past the sergeant before he had a chance to do anything, and stepped out into the corridor that led to the elevator.

"Lana!" Julie hissed urgently.

"They still don't know we've escaped," Lana said. "Just follow me, and act natural."

And with that, the reporter gave her best impression of a soldier's purposeful stride toward the guards.

Julie took position behind Kidewange and Carter, while Granger and Ramirez flanked them. Then they fell into formation behind Lana.

"There's no way that this is going to work," Ramirez said.

"I don't know if we have another choice," the sergeant said quietly back to her.

The soldiers at the lift faced their group, and his nervousness grew.

"Who's ordering you to move these two?" the marine demanded.

"That's classified," the sergeant responded with a glare, as if daring the man to question him.

"Well, we're still going to need to see your authorization. Give me your palm," the man said.

Granger tried to catch Ramirez's attention as he placed his palm on the reader. He didn't want any more killing than was necessary.

"So, he's not talking?" the guard said, nodding to Carter.

"Not as much as I should," Carter said.

Julie's hand crept down to the pistol strapped to her thigh, and she noticed that Ramirez had shifted her weight to spring forward. There were six marines on guard, and they all seemed alert and ready, but if she could take two of them out immediately, they might have a chance.

"Unauthorized!" the guard next to Granger cried.

Julie's pistol roared out from her holster. She fired, taking one guard in the leg and another in the arm, while the sergeant unslung his rifle and tried to stop the marines guarding the elevator from slipping into cover behind a set of nearby crates.

"I'll keep 'em pinned down!" he called to Julie. "You guys go!"

Julie ran for the elevator with Captain Carter. When they got there, she pounded the control with her fist and ducked down as a plasma bolt scorched the metal overhead.

"Get to the ship!" the sergeant cried as he laid down a stream of cover fire. Ramirez had taken cover behind a barrel, and was firing right along with him.

The lift's security doors opened. Carter and Julie ran inside, but Lana and Kidewange were still crouched together behind the identity station.

"Lana, come on!" Julie called. The reporter nodded, then stood and sprinted for them with Kidewange following right behind her, but Julie watched in horror as a ball of plasma struck the reporter in the stomach.

Lana stumbled and fell, skidding into the door. Julie pulled her inside just as the elevator doors closed. Carter slammed the button for sublevel two, and then knelt down to attend to Lana.

"Oh god, it hurts!" Lana gasped.

Her uniform was scorched at her right hip. The bolt had burned through her, and Julie could see black bone at her pelvis.

"Ms. Ford, we need to get her to the *Ninkovich* immediately if we're gonna have any chance of saving her," Carter panted.

"This is Ensign Ford to the *Ninkovich*," Julie called. "Does anyone read me? I have Captain Carter. We need immediate assistance. I say again..."

"Something's wrong. We're not stopping at the right floor!" Kidewange said.

Julie looked up and saw that he was right. Instead of sublevel two, the elevator was whisking them higher and higher through the tower.

"What's happening?" Lana gasped.

"I don't know. Hang in there," Julie said.

Julie readied her pistol again as the elevator slowed. Its doors sprang open, and she faced two dozen marines with drawn rifles. Captain Carter's hand covered her pistol, pushing it down to face the deck.

"Sir!" she cried.

"It's over, Julie. Getting yourself killed won't solve anything."

* * *

The Situation Room

"Do you see what you've done?" Cazador screamed.

Carter's worst fears were being realized on the room's holoscreens. The robin's egg blue of Uranus shone against the blackness of space as if it were a dab of watercolor on black canvas, but its delicate light was fading as the First Ones crawled through its atmosphere. The creatures breached and swam through the planet as if they were sharks in a feeding frenzy. As they swirled, Uranus' atmosphere drained and faded away. The creatures dug deeper, consuming the planet's milky center of ammonia and methane ice until the planet had been reduced to nothingness.

"They've cut through your outer defenses, haven't they?" Carter asked.

"Our ships didn't stand a chance. They're on their way to Saturn now," an SSC officer answered with a glare at Cazador.

"I told you what would happen if you tried to engage them," Carter said.

"You didn't give me the weapons," Cazador fumed. "You led them here."

"If you take me to the *Ninkovich,* I can stop those things," Carter said flatly.

In the light from the myriad holoscreens, Cazador's leathered face seemed lost. The man who had once thought that he had control over so many, who thought he'd risen to the pinnacle of power, was now seeing how foolish he had really been.

"Power comes from those around you...from their strength, not through fear," Carter said, desperate to make Cazador understand.

"You were always too good, weren't you?" Cazador spat. "You always pretended to know what would happen, but I own the world, little brother. It's mine."

"No one else needs to die. I can fix this, but you have to let me!" he said as he stared earnestly at Cazador, pleading with him to give up the revenge that had consumed him beyond the point of human decency.

"No," Cazador said, shaking his head. "No...we will fight and die together, Atlas Carter, just as we used to."

Chapter Thirteen

SSC Ship of the Line Lancer
In orbit around Saturn

Rear Admiral Bartomo had been promoted to command the *Lancer* two months ago. He'd worked hard at his profession, conscientiously following orders and working on details such as the logistics of supply, crew morale, and formation drills for various threats such as insurrection, Bwain swarms, and all manner of hybrid maneuvers. He considered himself a steady commander. He was still green, but he had planned to grow into his role over time as head of the Saturn Defense Force's vanguard.

That time was about to run out.

"Your orders, sir?" his comms officer asked again.

"What's the creatures' ETA?" he asked.

"I don't know. I can't give you an exact time," the nav officer answered. "It took them three hours to reach Uranus from Neptune. That's a distance of 10.88 AUs, which is…"

"Unprecedented…," the admiral said quietly.

"Yes, sir," the navigation officer acknowledged. "They're traveling faster than light, but I don't have enough data yet to say just how much faster."

"What's our best offensive scenario?" Bartomo asked his weapons officer.

"I'm not sure we have one, sir," the woman said as she checked the information flowing across her screen. "From the data the other ships sent, our weapons seem to have no effect on these things."

"So we can't fight them, and we can't outrun them," Bartomo observed matter-of-factly.

On his holoscreen, the faintest white glimmer wormed its way toward the ships he had positioned behind the planet. His job was to prevent any threat from entering the inner solar system, and yet he couldn't imagine how to execute his orders in any way that would represent a meaningful resistance. The only thing he could think of to try and stop them was to hide, and then possibly use his fleet's weaponry to ignite Saturn's hydrogen in an effort to burn the things. After watching them consume two planets and three battle groups however, he had very little hope that their fate would be any different.

"Send a message to Earth, messenger vessel, highest priority," Bartomo ordered.

"Ready, sir," his comms officer called from his nearby station.

"Rear Admiral Bartomo to SSC command. We are about to enter action against the alien threat. From previous fleet interaction, I do not anticipate success. My tactics will be to try and draw the creatures away from the antimatter station and mining colony so as to give them time to evacuate. Suggest that at this time you consider evacuating the Earth. Put as many people as you can onto ships, and head for other colonies. I do not consider this attack a survivable scenario for the planet."

He stopped, but had received no confirmation from his communications officer.

"Sir?" the sailor asked.

"Release the messenger."

"Yes, sir."

Bartomo sighed. It was, considering the circumstances, a sensible order in a situation that had been impossible to prepare for, yet now he had to go one step further.

"Open a channel to the fleet," Bartomo ordered.

"Open, sir."

"This is Rear Admiral Bartomo. In observing our tactical situation, I do not think we can defeat these creatures in combat. The only thing we can do is to give the people back on Earth more time. To that end, we'll run in random vectors away from Saturn in order to draw the creatures away. If one of them nears you, I want you to release every shuttle and fighter you have. Put them on programmed trajectories away from your ship. These things like to eat, so give them everything you can. Hopefully it'll buy enough time for at least some of us to survive this."

"Sir...," his science officer called.

"Not now," he said. Bartomo's mind was fixed on how much distance he could put between his ships and the civilians. He didn't have time for orbital fluctuations or any other minutiae.

"Sir, the aliens are here."

For a moment he couldn't believe the report.

"That's...they're getting even faster?"

"Yes, sir."

"How many?" Bartomo asked.

"It's hard to get a reading on their numbers. Maybe two-hundred? That number isn't exact."

Atlas' Final Approach

Bartomo had thirty-three ships. It would be a slaughter.

"Get the *Edinburgh* out, ASAP."

On the holoscreens, the fleet's fastest ship looped away from Saturn, spewing countermeasures and laser fire to try and draw the creatures' attention.

"I think it's working, sir!" his nav officer called.

Rather than rushing directly toward Saturn, the alien horde slowed. First, they massed together almost like a school of fish, then split into two streams. One group pursued the *Edinburgh* and the others resumed their press for Saturn.

"All ships, all hands, you understand what to do. Good luck," he transmitted.

On his holos he watched his fleet run in every conceivable direction away from Saturn, lighting up the space around them with every weapon they could fire. The creatures schooled again, seeming confused, until groups of them streaked in all directions after his ships. Bartomo watched in shock as the things snatched missiles out of the air, bathed in radiation clouds, and absorbed magna-cannon shots with trouble at all.

"It's almost as if they're playing," his weapons officer rasped.

"That's because they know we can't hurt 'em," Bartomo said. There wasn't much else that anyone could do at this point, other than stare helplessly at the streaks of horror and destruction.

The first of his ships to go was the *Gold Coast*. The ship was shooting nearly straight down below Saturn's orbital plane, and for some reason, ten of the creatures had decided to pursue it.

"Countermeasures firing," the *Gold Coast's* captain cried, "Magna-cannons on auto."

Successive rings of mirrors, chaff, and radiation bloomed from the frigate. Two or three of the aliens stopped, spreading wide wings and fins to slurp up the matter, but the others kept after their target.

"They're still coming! Releasing shuttles and fighters," its captain called.

Bartomo watched as the ship's entire compliment of fifty fighters and twenty-five shuttles shot out from either side of the frigate. Their courses were computer controlled as they arced outward in a series of spirals away from the *Gold Coast*.

As before, several of the creatures were distracted. Only two now pursued the ship itself. One of them resembled a whale with thousands of jellyfish stingers drifting from it, while the other could have been a bat with a dolphin's fins. Despite their ungainly appearance, they were mere kilometers from the *Gold Coast*.

"All crew, abandon ship!" the *Gold Coast's* captain ordered.

Bartomo zoomed his holos, hoping against hope that the maneuver would work. Thousands of escape pods fired in the opposite direction of the creatures, while the ship curved away from the pods. The ship was triggering its Alcubierre drive as well, which was a smart maneuver. Unfortunately, just as the sheath of bent space time was building around the *Gold Coast*, the bat creature smashed broadside into it. The effect was as if someone had taken a sudden bite out of the ship. The frigate wheeled over, losing momentum as the other creature's tentacles sunk deep through the superstructure, tearing it to pieces.

"No!" Bartomo's navigation officer moaned as he watched, horrified.

The whale creature combed through space around where the *Gold Coast* had been, its tentacles shooting out to scoop up the life pods that had been ejected.

"Sir, we need to tell the fleet," his weapons officer said.

"We already knew we didn't have a chance," Bartomo said.

All he could do was watch as ship after ship lost its race with the creatures.

"How are the civilian evacuations going?" he asked.

"Maybe a quarter of the population loaded," his comms officer reported.

"Tell them to move faster. We can't give 'em any more time."

"Twelve...no, thirteen ships down," his science officer called. "Sir..."

"Nav officer, get me another course. Try and find the maximum distance we can put between us and those things," Bartomo ordered.

"Sir..."

"I just need you to execute my orders, sailor!" Bartomo barked.

"No, sir...there's a new signature, just off our port bow."

"What? Show me."

Bartomo thought he was prepared for anything, but the sight of a Bwain ship arriving just in front of him somehow infuriated him.

"Target that ship. Give 'em everything we have," Bartomo snapped. "At least this time..."

"Sir, the Bwain ship is moving away. It's heading *toward* the creatures!" the officer reported.

As he watched, a glowing trail of energy shot from the Bwain ship toward one of the other aliens.

"Sir, the aliens are...they're leaving us! They're targeting the Bwain ship."

"My god...," Bartomo murmured as he watched the Bwain's projectiles tear into another of the other creatures. "We might just have a chance!"

* * *

The Bwainhome

When Hal had felt the telltale shifting of the *Bwainhome*'s course, at first he hadn't really thought anything of it. He'd been working on a formula for converting the garbage from the SSC ships into reusable parts and had been lost in the calculations when Granger grabbed his shoulder.

"I'm workin' here. Whadda ya want?" Hal complained as he slipped off his hologoggles.

"Come with me," Granger insisted.

"Why?" Hal barked, annoyed at having his work interrupted, but Granger was already running up the glowing ramp that led away from Hal's factories.

"Damn it," he said as he set his goggles down and jogged after the scientist. There had been a time when Hal's drinking had left him heavy and unable to run more than a few steps, but the constant walking through the massive *Bwainhome* had built his endurance, and soon enough he'd caught up to Granger.

Atlas' Final Approach

"Do you feel it?" Granger asked.

"Feel what?" Hal asked.

"The dimensional shift."

"You scientists sure are great at half-explaining things," Hal said. "Maybe this is why Pandith decided to stay on that gravity shuttle when we came over here scavenging."

Granger's pace slackened for a moment. His eyes widened at some internal realization.

"Oh, crap. I forgot. I'm the only one who knows," he said as he frowned in concentration.

"Who knows what?"

"We discovered that the Bwain can be tracked through Majorana radiation back before this ship came through The Gates. And since we've had some down time, I've made an experimental unit that tracks the radiation," he said as he tapped a small box that he'd affixed to his collar. "I'd hoped to be able to somehow reach out to Captain Carter, but what the box actually did was show me Majorana perturbations."

They were circling higher in the ship, winding through the living areas where Bwain frolicked and squawked, pushing through crowds of the creatures as they fluttered about on their arcane errands.

"The hell is a perturbation? You mean disturbances?" Hal asked.

"Yeah, exactly. I thought they were random, until I realized that they coincided with the Bwain fighters that the captain asked to guard Pandith. Each perturbation was a fighter in flight."

"You mean you can...what? You can sense when those things are moving?"

"Exactly, and the perturbation that just happened is bigger than any I've felt so far."

"So...what's that mean exactly?" Hal asked.

"It means the *Bwainhome* is moving," Granger said as they reached what passed for the craft's bridge. It was a darker room where swirls of color lined the deck overhead, and glowing controls floated in and out of existence before a group of focused Bwain.

"Well, so what? I mean, that happens all the time, right?" Hal asked, still not sure why Granger seemed so excited.

"No, it doesn't. It only happens when Captain Carter is on the ship," Granger said.

"So that means we've found him?" Hal asked, wishing that Granger would just get to the point already.

"Can you show me where we are?" Granger asked the closest Bwain. The creature shook its head, apparently distracted from studying an arced sphere that glittered with tiny lightning bolts.

"What about you? Can you show me where we are?" he tried again with another of the creatures. This one looked up and ruffled its feathers.

"Save," it croaked.

"Save?" Hal asked. "Save what?"

The Bwain's eyes flicked closed. Suddenly the ceiling above them glowed with a bright projection. The view was of a solar system with six planets, the outer one being a ringed gas giant.

"Oh my god, that's Saturn! But where are the other planets?" Granger gasped in shock.

"And this winged dot," Hal pointed up at a black oval that had just appeared next to the planet. "That's us?"

The alien nodded.

"And those are the First Ones," Hal murmured as the reality struck him with full force.

A swarm of white creatures was turning back from attacking a crippled fleet of human ships, and heading straight for the *Bwainhome*.

"So that's where the other planets went. I think the Bwain are going to war, and it looks like they're doin' it on their own," Hal said.

* * *

The Constantinople

One minute the *Bwainhome* was holding its position in front of the obelisk, and the next it was gone. The transition happened so suddenly that it took Mephista a few moments to even notice that the great black ship had disappeared.

"Ms. Hoff, confirm section 10-35 with direct visual," Mephista ordered.

Danielle trained one of the *Constantinople*'s telescopes on the area of space where the *Bwainhome* had previously been stationed, and suddenly sucked in a deep breath.

"Ma'am, the Bwain ship is..."

"It's gone," Mephista finished. A part of her heart swelled at the thought of what that departure might mean. After a week of tense waiting, Atlas might be coming back to her. Either that, or things might be much worse than she thought.

She had ordered the Bwain be kept on all SSC ship bridges, in spite of her growing annoyance at what had seemed more and more like the bird-creatures' independence. They rarely listened, and constantly got underfoot. They were possessed of a burgeoning curiosity that annoyed her officers to no end. Mephista needed to keep them in place though, in the hope that she would hear something from Atlas and learn what was going on. If only he would contact her and let her know what was happening.

"You," she said to the Bwain that was pecking at a railing in front of the captain's station. "Where did your ship go?"

The creature's feather's shifted into a martial red, then faded to its mottled gray.

"We fight," it said.

"You fight? Fight what? Where?"

"Fight First Ones," it answered. "Bwain strong. We fight."

"Comms, get me the rest of the fleet, have them standby," she ordered, and then she turned her attention back to the Bwain.

"Where are you fighting?"

The alien blinked, but said nothing.

"Where did your ship go" Mephista repeated.

"To fight," it answered.

"Ma'am, the comm channels are open to the fleet," her communications officer called.

"Copy that," she said. "To the fleet, this is Captain Mephista. The *Bwainhome* has disappeared, and the Bwain are telling me that it's gone to fight the First Ones. I'm trying to understand exactly where that is, but if any of you can get further intelligence, I'd greatly appreciate the help.

"Now, where were we?" she said as she turned back to the alien creature before her.

* * *

The Obelisk

Pandith had occupied his time with talking to the Aric and the Bwain, sometimes at the same time. It had been strange, staying on station by himself with only the Bwain to keep him occupied, waiting for an attack from the First Ones that may or may not come. If Granger had still been on the shuttle, he would have no doubt used the opportunity for more scientific exploration, but Pandith was an empathetic soul, and he was drawn to a different type of understanding.

"And when you get to your home planet, then what will you do?" Pandith asked the Bwain.

The creature was holding a ration bar in its claws, darting its purple tongue out to taste the human food.

"Live in trees and jungle, like before," it said.

"And that's all you want?" Pandith asked. "You've been living in space for thousands of years. You've carried more knowledge than anyone, and all you want is to live in the jungle?"

"Bwain are saved. Now want home."

Pandith heard Captain Mephista's message, and turned to study the alien beside him.

"Aric," he asked. "Did you hear that?"

"Yes," the strangely synthesized voice said into Pandith's earpiece. Pandith still shuddered to hear his former crew member's voice. Aric was in such obvious pain that Pandith couldn't even imagine what the man's horrible cyborg existence was like. He preferred the memory of Aric sacrificing his life so that Pandith could get the rest of the *Fates' Winds* crew out of the ship. Hearing his tormented soul as it existed now was pure agony, but he knew that more than anything, Aric Keith simply needed someone to talk to.

"Where would the First Ones go?"

"To Earth," Aric said.

"Is that where your ship went? To Earth?" Pandith asked the Bwain.

"What is Earth?" the creature squawked.

Pandith thought for a moment, then pulled up a holoimage of Earth.

"This planet, the third from the sun in this part of the galaxy," Pandith said as he pointed to the image on the screen.

The Bwain blinked, then shuffled closer to the holoimage.

Pandith zoomed further and further into the image until he was showing mountain, jungles, and oceans. The Bwain's claws raked through the image, distorting it, but the creature didn't seem to care.

"Met Bwainslayer here," it said.

"What?"

"Carter, met Carter here."

"That's impossible."

"Bwain travel far. Bwain know things. Bwain watch," the creature said as it picked absently at something of interest on the floor.

"You watched humans?" Pandith asked.

"We watch all. We know."

"Is that where the *Bwainhome* went?" Pandith asked.

"No," the creature squawked as it shook its head.

Frustrated, Pandith sat back. His gesture knocked the holoimage back into a long shot of the solar system. For all they knew, the First Ones were ravaging some other colony, and he was powerless to help.

"No, not Earth. Here," the creature added as it stretched out a claw to point at a different location.

*   *   *

Saturnian Orbit
The Bwainhome

Hal had already been in more space battles than he'd ever care to remember. In each one of them, he'd fixated on a different way to die.

They were scenarios that had run through his mind while he'd been on board the human ships, and as such, he'd been able to bury himself in his work to try and cope, even as ships around him were destroyed. He'd worked in a near panic because he wanted to live, and now he realized...so did the Bwain.

Rather than the fumbling, childish aliens they'd been for so long, the creatures worked with a new-found sense of organization and discipline. The battle was hard to follow from the strange markings and screens that floated seemingly at random through the bridge, but an overhead image centered around a depiction that was clearly Saturn made things easier.

The Bwain deployed their dimensional fighters in one massive wing, but the craft didn't surge toward the cluster of First Ones that were feasting on Saturn's rings. Rather, the fighters shot toward the creatures that were attacking the human ships. Each individual fighter had no chance of taking down a First One with its small weaponry, but collectively they succeeded in drawing the creatures' attention.

"My god, they're protecting the navy!" Granger exclaimed.

The First Ones peeled away from the human ships and began following the Bwain fighters as the craft raced back to the *Bwainhome,* and it was here that Hal saw the strength of their plan. What felt like static electricity crackled through the bridge area, causing Hal's hair to lift from his shoulders, and then all hell broke loose.

The *Bwainhome* launched a series of transdimensional projectiles at the approaching First Ones. Some of the creatures were able to dodge, but those that didn't were struck and torn apart. Hal watched one impact cleave one of the monstrosities nearly in two. Inside the thing was simply a white shuddering blankness that dissolved and faded to gray smoke.

"So this is what they did with all my material," Hal said as he stared in disbelief. "They were making bullets!"

The First Ones gathered themselves into a furious spiral, darting and weaving and disappearing in the blink of an eye.

"The First Ones have adapted their defenses. That's not good," Granger commented as he watched the images before him.

For all the martial confidence and tactics that the Bwain had learned from Captain Carter, the aliens were still slow to adapt. They tried firing their new weapons at the formation, but many of the projectiles missed and spewed harmlessly into empty space. Their fighters tried to pepper the outer edges of the First Ones' formation, but tentacles and projectiles stretched toward the craft and swept them from existence.

"Come on little guys," Hal pleaded through clenched teeth. "Come on!"

Suddenly the First Ones exploded, sending individual creatures in a dizzying array of directions. The things were so fast the *Bwainhome* couldn't keep up. Hal's neck twisted trying to follow the action above him.

"What are they doing?" he asked.

"Look there!" Granger called. The First Ones were barreling toward a group of SSC ships that had just appeared after an Alcubierre jump. Their navigation officers were trying to take what looked like a wall formation, but they wouldn't have any time to react.

"They're gonna get slaughtered!"

Hal wondered what the creatures actually thought about what they were doing. Was there any mercy or understanding, or was their drive to consume was all-encompassing? There was no way of knowing, but from their actions, the answer was fairly clear.

"Look!" Granger said, as the pointed at the images.

The lead First One shuddered, flaring red and pink for just a brief moment, and then it collapsed in on itself.

"Zoom in! Or...damn it, I need to see what ship that is." Granger shouted excitedly.

Watching the fleet maneuver and fight back against the First Ones, and seeing creature after creature split apart against their onslaught, the answer soon became clear.

"It's Mephista! They found us!" Hal said, let out an excited shout of his own. "But how'd they get here so fast?"

"It must have been the *Gravity Drive*! Pandith figured it out!" Granger said as his eyes tried to take in everything that was going on all at once.

Just then, the *Bwainhome* rocked backward, sending Hal and Granger skidding along the floor with some of the Bwain. Some of the other Bwain flapped up into the air, squawking anxiously, and the color in the room flashed, taking on a pained purple once more.

"What happened?" Granger asked.

Hal had landed on his back, and was looking straight up at the display. He pointed at the hideous shape that had caught the *Bwainhome* and was washing over its hull like an angry wave.

"One of 'em got us," he said.

*   *   *

Earth

It took the light from Saturn eighty-nine minutes to reach Earth, and so Atlas Carter knew when he saw the First One fix itself to the *Bwainhome*'s hull that their only hope might already be gone, and the emptiness he felt without his contact with the ship throbbed like an exposed nerve.

"You gotta get me on that ship!" Carter barked. "It's the only way that you, or any of us will survive."

"The last thing I'll do is put you in a position to harm...," Cazador began.

"You're the one who's harming everything!" Atlas bellowed. "You've been blind to everything you've done. All you know is how to kill and fight. That's why we're different...because I believe in something better, and that's exactly the reason why you can't stand me. I chose a better life. I chose to take responsibility for my own actions...to be better than I was, but you're just the same old man you always were. You're just a soulless, pathetic excuse for a human being!"

"No," Cazador said. His smile was a pained grimace. "It's because you were weak and should have been stronger. Now, as much as I've appreciated our little reunion, it's time to say goodbye."

Cazador lifted his pistol and squeezed the trigger. Carter ducked away from the shot just in time, but the sizzling plasma grazed the side of his head. He slumped to his knees with the charred meat of his own scalp filling his nostrils.

"Captain!" he heard Julie cry out, but there were suddenly other voices too. It was like a shimmering chorus bound by a deeper bass throb that sang of the end of its journey after a millennia of searching.

"I'm here," Atlas called to them.

"But not for long," Cazador answered.

The president was three feet from Carter. It would be impossible for him to miss at this range, but when he raised his hand and squeezed the trigger, the air in front of him exploded.

A Bwain with half its chest torn apart fell to the ground, writhing in agony between the two men. Cazador stepped back, startled at what had just occurred.

Carter rose to his feet as dozens more of the creatures exposed themselves. Human officers drew their weapons, but the Bwain had stationed themselves in between each one, and there was nothing that could be done.

"They won't hurt you!" Carter called to the officers.

"Traitor!" Cazador shouted. He spun and fired at the Bwain, catching one of the aliens in the throat. Enraged, Atlas leaped forward, tackling his nemesis to the ground and knocking the pistol away from him. Cazador's good eye lit with fury.

"When your wife died in my arms, I told her that you never loved her," he sneered.

Carter roared, pounding Cazador's face and body. Months of loneliness, of anger and hurt poured out of him. Skin split, bones cracked, and blood spattered in crimson droplets. Carter swung and swung until he felt both human and Bwain arms pulling him off of his childhood friend.

"No!" Atlas screamed.

"That's enough, sir," Julie said.

"Save," a Bwain squawked.

Looking down, he saw that Cazador's face was a shattered mass. The *Narco*'s broken jaw still worked under the mutilated skin.

"You've...learned well," the *Narco* gasped. "Now finish it."

"Save," another Bwain squawked.

Atlas looked around him, and finally focused on Julie's battered face.

"Nothing is worth killing," she said. "You taught me that."

Cazador made a wet sucking sound, which after a moment Atlas realized was laughter.

"You're...too...weak," the *Narco* taunted him.

"It takes more strength to live," Atlas said.

Then he turned to the Bwain. The moment Cazador's pistol shot had torn open the lattice that had been shielding Carter's thoughts, they'd come via their dimensional fighters. They'd been hunting him for days, trying to bring him back to the *Bwainhome*. He felt their anxiety, their pride, their pain once more as his own.

"Take me home," he said to the creatures.

*   *   *

Saturn

The Ancient's claws skittered over the *Bwainhome*'s hull. In the space around him, the dimensional weapons stabbed into his brethren, flaying their limbs and cleaving their bodies. Roaring in pain and fury that these pathetic creatures would dare try and stop them, the First Ones redoubled their efforts. The knowledge that they could be hurt, that they could be sent back and doomed to wander inchoate through the upper dimensions for all eternity was too much. It would be because of Atlas Carter, the human that hid in this pathetic, withered husk.

The ship turned its hateful armament toward him. The Ancient lifted from the *Bwainhome*, spinning himself away from the shots that tore off into the blackness.

"PROTECT ME, BROTHERS!" The Ancient cried.

Two First Ones swung in, raking their tentacles across the *Bwainhome*'s hull. Its weaponry disintegrated at their touch, but the hull itself held firm against their grasp. The Ancient dove once more against the black armor, digging with the thousands of legs that writhed under its caterpillar body. The Ancient needed only to drill deep into the ship and tear it apart so it could guzzle its innards, and Carter's ability to resist him would be ended.

Making no progress at the craft's stern, The Ancient scrabbled toward the oblong ship's center. The First Ones saw matter differently, observing how it pulled and stretched against the forces of gravity, how it oscillated between other universes and other dimensions. They could see the quantum possibilities like breadcrumbs that led to more food, more sustenance to keep out the crushing weight of gravity. There at the crest of the Bwain ship rose a strange disturbance. Drawn by a dim memory, as well as his hunger, he crept toward the oddly familiar shape that seemed to radiate eternal sustenance.

When he reached his destination, The Ancient drove his forward claws deep into the ship's black carapace. Cutting through years of armor and scaling, he scraped more and more deeply as his limitless muscles pushed with the strength of all they'd consumed. He burrowed for so long that the whisper calling to him did not even rouse him for a time.

"What are you doing brother?

The Ancient stopped its attack, momentarily startled. Casting its awareness around itself, The Ancient felt its other brothers locked in vicious combat with the new human ships that had arrived with their own dimensional weapons. The gravity weapon lashed out at them over and over again, but they could avoid it if they were careful.

None of his brethren had called him. Consumed by his quest, he turned his drilling mouthparts to the task of burrowing into the *Bwainhome*. The ship had had a dimly remembered taste, something long forgotten that hinted of white purity.

"What are you doing brother?" he heard again.

"I AM NOT YOUR BROTHER!" The Ancient growled. He shook his head as a dog might, trying to snap its prey's neck.

"What do you seek?"

The Ancient ground its feeder legs against the implacable hull. Layer by layer, he scraped the craft open until the first puffs of atmosphere through the ruptured hull whisked against his skin.

"You are different than before."

"STOP SPEAKING!" The Ancient bellowed. *"YOU WERE WEAK, LEFT BEHIND! YOU WERE THE KEEPER OF THE KNOT, AND YOU FAILED US!"*

"I am the keeper," the Bwainhome whispered.

Desperate now, The Ancient worked to widen its penetration. Around him, the other First Ones either consumed their enemies, or fell to their weapons and dissipated, returning once again to the great obelisk. Hunger was their purgatory, their drive, the only emotion in their soul, and it would plague them until they rejoined the Knot. They had tied it so that only they could untie it to recover what had been.

"YOU CANNOT LET CARTER CONTROL YOU!" The Ancient howled.

"You are not as you were."

"I AM LIFE!" The Ancient growled. *"I AM ALL THAT WAS AND IS."*

"Not anymore," a new voice said.

"THE CARTER!" The Ancient roared in fury.

* * *

The Constantinople

"Mr. Purcell, see if you can drive that group away from the antimatter station," Mephista called to her fighter squadron.

"Copy, ma'am," the weapons officer acknowledged. On the holos, his hundred-odd vessels shot toward a cluster of First Ones that was feasting on the remains of an SSC ship just before reaching the station. Their weapons bloomed, scattering the First Ones away from the civilians.

"Beta wing, bring yourselves around on heading toward .12.857.345," she ordered. "I want you to try and sweep anything you find in that area toward the *Bwainhome*."

"Yes, ma'am," her captains responded. A third of her fleet then swung as if closing a gate, firing their new weaponry as quickly as they could against the encroaching First Ones as they drove them away from Saturn. Mephista felt alive for the first time, losing herself in the ebb and flow of battle. She hadn't said goodbye to Atlas just yet, and she didn't intend to.

"They're doing something different. I'm not sure what...," the *Kuwait*'s captain called.

"Transmission lost, ma'am."

On the holos, she saw the ship crumple and fold at the middle.

"What happened?" she demanded, as she studied the images before her.

"It looks like they're using some sort of a new strategy. I think they're using suicide attacks against us," Danielle said as she rapidly brought up a series of new images for the captain.

"Ma'am, it's Lieutenant Xiao," Danny called. The supply officer was in command of another one of the shuttle wings. "You need to get to the *Bwainhome*. I think it's in trouble."

* * *

"That's the way to hit 'em!" Bryon cried out. The Bwain sitting behind him in the cramped fighter cabin squawked in excitement as a First One that had been just about to cleave through his line of fighters shuddered and flashed a rainbow of colors before crumbling in on itself.

"Thanks, Lieutenant," one of the pilots' called back to him over the comms channel.

"Don't mention it," Danny answered. "Now, let's make sure that... Oh crap!"

On his holos, a disgustingly engorged First One streaked from Saturn's rings straight toward the station.

"Hit that thing before it...," he started to say, but the creature moved so fast their shots fell wide and short before it slammed into the station. Rather than come out the opposite side, it wormed its way inside, consuming everything it could.

"There are five hundred people in there!" someone gasped on the open channel.

278

"Shuttle wing Tango, open fire on that station with everything you have," Purcell answered.

The Bwain behind him stilled, closed its eyes, and a bulb of lavender plasma shot toward the station. Many of the weapons impacted harmlessly on the station's surface, and Bryon wondered for a moment if the First Ones had become smarter. In the end however, the creature was betrayed by its own body. As it dissolved more and more of the station, it became a bigger target and was soon a writhing ghost fading back to oblivion as the fighters concentrated their fire.

"*Constantinople*, be advised that primary protection duty is ended with the asset's loss," Bryon called. "We..."

"Get to the *Bwainhome!*" Mephista nearly shouted in his ear. "All ships, all craft, concentrate on the *Bwainhome!*"

Bryon was wrenching his controls before the order finished. He swung his view and centered it on the *Bwainhome*, which was under heavy assault from the First Ones.

"One of those things is on top of it," someone said.

At first Bryon couldn't be sure what he was seeing. Everything else the First Ones touched dissolved almost instantaneously, but it looked like the creatures were digging at the *Bwainhome* with their claws, tentacles, and other appendages. One of them, the biggest, seemed to be burrowing inside of what would have been the ship's spine.

"Let's peel that thing off for the captain," Bryon said. "Go ahead, little buddy."

But no shot came. Bryon glanced back, expecting the Bwain to be down on the floor and a replacement taking its place, but his same copilot was sitting there.

"What's goin' on?" he shouted. "Fire!"

"Will hurt home," the creature said.

"Why is no one firing?" Mephista asked.

"That thing is hurting your home!" Bryon shouted at his copilot, but the Bwain just sat there shaking its head.

"Will hurt home," it said again. "Can't shoot."

"Oh, Jesus!" Bryon groaned. "Captain, we've got a problem."

* * *

The Bwainhome

The *Bwainhome* was dying. After so many millennia, just as it had been about to be reborn, the ship of years was being torn apart. Captain Carter could *feel* the ravenous First Ones just beyond him, while at the same time he could sense the *Bwainhome*'s terror and resignation.

The Bwain fighter he rode in flashed through space and time in an instant and deposited him in the shuttle bay. He sprinted forward in a strange fugue of his own body and the *Bwainhome*'s mind. Up and up he rose, pumping his legs, and leaving the pain of Cazador's beating behind until at last he reached the Endless Knot's chamber.

He thrust his hand into the Endless Knot as he had once before, only this time it was because he wanted to live.

Chapter Fourteen

Atlas' skin was on fire, but it wasn't his skin that was the source of the sensation, it was the *Bwainhome*'s hull. The Ancient, who'd once been like him, who had ordered him to carry the Knot until the First Ones' return, was trying to kill him.

The Endless Knot had been placed inside the breast of one of the First Ones, given to a chosen guardian for safe keeping in the event of the First Ones' return. It was the key that would allow them to fully reclaim their physical existence, but the *Bwainhome*'s kindred had been gone for far too long. They had changed. The Knot was a force that bound all life, the very essence of the universe. The Bwain had taught it to the first peoples on Earth. It had twisted and contorted itself for millennia, sentient but not alive, it was a distillation of everything that the First Ones had learned, and in that time, it had come to think for itself.

All barriers of time and space and understanding were stripped away from him. He could see through the eons of the past. He felt the constant loneliness, the fear and the hurt, the spark of the First Ones, their knowledge and warmth, then their self-centered quest for knowledge, and their abandonment of the world they had created. He remembered everything.

"You cannot do this," some of the First Ones had argued. *"What of the Bwain?"*

"What of them? They are slaves."

That had been all that the Bwain had known. Until Carter's arrival on the *Bwainhome*, it was all they'd ever been.

The Ancient wanted them to be slaves again. It wanted the Knot for itself, but Atlas had other plans.

His skin caught fire. White lightning sprung from the Knot, leaping above him in a rush like a reverse waterfall. The flames rose and grew until there was only a cool whiteness. In the impossible light, he felt himself shed what had been. The universe fell away, and he existed in a timeless instant.

Then, a small voice rose to him. One he remembered, longed for, and sought after.

"Aida?" Atlas asked.

* * *

The Constantinople

Mephista tried to use her hand to block out the brilliant white flash that erupted from the *Bwainhome,* but it overloaded her retinas and for a moment and she could see nothing at all. Her fear for Atlas' safety had her heart pounding hard in her chest. If the *Bwainhome* had been destroyed, if Atlas had perished...

A small hand clutched hers. She felt the hard scales of a Bwain's palm in her own.

"Look," the creature hissed.

"Ma'am, I'm reading supernova-level brightness," Danielle warned. "We may need to try and run."

As she blinked away the afterimage, Mephista saw that it was too late. The white explosion ripping through the space around Saturn was moving too quickly. All she could do was close her eyes and pray.

"Brace for impact!" she ordered.

* * *

Bryon expected to feel the explosion tear apart his fighter. He closed his eyes, hoping against hope that somehow his EVO suit would protect him. He'd expected a sudden depressurization, or a wave of debris that would tear his ship apart, but instead, nothing happened. Peeking out of one eye, he saw a bright whiteness that was draining the color from everything except the Bwain behind him. The creature had left its seat and was standing on Bryon's lap, flickering with deep greens and browns interspersed with white. The alien was silent, and then bowed its head and raised its wings.

"What are you doin'?" Bryon asked, but the alien didn't answer.

Blinking, he hunched forward to see around the Bwain. When the light faded and he could see far enough into the distance, Bryon realized exactly what the creature was doing.

"You're...praying?" he whispered to himself, awed by what he was seeing.

* * *

Earth

The Bwain surrounding the presidential tower's situation room suddenly stilled. They'd been squawking and pacing around the circular installation, pecking now and then at any of the marines who seemed too aggressive. Suddenly, in unison, their color rose to a brilliant emerald. Somehow, Julie felt the rush of humid air across her neck, and the feeling of cool water flowing down her throat. There was the warmth of the jungle, the soaring sky...but where was this?

"What's happening?" Cazador said, coughing roughly as he struggled to get the words out.

On the holoscreens, the desperate battle with the First Ones played out an hour behind reality.

"They're attacking the *Bwainhome!*" Julie exclaimed.

"I...told him," Cazador wheezed.

Then she glanced down at Lana, who was hunched over her wound while the medics worked on her. What had been the reporter's hip and abdomen had been reduced to charred flesh, but she was spasming now.

"You have to let them help you, Lana," Julie said, almost desperately. "You have to..."

"What the...? I don't understand," one of the medics said in a bewildered voice.

A white glow shone from the wound, and as Julie watched, the flesh began knitting itself back together. Lana looked down at herself, as startled as everyone else by what she was seeing.

"What is it?" she asked.

"Save," the Bwain said. "Save! Save!"

It's the captain!" Julie said. "I think he's won!"

* * *

The Bwainhome

"This thing's shaking itself apart!" Hal called. "We gotta get back to the shuttle bay!"

Granger was struggling to his feet, trying to keep his balance while the deck below him pitched and rolled like a ship crossing heavy swells. Granger expected the Bwain around them to be panicking, collapsing in fear at the sight of the First One that had latched on to them; but, if anything, they seemed calm.

"Something else is goin' on here," he said as he motioned toward the Bwain. "Look at 'em."

As one, the creatures' pigmentation had shifted to a brilliant white, with waves of silver and gold rippling across their abdomens.

"I don't care what color they are," Hal said as they regained their footing and looked up at the image above them. "We gotta get the hell off this ship First One digs any deeper."

For a moment, Granger resisted. The scientific observer part of him wanted to stay and document the only time the Bwain were ever seen like this. Were the creatures preparing for death? Were they trying to resist? It appeared that the largest First One had pierced the *Bwainhome*'s top deck, so were they trying to repair the ship that had been their race's home for close to eternity?

"Come on! You stupid scientists are all alive, but there's no studying if you're dead!" Hal called urgently as he turned to run.

Reluctantly, Granger followed him down the sloping ramp that led toward the shuttle bay. Suddenly, a massive boom sounded through the ship. Hal flew sideways against a wall that throbbed in orange and pearl, while Granger fell to one knee. A second boom sounded, and then the ship stilled.

Granger helped Hal up, and they turned back toward the spiraling path that led down to the shuttle bay.

More booming sounds echoed throughout the ship, shifting the deck under them so sharply that they both fell to their knees.

"That thing's breaking through!" Hal screamed as he continued on, crawling on his hands and knees just as fast as he could, but Granger knew there'd be no escape once the First One reached inside. The observer's desire overtook him, and he rolled onto his back.

"Hal!" Granger called amidst the booms.

From where he lay he could see the path leading to the Endless Knot. A brilliant glow was streaming from the chamber and flowing across the ceiling.

"Hal, it's not what you think!"

* * *

The *Bwainhome* remembered. The *Bwainhome* always had. Its job was to keep the Endless Knot safe until someone arrived who understood both the Knot's power, and its extreme complexity. Atlas Carter was that person.

The Knot was not to be used for violence, or greed, or savagery. When they left, the First Ones had put these safeguards in place to ensure that civilized life, life with compassion would evolve.

He was the only one who understood. He was the only one with the fighter' strength, mixed with the despair of loss, and so the *Bwainhome* had helped him because those he fought against those who were not worthy. When the *Bwainhome* called Carter to itself a final time, they became one, and the Endless Knot was unlocked.

On top of the *Bwainhome*, the quantum forces that had sustained The Ancient were torn apart by the wave of gravitational pressure that erupted from the Endless Knot. Shrieking, the First One tried to flee but was shredded by gravity's oscillations. The waves trapped the other First Ones, pinned them in place, and stripped their essence from the universe.

The explosion gathered speed as it raced through the solar system, traveling faster and faster until it reached the other Bwain fleets at the farthest reaches of the galaxy. Each colony heard the siren call, and turned their ships in the direction of a new beginning.

On the *Bwainhome* itself, Atlas Carter's body lay still while the Endless Knot circled above him like a shroud.

Chapter Fifteen

Earth

In Belize City as a youth, Cazador had once been backed into a corner of a half-collapsed house by the older *Narcos*. It had smelled of damp cinderblocks and mold, and he'd been sweating in the humidity as the men circled him like a pack of dogs. He was fourteen-years-old, and had stolen a motorcycle from one of them when the man had fallen asleep drunk. Now they had come for their revenge.

Each of them had a gun, but they laid their weapons behind them. Instead, they came at him with open hands, grinning with teeth that had been capped with gold or filed sharp. They thought they were showing their toughness. They thought he was not a threat, but they were mistaken. He drew a hooked knife from his trousers, wrapped his fingers through the brass knuckle hilt, and waved them onward.

"Come on!" he cried. "You think I'm just some weak, defenseless prey, but you'll find out. I'm the hunter, and you're all about to die!"

From the moment he walked out of that ruined house covered in blood that was not his own, Cazador had vowed never to be weak again. When the Bwain were distracted and no one was watching him, he ripped two plasma pistols from under his suit and showered the Bwain with hellish energy.

His aim was poor, hurt by his ruined face. Marines and aliens alike clutched at their brutal wounds, screaming and falling around him. None of them mattered. They were like Aída and Carter, collateral damage in the quest for power. Two of the Bwain clawed at his leg, trying to stop him. The creatures had weapons, but weren't trying to kill him. This was always Carter's weakness, and it sickened him.

He kicked the bird things back, shot one's head off and hit the other under its wing. The headless one staggered back and forth, like a chicken in a yard not yet knowing it was about to become dinner. Cazador lurched for the elevator.

Arms clamped down over his. It was a marine that wasn't too happy about seeing his squad mates murdered. The hunter was still full of surprises, and he snapped his damaged head back against the soldier's nose. He felt the bone break and sink into the man's face, and when Cazador spun, his pistols took out two more marines and another Bwain.

They were all trying to capture him. Their mercy made them weak. He needed only to get to a shuttle so he could return to Belize. The *Narcos* were still strong, even if they didn't yet rule the galaxy. The people still knew him as president. He would make a triumphant broadcast about what had happened in the outer system. He would gather the planet and all her colonies to him, and they would know his power.

Suddenly, a light brighter than the sun ripped through his chest. He clutched the gaping hole where his heart had been, trying to gasp a breath. A blurred figure appeared in front of him as he fell backward.

"That's for Captain Carter," Julie said, and then she aimed the pistol at his face and squeezed the trigger. "And this is for me!"

All was blackness and burning, and the hunter's days had finally reached their end.

* * *

The Constantinople
Saturn

Mephista collapsed back into her captain's chair, as a stunned silence hung over the bridge. Whatever had emanated from the

Bwainhome and torn the First Ones from this universe seemed to have carried a profoundly contemplative mood with it. The ship's communications channels were silent in her ear. The crew were motionless at their stations, just staring at the holoscreen. Static electricity filled the air, as if everything was connected and the very molecules themselves were alive. Mephista's legs itched, and the first thing she did after sitting down was to rub one of her boots against her calf.

The Bwain on the bridge had settled into an odd posture, resting on their knees with their heads bowed and their wings in the air, almost as if the ungainly things were ready to leap upwards. Whites and golds and silvers rippled across their feathers, but aside from the coloration changes, they too were still. The tingling rose up Mephista's legs and curled through her spine. She twisted in her chair, rubbing her lower back where the strange feeling seemed to gather and build.

"Bring...," she started, and then she paused, considering the magnitude of the battle they had just won. "Bring the fighters back."

"Yes, ma'am," Danielle responded.

"Comms."

"Ma'am?" a distracted ensign asked after a long pause.

She reached down, scratching at her shin, then pulled her leg up higher.

"I want you to open every transmission signal we have to every ship in the fleet. I want you...no, I want everyone...every crewman to call Earth, or their home colony, or anyone who'll listen."

"What do you want 'em to say, ma'am?" the ensign asked. It could have been sarcastic, but she knew it wasn't. The ensign felt the same thing that she did.

"I want them to tell everyone what happened out here," Mephista said as she gathered her strength and pushed down on the arms of her captain's chair. "I want them to talk about this feeling."

"Yes, ma'am," the ensign acknowledged.

"The shuttles are returning," Danielle said.

"I have messages from Saturn, from Earth, from the defense force..."

"They can wait," Mephista said. Her voice was quivering, and she spoke with a new uncertainty.

One of the Bwain's heads rose and turned toward her.

"It's alright," the creature said in a hiss that could have been a whisper.

Letting go of the handrails on her captain's chair, Mephista put her weight on her legs for the first time in three years. They were weak and atrophied from lack of use, but they held. She felt her muscles trembling with the energy that had flooded through everything, and tears burst down her face.

"Oh, Atlas...," she whispered to herself as she turned and made her was unsteadily toward the airlock.

"Ma'am, where are you going?" her deck officer asked. That caused her to pause for a moment. Abandoning her post while under threat was an offense that would result in an instant court-martial, punishable by death for a captain, but she no longer feared death, and there was no longer any threat.

"I'm going to see my friends," she said before continuing on her way.

* * *

Danny had made it to the ramp of his fighter before sitting down hard on the metal gangway. The sense of relief coursing through him was indescribable, a kind of calmness in his heart that felt as if he'd just finished a long meditation. He reached up, unsealed his helmet, and let it drop beside him. It rolled down the ramp and skidded a meter or two farther on the shuttle bay's deck. All around him shuttle pilots and Bwain were disembarking, tottering with a stunned aimlessness.

The Bwain in his own fighter hadn't disembarked. Danny stood on rubbery legs, going to check on the aliens who were still sitting quietly in the craft, appearing almost as if they were in prayer. A flash of light caught his eye. The nanobots on the shuttle were working at something wedged in a seam next to the fighter's hull. He reached in with his glove, found the foreign body, and leaned back. For a moment, it wouldn't release, but then it gave way and he stumbled back two paces.

Glittering in his glove was a piece of mirrored chaff, part of the laser countermeasures released by one of the doomed SSC ships. In the polished glass, Danny could see his face. He was no longer the bitter, round-faced supply officer. A new maturity had hardened in him. He'd lost weight but felt more substantial.

"Did you lose something?" Bryon asked as Danny stood there examining the mirror.

The weapons officer stood at the foot of the ramp, holding up Danny's helmet. A cluster of Bwain stood in a swaying circle behind him, occasionally pecking at his EVO suit.

"No, I don't think I did," Danny answered. "Just the opposite actually."

* * *

Bryon sat down next to Danny on the ramp. For a time, neither of them spoke. They simply watched as the other shuttles made their way through the electroshield and into the shuttle bay. It was as if some invisible snowfall had muffled all sound. The inducers, the warning tones of the bay doors, and the march of boots across the deck all came from an unknown depth.

"I wish Kaylee was here," Bryon said. "Threed too."

Danny didn't answer for a while. He just kept turning the mirror over and over in his hands.

"Maybe they are," he finally said. Bryon had to admit that Danny might be right.

"You know, when I first went after these things with Threed, I thought I was gonna die, but it was all right if I did, because at least I'd be helping you guys," Bryon said.

"You were afraid?" Danny asked.

"Nothing a good weapons officer would ever admit, but yeah. I was pretty scared. I just did my best not to show it."

"How about now?" Danny asked.

"No," Bryon replied. "And you know, to be honest...I don't think I'll ever be afraid again."

A strange shuffling sounded behind him. Bryon glanced at the Bwain, but they were all nestled together, almost asleep.

"What will you do now?" Bryon asked.

"I dunno. I think I might go back to China to visit my sister's grave. I'll have to find out where Tannin's people buried her."

"Yeah, that sounds like a good idea. I think we should all take some personal time," Bryon said.

"I hope you guys can put off your vacations for just a little while longer, because I've got one last request," Mephista said.

When Bryon looked up, he was absolutely stunned at what he saw. The captain was standing, leaning on what looked like a spider steel cane while resting her other hand on Danielle's shoulder for support.

"Your legs!" Bryon gasped in shock.

"They're back, and I'd like to thank the man who gave 'em to me." Mephista said with the most genuine smile that any of them had ever seen from her.

* * *

The Bwainhome

When the wave of milky light washed over him, Hal had thought he was rising to the Great Spirit. He closed his eyes and felt the wind over the Oklahoma plains caress his skin, smelled the dust from the fields tinged with fertilizer, and tasted the kiss of a humid night.

"My son," Granger coughed.

When he heard the sound of Granger's voice beside him, Hal knew he wasn't dead, but he couldn't understand what he was feeling. As he got to his feet, he could almost see Gertie's rolling hills again, intermixed with the home he'd locked for the last time in a drunken haze before taking the bus to the spaceport and boarding the first colony ship that would have him.

"It's time to go home," he said as he helped the science officer to his feet.

As Granger dusted himself off, Hal's eyes wandered to the chamber above.

"Did it sound like a heartbeat to you?" he asked.

"It sounded like everything," Granger said.

"Then I think we need to see what it is. For science."

They climbed in silence. The *Bwainhome* had changed once more. Where before the hardened bulkheads and decks had been stiff and frozen, now they felt warm, almost growing. The ship was alive, of that there was no doubt, but what kind of life did it harbor?

Inside the Endless Knot's chamber, the white light should have blinded them, burned their skin, but somehow Hal found that he could still see. In fact, he felt as if his sight was joined with not only the Bwain in the room, but with all the other creatures on all the other planets in the universe, and that was how he knew that Atlas Carter was dying.

* * *

"I don't feel as bad as I look," Atlas said with as much of a smile as he could muster when Hal and Granger helped him to sit up.

"That's uhhh...that's good...I guess," Granger said.

Atlas' consciousness felt stuffed into too small a vessel. His body was familiar but outgrown, and yet he needed it for a little while longer to communicate with these men who'd become his friends. He reached for Hal to pat him on the shoulder and saw that his arm, the arm that he'd thrust into the Endless Knot, had sprouted the same glassy tendrils that Hal's weapons had grown. Granger's eyes widened when he saw what had happened to the captain's arm, but he tried not to show it.

"I can't go back," Atlas said. It was the only explanation he could think of, and it said everything.

"Captain, what happened?" Granger asked.

"This ship...you were right. It's alive, but more alive than you could ever imagine."

The words felt strange, foreign and unwieldy from his lips, tongue, and throat. He preferred psychic communication, where he could paint a picture with images and emotion that could instantly be understood across the galaxy. Yet he had only a little while longer to remain in this form.

"The First Ones were never the first. There was life before them. At least, a kind of life," he said, and then paused to catch his breath.

"The Knot?" Granger asked.

"Yeah."

"But what is it?"

"I thought it was what the First Ones used to control the Bwain, and to enslave them the way they did. In a way it was, but it was so much more than that. The Knot is the foundation of our universe. It's an intelligence that exists in a way that I don't even know if the First Ones or the *Bwainhome* ever understood. The best way that I can describe it is that it acts to keep things in balance. The First Ones made it the key to their power. It was so important to them that they placed it inside the body of one of their most respected leaders."

"The Bwainhome," Granger said.

When Carter nodded, his head felt impossibly heavy. His face was still swollen from Cazador's fists, but pain no longer seemed to matter as much.

"The *Bwainhome* agreed to become sustenance for the First Ones' slaves, and to keep the Endless Knot for the First Ones, should they ever return. Over thousands of years it fell into a deep sleep, and when the First Ones returned, it realized that its former cousins were not the same beings that it had been dreaming of."

"What does the *Bwainhome* want?" Hal asked.

"To wake up. To live as it once did," Atlas said. He coughed for a moment, and then wiped a weak hand across his battered face.

"It's not going to eat any planets, is it?" a voice asked.

Danny, Bryon, Mephista, and Danielle were entering the chamber.

"Help me up," Atlas said to Hal and Granger. They pulled him upright, and he greeted Mephista with a hug.

"You're shorter than I expected," he said with a slight grin.

"And you look like hell," she said, smiling back at him.

They held each other for a long moment before Mephista finally released him.

"Thank you," she whispered, as she wiped a tear from the corner of her eye. "For everything."

"Captain, if you don't mind me asking, does this mean we can all we go home now? Being inside a living thing's guts kinda gives me the creeps," Bryon quipped. Atlas couldn't help but laugh.

Atlas' Final Approach

"As your commanding officer, my last act is to hereby give all of you a lifetime of leave."

"Does that mean you'll have some vacation time as well?" Mephista asked.

The sadness that he'd been holding back finally flooded through him, and the group stilled in quiet reflection.

"No, I'm afraid not. My mission hasn't changed, but I've still got one last thing to do."

* * *

The Fates' Winds

The only light in Aric Keith's world came from the obelisk. He'd spent hours staring at it, wondering when The Ancient would return, until the strange white light had roared through his empty system and freed him. He could not explain the sensation, but knew somehow that his life was once more his own. He stood, walked, floated, and no pain or screaming came to him.

Freed for the first time to wander the broken ship, Aric found himself drawn to the dayroom. It had once been a garden of green and growing things where the crew would come to relax. When the ship had been hulled, the atmosphere vented, and much of what had been was sucked into space. Just a few frozen tree trunks from the orchard remained. The path that led from the river to the marsh, and a bench where he could sit and stare out into the stars.

This was where he was sitting, thinking of ways to fix the ship and sail onward, when another light arrived in the system.

"Does anyone know a good engineer?" Atlas Carter's voice asked. "I could use one where I'm going."

* * *

"So, this is it?" Mephista asked.

They stood alone in the chamber of the Endless Knot. The Bwain and Carter's other crew had given them their privacy to say their final goodbyes. Atlas held her awkwardly, his one arm transformed, and the strength in his body fading. She could already feel that parts of him were no longer with her.

"I can't stay here."

"I know," she said, wiping her tears away. "And I want you to know that I understand about your wife."

"I had to know the truth."

"She's why you came out here. I never would have met you otherwise," Mephista said.

He nodded, because there was nothing more to say, and then he gently released her. The Endless Knot was churning behind him like an eternal ocean. His eyes flickered with the same light.

"Whatever happens afterward, I'll never forget you," Atlas said as he stared into her eyes. He ran his hand along her cheek, as if permanently etching the memory of her into his mind.

"Who knows? Maybe if I go back to being a pirate, I'll find you again someday at the other end of the galaxy," she said, smiling bravely as a wave of memories washed over her.

His smile was the last she saw of him before she turned to take the long walk down to the shuttle bay. There, the last human shuttle waited to take her and the others back to what was left of the fleet.

Atlas' Final Approach

As they slipped from the *Bwainhome* for the final time, she held her hand against the electroglass. Though once she'd felt only cold on the other side, now the space between them felt warm, and for the first time since she could remember, she actually laughed.

Epilogue

If you were watching the *Bwainhome* from above, you would have seen its roof split like a flower's bloom. The Endless Knot spun faster and faster, its glow building until it shone through the blackness of space brighter than any sun. A single figure could be made out at its center, a man whose shape flickered in and out of view. The Knot drifted toward the obelisk, detouring slightly to swing over the wreckage of the *Fates' Winds*, where it rendezvoused with the battered ship's last loyal crewman.

With incredible speed, the Knot pulled away from the *Fates' Winds* and headed directly toward the obelisk. There was a blinding flash, and then nothing but the emptiness of space.

* * *

Once more, Atlas Carter was flying. The air over Belize City was a crisp blue, and the smoke that filled the air from dozens of fires drifted far below him. He pushed his stick forward, ducking under clouds until he was winging over the rooftops. There was the gym where he'd trained, and farther over was the cafe where Aída would stagger over the cobblestoned streets in her heels to bring him coffee and empanadas for breakfast.

His helicopter chopped the air. The vibration threatened to pull him apart, but he was almost home.

A figure dressed in red stood on the rooftop. She was waving, her hair streaming back from his wake. He set down his heavy craft beside her and turned off its engines, left his pilot's chair for the last time, and lost himself in Aída's loving embrace.

His journey had finally come to an end. He was home.

About the Author

J. Channing is an engineer and manager for a semiconductor company in Boise, Idaho by day and a dedicated entrepreneur and freelance writer by night. Born in Butte, Montana, he spent most of his childhood roaming around the northwest, living in eighteen different locations before getting through high school. When not at his day or night job, Channing is also actively involved in the community, with his church, and as a small business owner. He utilizes his business ties and proceeds to give back to the local community, having raised funds for Boise area charities.

J. Channing has been interested in military history, time travel, World War II, and weapons technology since he was a small child. The original story concept for *Forever* was outlined on one of his many solo bus rides from the Seattle area to Helena, Montana. It was adjusted and improved over decades and was finally, as a labor of love, completed. The book is a fulfillment of a story that has played out in his head hundreds of times; he hopes the world enjoys it as much as he always has.